BEYOND RECOGNITION

David Berardelli

BEYOND RECOGNITION

GRAVESTONE PRESS

ISBN: 978 1 78695 718 4

Gravestone Press
is an imprint of
Fiction4All
www.fiction4all.com

This Edition
Published 2022

Cover Art: Linda York

PART 1 - *Prey*

CHAPTER ONE

THURSDAY P.M.

Desmond Roth got off the plane at Pittsburgh International and joined the long procession of passengers shuffling toward the landside terminal at the other end of the sprawling complex. The brightly lit area, chaotic with nervous humanity, provided direct access for everyone scrambling to get on their flights or coming off them.

Roth walked briskly toward the front of the building, avoiding eye contact as much as possible. Anonymity had been his way of life the last few years, but after his close call in Orlando one year ago, staying under the radar had become an issue of life and death.

People slouched on stools at the food court, chowing down burgers and subs and drinking coffee and beer. He kept a close watch on the activity, his finely tuned senses picking up quick images. Family reunions. Loved ones departing. An impending funeral. An important business convention. As always, he checked for eyes following him, as well as eyes turning away a little too quickly.

He saw no sign, sensed no danger or tension.

As he reached the last leg of his trip through the terminal, where the ticket and car rental agencies awaited him, he caught someone eyeing him from the approaching crowd. A sloppy-dressed guy with wild black hair and a three-day growth of beard. The man quickly averted his eyes and then looked down at his feet as he kept coming.

Roth caught a bright image: a flash of hands, an instant's distraction.

A pickpocket. I really don't have time for this.

The man sidestepped at the last possible moment. His left shoulder bumped lightly into Roth an instant before he moved away.

Feeling the microscopic pressure touching his breast pocket at that same instant, Roth spun around. His right arm shot out, his hand latching on to the man's shoulder.

The man froze.

Roth focused on the man's bloodshot eyes. Roth held out his left hand.

Trembling, the other man reached inside his jacket, removed the tan camel-skin billfold, and handed it over.

"Pl-Please...*please* don't call the cops..."

This man had obviously been a victim of hard times. His shirt and jeans clung to him. He'd either taken them from the local Goodwill box or had recently lost a considerable amount of weight.

Keeping his hand on the man's shoulder, Roth glimpsed more images. This man had spent half his adult life in jail--petty theft, picking pockets, purse-snatching, burglary, grand theft auto. Booze and endless lines of coke also came into the picture.

"How many others have you taken today?" Roth asked.

The man shrugged.

"A shrug doesn't tell me much. I prefer a number."

"Three..."

"Take what you've got to the nearest church and leave it. They won't ask questions if you just walk in, dump it in their office, and leave. Understand?"

"Yes, sir."

Roth released the man's shoulder. The man seemed to be in some sort of daze. He began staring at Roth's hand.

Roth hurried away, toward the EXIT doors on the other side of the big building.

Twenty minutes later, Roth slipped behind the wheel of a gray Dodge Challenger he'd rented from one of the agencies he'd passed on his way out of the terminal. He glanced at his watch. The pickpocket had only cost him three minutes or so. He'd make it up on the road.

Ten minutes later, he separated from the heavy flow heading for Pittsburgh, got on I-70 and headed west.

His destination was Manville, Ohio. According to his friend, this trip would take about half an hour.

***

Her eyes glazed over from staring at the computer screen the last four long hours, Laura Neilson closed the laptop and pushed her chair back from the metal desk, where she and Maddie did the books and tallied the day's profits.

It was almost six, and Laura was tired. Good thing it was the end of the workday. Carl Gibson,

Maddie's husband and co-owner of Coffee Masters, had no doubt already flipped the sign on the front door from *OPEN* to *CLOSED*.

The coffeehouse had been nearly empty since around five. It had been a normal day, the customers trickling in shortly after nine, when the place opened. Activity stayed high from the time the lunch crowd staggered in shortly after eleven, remaining busy until four, when the work force went home for the day.

Laura had been working for Maddie and Carl nearly one year. She'd started just a few days after receiving her clean bill of health. Just two years earlier, she'd been involved in a near-fatal accident on I-70, when an idiot in a Ford F-350 pickup rear-ended her at nearly 100 miles an hour. The collision sent her silver Dodge Charger into a quarter-mile skid, causing it to flip over, roll off the Interstate and land in a ditch. The driver of the truck, a nineteen-year-old high school dropout wasted on meth, had no driver's license or insurance, no permission to drive his uncle's truck, and disappeared the moment he was released on bail.

The accident left Laura with two smashed vertebrae, dislocated pelvis, three cracked ribs, a broken jaw and a broken arm. The Charger was totaled. The dream car Momma had bought for Laura for graduating from Ohio University less than a month before the accident was gone forever.

Laura carefully pushed herself up from the desk. She considered herself fortunate that she could perform such a simple task. It had taken her many months to learn to walk all over again. Now, after nearly two years, she could walk almost normally, her pronounced limp giving her character, as Momma had said several times.

Sliding the thick strap of her lightweight tan leather tote bag carefully over her right shoulder, she left the cluttered office and shuffled stiffly down the hall and into the bathroom to wash her face and fix her hair.

Under the flickering overhead fluorescent, she stepped in front of the smudged mirror. Leaning against the sink to support her back, she splashed her face with warm water. After dabbing her cheeks with paper towels, she applied fresh lipstick and then carefully unwound the red rope that held the bun she wore during working hours. Her heavy dark-brown locks thumped onto her shoulders and slid down her front. For the next few minutes, she applied the large green pick to free the knots and clumps. After some furious tugging and pulling, she grabbed the hairbrush.

Maddie came in looking tired as usual, her fine features drawn, her cornflower blue eyes slightly veined. Judging by her sour expression, she'd either been to the bank or had another argument with Carl. Their eight-year marriage was solid, but they frequently argued about how the shop should be run. Maddie had put up the money for the down payment and had the final say. Carl ached to have a free hand in running the business. Unluckily for him, Maddie was strong-willed and fiercely independent, insisting on doing things her own way. Luckily for both of them, Maddie had good business sense.

"How'd we do today?" Maddie pushed some heavy red strands away from her cheek and gave herself a quick look of disapproval in the mirror.

"The after-lunch lull seemed longer than usual."

"It started earlier, too. Business didn't pick up again until much later."

"That new buffet restaurant that just opened in St. Clairsville could be slamming us."

"It shouldn't affect us *that* much. Hungry people don't go to a place that sells coffee and croissants. We cater to the Mall shoppers."

"I wouldn't worry. Once the new wears off, it'll pick up again."

Maddie shook her head. "Why are you always so damned optimistic?"

Laura could never understand why Maddie always chose the gloomy side of everything. "It beats being depressed, doesn't it?"

"Honey, *you're* the one who almost died, remember?"

Laura smiled. "The accident made me see things in a much clearer perspective, I guess."

"What you went through would definitely put a new slant on things. Call me weird, but I'd rather keep my negativity than go through something like that."

"I honestly don't recommend being rear-ended, believe me--especially at a hundred miles an hour."

"I'll take your word for it. While we're on the subject, I've been wondering. Everything okay at home?"

"Why do you ask?"

"I saw your mom the other day in town. She seemed really deep in thought. I was just wondering if--well, if something was going on…"

"We're both okay."

Maddie watched her for a moment; she obviously had something on her mind. "I guess I'm just wondering if…well, I don't know how to--"

"Just ask, Maddie."

"All righty. You haven't, by some strange coincidence, heard from your father, have you?"

The question took her completely by surprise. "Now why would you ask me that?"

"It was your birthday last week. I just thought--"

"You thought wrong."

"I'm sorry, honey."

"It's all right."

"You're sure? I know I've never been one to mind my own business… I'm just a little concerned."

"It's been five years since Dad left, and still no word. I've grown used to it. So has Momma."

"He didn't come see you at all in the hospital?"

"He was in Florida at the time. I don't know how he even heard about it, but he called a couple of days after I was brought in. I couldn't talk to him because I was all doped up. Even if I'd been awake, I couldn't talk very well with my jaw wired shut.

Apparently he only called that one time. I never heard from him after that."

"Never?"

"He never called again."

"My father did his share of crap, too. I saw him once or twice after I left home, but there was no love lost between us. When he died, I discovered that I couldn't even mourn. I obviously had no feelings left for him."

"I didn't know, Maddie. I'm sorry."

"I'm over it. I can tell by what I see in your eyes that you're over it, too. But he should've at least visited you in the hospital, for crying out loud."

Laura tried once again to force away the hurt. It was tough. She'd been so angry and upset when Dad had left. Because of his actions, she'd harbored a deep resentment for all men and feared she'd never be able to trust anyone again. She'd known a few decent guys, even dated a couple of them before her accident. Even so, she remained uncomfortable in their presence and blamed it on the pain and distrust she'd developed from her father's abandonment.

"I don't know if I'm fully over it," she told Maddie. "I don't know if I'll ever be."

"Well, if you ever need to talk, Carl and I live upstairs. And we keep late hours." Maddie patted her shoulder and slipped into the stall.

Laura shuffled outside through the rear entrance, where she'd parked her ten-year-old light-blue Honda Civic in the side lot facing the Ohio Valley Mall on the other side of the open thoroughfare. The Civic was a far cry from her beloved Charger, but she wasn't making much money and had very little in her savings account. Economy had become her only option.

She slid very carefully behind the wheel, wincing at the sharp stab of bright pain. *Not quite right.* Gently she situated herself in the seat, giving her bones plenty of time to arrange themselves for the trip ahead. *There.* The pain slowly ebbed into a distant hum.

She pulled out of her space, coasted down Mall Road and got onto I-70. Traffic was heavy as usual, the rush hour still in full swing. Although she regularly used the same stretch of highway that had nearly killed her, she knew not to let such things haunt her. It was never very bright to keep looking back. It prevented you from seeing what you should be facing in the present. She'd read that in a book a while back, liked the way it sounded and never forgot it.

The drive to Manville, where she and Momma lived, was only ten miles. She pulled onto the first Manville exit and drove about a quarter of a mile down the straight stretch that went directly to town, before slowing and stopping at the red light. A dirty white van eased to a stop behind her. The driver's visor was pulled down. She had the eerie feeling that the driver was watching her.

Your imagination, kiddo... She'd just seen a really tense thriller on Netflix, where Jennifer Lopez was being stalked. *You don't wanna think of something like that right now.* She was being silly.

There was no need to panic just because someone had gotten close to her in traffic.

Five minutes later, Laura pulled off the main road and eased up the two-lane street that brought her to their two-story brick house on South Elm. She pulled up the short concrete drive in front of the garage, next to Momma's maroon Crown Vic, and killed the ignition.

It was six-thirty. She gingerly got out of the car and hobbled up the concrete walk leading to the front stoop. Before slipping the key into the slot on the front door, a strange tingling at the base of her neck made her stiffen. Mindful of her balance, she turned around.

The dirty white van *hadn't* turned off. Sometime during the trip home, traffic had separated them, giving her the illusion it was gone. It sat directly across the street, next to their neighbor's faded gray mailbox, and didn't move away until she'd backed up against the door and dropped her keys on the concrete stoop.

***

"Everything okay, baby?"

Momma appeared in the kitchen archway, munching on a carrot stick. She'd already changed into her light-blue bathrobe.

Laura immediately flicked on a bright smile and forced herself to ignore the all-too-familiar stabbing of bright flame racing up her spine. In her panic, she'd twisted around out on the porch, shot awkwardly through the doorway and slammed the door behind her. Now she stood with her back braced against the door, holding her breath while remaining totally still, waiting for the tremors to subside.

And now she had to find some way to convince Momma that nothing was wrong.

"I'm fine. Why?"

"Why're you standing there like that? Is your back acting up again?"

"I sort of stumbled…when I came in."

"I wondered why I heard the door slam."

"Sorry about that. I bumped into it before I could close it."

"You need to be more careful. Are you sure you didn't hurt yourself?"

"I'm sure."

Momma went back into the kitchen.

As the pain gradually became a distant throbbing, Laura began thinking clearly again.

Someone had followed her home.

The very idea was silly. She drove an old Honda, did the books at a local coffee shop, maintained a savings account that barely covered the bank's $8 monthly service fee, and wore reasonably priced, off-the-rack clothing.

Why would anyone be interested in someone like her?

Who would want to bother with someone who took half an hour to get out of her clothes, hobbled around and screamed in agony whenever she stumbled or raised her leg an inch too high while getting out of the tub?

Was it because she was a slender young female? Because most people thought she was pretty? Was it her thick head of hair that looked fairly good most of the time, if she brushed it just right and let it do what it wanted?

Was that what stalkers looked for these days?

She needed to stop letting her imagination run wild. Even if there really was someone following her, that didn't mean they were actually interested in *her*, did it?

Momma would be a much better candidate. She was attractive and in great shape for her age, and pretty much financially independent since the house had been paid for. And, of course, her job working for Sam more than paid the bills...

Enough. This was beginning to wear on her nerves.

She straightened very carefully and slowly turned around. Trembling slightly, she moved closer to the peephole.

The street was empty.

She wanted to slap herself. Just because she'd seen a dirty white van parked across the street didn't mean it was the one she'd seen before. There were certainly more than one or two dirty white vans in town. Even an idiot could figure *that* one out...

Laura suddenly noticed the thick, tangy aroma of Momma's legendary beef stew. Her mouth watered, and the subject of the van and her imaginary stalker instantly dissolved.

She dropped her bag on the recliner on her way to the kitchen and hung her keys on the pegboard fastened to the kitchen wall. She shuffled over to the simmering coffeepot. "How was your day?"

Momma just shrugged and went over to the stove, where the stew popped and bubbled in the large blue spatterware pot.

Laura knew better than press the issue. "Maddie asked about you."

Momma stirred the stew gently with the ladle. "How's she doing?"

"She and Carl are both doing well."

"Tell them I said hi."

Laura had a swallow of coffee. She began thinking about the van again. She wanted to ask Momma if she knew anyone who drove one but knew that would be a mistake. Momma would want to know what was wrong and Laura would have to lie. Laura was a terrible liar. Besides, suggesting someone might be stalking them would not be very bright.

"Well, I'd better get out of these clothes. How's Sam, by the way?"

"I haven't seen him. He's in Wheeling and probably won't even be in town for the next few days."

Laura grabbed her bag as she crossed the living room. Her back still ached; she'd probably have to take a pain pill after dinner.

Before she went over to the stair lift, she had another peek at the peephole.

Still no sign of the van.

***

Crouched behind the wheel of the van, Earl Hinkley squinted into a pair of second-hand Nikon Action Binoculars he'd found at a local yard sale in St. Clairsville a couple of days ago.

He'd parked about half a block down from the Neilson house, on the other side of the street. From his vantage point, the tall rosebush out front blocked part of the front porch; the bushes pressing against the corner of the house concealed the front door. The driveway sat in full view. So did the girl's Honda and the mother's Crown Victoria. The street light at the corner had already come on. Despite the approaching darkness, he could clearly see if anyone came out of the garage.

He'd pulled a giant boner by letting the girl see him. Mr. M had told him to keep the girl and her mother in sight, but under no circumstances should he be seen.

He laid the binoculars on the seat beside him, pulled a crumpled pack of Marlboros from his shirt pocket and shook one loose. He didn't smoke much--usually when he was nervous and didn't have any weed with him. It didn't take a rocket scientist to know that bringing along a blunt for this would be seriously stupid. He was toast if Mr. M found out. Best be extra careful. Maybe she'd forget about him if he laid low for a while. His best bet was to grab a different set of wheels. If she didn't see the van again, she'd probably think she'd only imagined someone following her.

The buzzing of his cell made him jump. Cursing himself for being such a wuss, he grabbed the phone.

The display said, *Unknown Caller*.

Damn. It was probably Mr. M.

He took a deep breath and told himself to hold it together. He didn't want to sound like he was about to lose his lunch. Mr. M could smell fear like a hungry wolf and would know something was wrong.

"Yes, sir."

"Progress report," the low-pitched voice said.

"I'm watching the house right now. The women…they're both there."

"You weren't spotted?"

He shivered. "Not a chance."

"See that you aren't. Just keep a close eye on them. The moment you see anyone wandering around, you know what to do." *Click.*

Yeah. He knew exactly what to do.

He glanced at his watch. It was nearly seven. The women were probably home for the evening and wouldn't go back out until morning.

He'd keep an eye on the house until he was sure they'd gone to bed. Hopefully they wouldn't have visitors. Mr. M said they usually didn't, but you just never knew what women were up to…

He flicked his spent smoke out the window and fired up the van. He'd find a good place down the street to hide the van, come back and sit in the bushes at the corner with his binoculars. He hated sitting on the cold ground, especially at night, but two thousand bucks was good money for a couple of days' work. It would take him six weeks busing tables at the Buffet Garden to earn that much.

Besides, he only had to stay until all the lights in the house went dark.

He had to do this right. You didn't want to cross someone like Mr. M.

CHAPTER TWO

FRIDAY A.M.

At nine-fifteen in the morning, the van was returned to Ralph's Rent-A-Relic on the outskirts of St. Clairsville and replaced with the faded blue '97 Ford pickup Earl Hinkley had been driving since his old man had abandoned it when he'd left town three years earlier. It was unremarkable in appearance and, like dozens of others in the area, butt-ugly--something folks didn't like looking at.

Earl was determined not to fuck up again. He hadn't applied himself in school and dropped out halfway through his eleventh year. He'd done a little time last year, when he got drunk one night and left the local 7-Eleven with a couple of graphic comics tucked under his jacket. Even though Mr. Porter had done him a favor by hiring him to bus the tables at the Buffet Garden six months ago, Earl still occasionally reverted to his old habits by snatching up tips during hectic times.

Sometimes a guy just couldn't resist temptation.

But no more of that shit. This job would give him a fresh start.

Neither the Crown Victoria nor the Honda was parked in front of the Neilson house on South Elm at 9:45. Earl knew not to panic. The daughter worked at that coffee place down the road from the Mall, the mother for some big shot developer in Manville. Mr. M said the mother was good friends with the developer and actually ran the office. She

20

wasn't young but still looked good. Earl figured she might have boffed her boss to get the job.

Hot-looking babes had it made--it was that simple. With guys, it was more complicated. Unless you were rich or famous, or drinking buddies with the boss, you were SOL. Earl's old man had told him about life a long time ago. The old man stayed drunk and sloppy most of the time back then, but he sure was right-on about shit like that.

Earl drove back to Manville and headed straight for the Savings & Loan, where the mother worked. He parked along the curb on First Street, two spaces down from the intersection, where the Corner Newsstand anchored the block. The Savings & Loan sat directly across the street. He decided to buy something to read to pass the time. He'd already had breakfast, so he was okay. He might need a root beer shortly, but he'd worry about that when the time came.

Inside the dimly lit store, a pot-bellied old dude sat behind the counter on a metal stool, sweating over a crossword puzzle. The toothpick half-buried between his fat lips inched slowly from one side of his mouth to the other. He didn't look up when Earl came in.

Earl examined the shelves, passing on the girlie mags. He wanted mindless material. He enjoyed salivating over pages of naked babes just as much as the next guy, but dealing with a boner right now would distract him too much.

He grabbed an old *Spiderman* issue, paid, went back outside and climbed back in the truck. Then he squirmed into a comfortable position and opened the comic book. Just when he'd got it spread out just right over the steering wheel, he raised his eyes and saw Barbara Neilson coming out of the Savings & Loan Building.

***

The Manville Drugstore was practically empty when Barbara Neilson walked in and went down the long aisle that led to the pharmacy counter in the rear of the large brightly lit room.

It was time for Laura's refill. Besides, the morning had been hectic, and Barbara needed a few minutes to stretch her legs. It was just one block from the Savings & Loan to the drugstore--a three-minute walk, tops. She'd be back long before she was even missed.

Alicia, the sweet young thing who'd known Laura in high school, appeared behind the pharmacy window, smiling brightly. "Mornin', Miss Barbara. Help you?"

"Yes, Ali. Laura's out of meds. How soon can you have a refill ready?"

"Gimme five minutes."

"Thanks."

"How's she doing?"

"Pretty good, actually."

"Saw her the other day. Her limp's much less noticeable."

"She's definitely getting stronger by the day."

"Glad to hear it. Be right back."

Barbara went down the aisle and began checking out the assortment of hairsprays and perfumes sitting on glass shelves. She picked up a bottle of *Tabu* and examined it. When she put it back, she suddenly discovered that she had no idea where she was.

Great. I've zoned out again...

The last she remembered, she'd just talked on the phone with Sam, who was now in Pittsburgh, working on a land deal. Knowing Sam as she did, she guessed he'd be there all day but would probably call at least three more times before she left the office for the day.

The last few days, she'd been thinking more and more of her ex-husband Joe. It was probably because of the dream she'd had two weeks ago. She couldn't imagine why she'd dreamed of him after all this time. He'd walked out of their lives five years ago.

Could Joe have been thinking of her? Why would a man think about a woman he'd deserted? Was this a guilt thing? Was he ill? Had he been told by his doctor that he should get his affairs in order?

It didn't matter, did it? He'd made his choice and acted on it. Entirely too many tears had already been shed. There was no reason to re-evaluate things at this point. It was over. She had to move on.

And she *had* moved on. When Sam hired her to work in his Manville office, things gradually settled into a more or less comfortable routine. They had dinner a few times, but it was never a romance thing. Sam had been married and divorced three times. At forty-five, he was much too old and settled in his ways to start another family.

It was the same with Barbara. She'd given birth to a beautiful daughter who'd grown into a wonderful, intelligent young woman. She wouldn't trade their relationship for anything in the world and didn't want anyone new coming into their lives to change the status quo.

She tried once again to analyze her dream. In it, Joe was talking, but his voice sounded muffled. Judging by his tense expression, his message was important, but she decided it was just her imagination kicking in and shouldn't be taken seriously. She'd read that dreams were disposable material the brain processed while the conscious mind was at rest. It made no sense to regard such things as anything but lingering bits of trash the mind hadn't yet gotten rid of.

Apparently the brain took its time dumping certain bits of trash.

Laura's meds were ready by the time Barbara went back to the window. She paid and hurried out of the drugstore.

***

Hidden behind a metal tree crammed with birthday cards, Desmond Roth watched Barbara Neilson leaving the drugstore. One last quick glance at her profile convinced him she was the woman he'd been told about. The photos he'd studied matched her perfectly.

Just ten minutes earlier, she'd come inside and gone directly to the pharmacy area. After speaking to the tiny young redhead behind the window, Barbara began browsing the shelves. She suddenly stopped moving and stared at something on the

24

shelf. She was apparently daydreaming or thinking of something she might have forgotten to tend to. She finally snapped out of it and went back to browsing the shelves. A few minutes later, she went back to the window, picked up a small white bag and left the store.

Meds for her daughter, most likely.

Following her outside and keeping a distance of twenty yards between them, Roth maintained a casual pace as she hurried down the street. When the light changed, she crossed the street, stepped onto the sidewalk, and disappeared inside the Savings & Loan building.

Roth went up to the intersection at the corner. For nearly a minute he stared at the building and wondered if he should follow her inside. Logic told him to wait until she was with her daughter. His trip here involved both the mother and the daughter.

Something began nipping at his senses. It was his gut warning him of impending danger.

Someone's watching me...

Roth had escaped too many close calls to dismiss anything his gut told him. And since last year, when his senses were suddenly enhanced a hundredfold, he knew to pay even closer attention.

Time to find out if someone really *was* watching...

He turned around and hurried back down the street, where the Challenger was parked along East Main.

***

Squinting behind his binoculars, Earl Hinkley scrunched down in his seat.

The dude walking behind the mother stopped at the corner, but instead of crossing the street, he just stood there, watching. Once the mother reached the other side of the street, she went inside the Savings & Loan building. The dude behind her stopped at the corner and stared at the building.

Earl laid *Spiderman* on the seat beside him. By the time he gave the binoculars another try, the dude was gone.

Shit. Earl scratched the back of his skinny neck. This was spooky. There was no way a dude could disappear that fast. No way in hell.

He pushed open the door, jumped down and trotted up the sidewalk. When he reached the end of the block, he peered around the corner.

A bunch of people were coming out of stores. Others crossed the street or got out of their cars. Some sloppy-dressed old dude with long gray hair and a white beard hunkered down at the other end of the block, hawking something brown into the storm drain.

Earl caught a glimpse of the dark-haired dude getting into a gray Challenger about halfway down the block, in front of Dottie's Meat Place. At the first break in traffic, the Challenger pulled out.

Earl bolted back to the truck, climbed in and picked up the binoculars. The light at the intersection changed. The Challenger came to a stop.

He put the binoculars back on the seat. Why would this dude follow the mother, stop when she crossed the street, then turn around, get in his car and leave town?

The light changed. The Challenger went through the intersection and headed east.

Earl fired up the truck, slammed it in gear and rushed up to the red light. While he waited, he picked up his phone and pressed the number on speed dial.

"Wheeling Investments," said the lady answering the phone. "How may I direct your call?"

Earl tried hard to remember what Mr. M had told him to say when he called. *Manville business. And no names. Above all else, don't mention any names.* "I'm calling to talk about the Manville business."

"One moment…"

Click. Another *click*, then:

"Whaddya have for me?"

"Well, sir, I think there might be somethin' goin' on…"

"Call you right back." *Click.*

Earl waited. Mr. M was probably switching to another phone, like those shady characters did in mob movies. This was something he didn't need cluttering up his head. *The less I know, the healthier I glow.*

The light changed. Earl made the left and pointed the truck east. He spotted the Challenger about half a mile ahead, following an old SUV going slightly below the speed limit. Good deal.

His line buzzed. He pressed the cell to his ear.

Mr. M said, "Talk to me."

27

"I think I spotted someone, sir. I'm followin' him right now on East Main."

A pause. "Go on…"

Earl could tell Mr. M was interested, but it made him wonder if he'd jumped the gun. After all, what had he seen? Some dude out there in the street. So what? And so what if he was following the mother? He hadn't actually *talked* to her, had he? He hadn't even followed her across the street or gone inside with her. What was the big deal?

His eye twitched. *Damn, damn, damn. I hope I didn't fuck up again…*

Then he remembered what Mr. M had told him. *Report anything suspicious.* Well, this sure felt suspicious.

"Some dude followed the mother to her building."

"Did he go inside?"

"No, sir…"

"What happened?"

"I dunno. I was watching him, but by the time I picked up my binoculars for a better look, he was gone."

A sudden silence. The big man was probably thinking it over. Earl figured it was good if you told Mr. M something that made him think. *If he thought I fucked up, he would've already said so-- right?*

"Where are you on East Main?"

"I'm about a mile east of downtown."

"Tell me exactly what you saw."

"He was walking about ten feet or so behind her to the end of the block, across from the Savings

& Loan, but when she crossed, he just stood there. He stared at the building for a little while. Then he turned around, went back down the street and got in his car."

"And you're sure he didn't say anything to her?"

"I didn't even see them look at one another, sir."

Another pause, this one longer.

Earl tensed up in the seat. He really hoped he'd done what he was supposed to.

"Keep up the shadow. Let me know where you end up. I'll have someone relieve you fifteen minutes after your next call."

"Yes, sir."

"By the way, what vehicle is he using?"

"He's in a gray Challenger. It looks brand-new."

"Could be a rental. What about you?"

"I'm in a beat-up blue '97 Ford pickup."

"Keep me posted." *Click.*

***

Edna was on the phone in the reception area, talking softly while poring over a file. Her head was down; she was immersed in the conversation.

Barbara tiptoed across the room and quietly closed her office door. She dropped her bag in her desk drawer. Her cell phone buzzed. Only then did she realize that she'd left it on her desk. She picked it up. It was Laura.

"Hi, baby. What's up?"

"Were you out of the office?"

She sank in her seat. "I just stepped out for a minute."

"You sound out of breath."

"Just came back this second. I got you a refill for your meds at the drugstore."

"Thanks, Momma. I just discovered a few minutes ago that I don't have any left. How'd you know?"

"Just a lucky guess."

"You're not worried, are you?"

"About what?"

"Last night, when I stumbled into the house."

"Well, that did concern me."

"I stumble a lot, you know."

"Not nearly as much as you used to. Anyway, I had a few minutes free this morning, so I decided to stretch my legs."

"Well, I called about twenty minutes ago, but you weren't there. It switched over to Edna, and she didn't even know you'd gone. It was kind of weird. I wanted to try your cell but decided to wait a few minutes. I know you don't like me calling you at the office, but I was a little worried."

"I'm sorry, baby. Like I said, I just stepped out for a minute. And you know Edna. She gets so involved in office stuff that she doesn't even know what day of the week it is. What's up?"

"I just wanted to ask if you'd like to meet at the Mall for lunch. There's a really terrific May sale going on at the jeweler's. They've got that gold horseshoe ring I've been lusting over. It's twenty percent off--can you believe that?"

"You've had your eye on that ring for months."

"Well? How about it?"

"Actually, Sam asked me to run over to the Land Office. It's a time-sensitive errand, so I've got to treat it as a priority as soon as he faxes the material over."

"Where's Sam?"

"He's in Pittsburgh."

"How about if we meet a little later? One o'clock, maybe? Maddie won't mind."

Barbara really wanted Laura to have that ring but knew she wouldn't be very good company. Her dream about Joe had unnerved her more than she realized, and she just didn't want to talk about it. She was relieved that she could use Sam's errand to bow out of this without hurting Laura's feelings. "Can we please do this another time, baby? How long's the sale good for?"

"Just today and tomorrow."

"We could run over there tomorrow morning..."

She heard Laura sigh. "I was kind of looking forward to doing it as soon as possible. I just found out about the sale a little while ago. Maddie had the paper lying on her desk. And the store only has that one ring, so..."

"Sorry, baby, but I've really got to take care of this. I'll make it up to you, I promise. If you decide on tomorrow morning, I'll make sure we get there as soon as the stores open."

"If you're gonna be busy, I understand."

"Thanks, baby."

"See you when I get home, then." *Click.*

A soft knock. The door eased open.

Edna poked her tiny birdlike face through the six-inch gap. "I didn't realize you were back, Ms. Barbara..."

"I only just got back a minute ago."

Edna blinked behind her reading glasses. "Why didn't I hear you come in?"

"You were on the phone. I didn't want to disturb you."

"Mr. Albright just called."

Barbara glanced at her console. The lines were all dead. "How long ago?"

"Just a few minutes. He was waiting for me to put you on the line when he received another call."

"Does he want me to call him?"

"He told me to give him ten minutes. Then he'll call you back."

"Thanks."

Edna pulled her head back. The door closed softly.

***

The gray Challenger pulled up in front of the First Catholic Church of Manville. The dark-haired dude got out and went up the walk, toward the stone archway.

Earl parked about a block west of the building and kept the pickup close to a bunch of trimmed hedges a few feet from the curb. He stayed in the truck and tried once again to reason this all out. The way Mr. M had explained it, he was interested in anyone who tried getting chummy with the Neilson lady. Mr. M hadn't said what was going on, but Earl suspected this had something to do with the Wheeling Mob. Nothing else made any sense.

If it hadn't been for the two thousand bucks, Earl wouldn't have accepted this job. He'd heard stories about the Mob and how bad those guys were. But Mr. M had assured him there would be very little risk as long as Earl stayed out of sight and just observed what was going on.

Mr. M had told him the lady's boss was an important developer. Earl wondered if there was some sort of power struggle going on like in those mob flicks he'd seen on TV. Earl had seen enough crime shows to know the Mob liked strong-arming people. They probably wanted some land the developer owned. Or maybe they wanted to blackmail the Neilson lady into betraying her boss or getting him to do something for them. The daughter could even be pushed around if the mother didn't want to cooperate. It would be easy to strong-arm a crippled chick.

But if that dude was after the mother, why hadn't he approached her? Why'd he walk away? Why'd he get back in his car and drive out of town?

And why drive to a church?

It's kind of hard to strong-arm someone if you walk away from them.

Once again, Earl wondered how much of what Mr. M had said was true. Mr. M wasn't exactly an honest dude. Earl figured that out when Mr. M took him outside the Buffet Garden and offered him two thousand bucks for this job. Earl was no genius but knew that was too much money for doing something honest. The job was simple: drive around for a couple of days, keep an eye on the mother, and call him when someone approached her and took her somewhere private. Mr. M would take care of the rest.

Earl sure didn't want to get on Mr. M's bad side. The man ran a bunch of businesses in Wheeling and had shitloads of people on his payroll. Everyone did as he said. For all Earl knew, Mr. M could be one of the big guys running the Mob.

When Mr. M came into the Buffet Garden last week, two other dudes were with him. All three wore expensive suits. Anyone could tell they all had money. Mr. M wore shiny jewelry and a ginormous wristwatch covered in jewels. One of his friends looked like the guy who did commercials for that Wheeling Corvette dealership.

Aaron, one of the busboys, said he'd seen them drive up in one of those shiny stretch limos celebrity athletes run around in. One of the meat cutters had seen them a couple of times but only noticed the jewelry and the pricey clothes when they brought over their plates for the roast beef entrees.

The three dudes acted really secretive as they sat in their window booth at the far end of the big room. Every time someone passed, they stopped talking and smiled, but didn't continue their conversation until they were alone again. Mr. M always flashed a gleaming grin whenever he spoke. He'd even grinned when he'd asked Earl to come over to their booth. The only time Mr. M *hadn't* grinned was when he took Earl outside later on and told him what he wanted him to do.

Once again, Earl wondered about the dude who'd just walked into the church.

What the hell was he *doing* in there?

Mr. M needed to be told about this. Let the big man figure it all out.

Earl grabbed his cell phone.

***

"A *church*? You followed this man to a *church*?"

"I watched him go inside, sir," the busboy said. "The Catholic church on East Main. It's about two or three miles from town, and--"

"I know where the hell it is." From his sixth floor office window, Miles Lester watched the Interstate-bound traffic soaring down North Main. What the busboy just said made no sense whatsoever. Lester didn't like it when things made no sense. It confused him, made him angry and nauseous. Confusion was something only losers and idiots had to deal with. Confusion complicated things, made it impossible to take care of business. It sure as hell didn't belong in this office.

"You're sure this is the same man you saw in town?"

"Yes, sir."

"And you're positive he didn't see you?"

"He didn't see me, sir."

A church... What the hell was going on?

"Sir, I could go inside. Maybe if I see what he's doin', I could--"

"Stay where you are." Lester scratched his jaw. No need for this to get any weirder. For all they knew, some innocent schmuck could have been walking up to the light just a few steps behind the Neilson woman when he suddenly remembered something important. Or maybe he got an emergency call on his cell.

But why drive to a church?

In any event, it had to be checked out. It just seemed suspicious that some innocent schmuck would watch the Neilson woman walk into a building before deciding to turn around and walk away. If the busboy was right, this schmuck was indeed following the Neilson woman.

"Where are you now?"

"I'm parked half a block down, on the main stretch, in some bushes. I can barely see his car through the trees."

At least the idiot had done *that* right.

"You're hidden from view, then?"

"Yes, sir."

"And you parked *after* he'd already pulled into the lot? Not before?"

"I was a block away when I saw him pull off."

Hopefully the busboy wasn't giving him a line. All kids were pathological liars. And when they didn't want to look or sound stupid, they lied even worse. "Like I said, stay in your vehicle. I'll have someone meet you there in fifteen minutes."

"Yes, sir."

Lester cracked open the phone, removed the SIM card and dropped the pieces in the wastebasket. He grabbed another burner from the pile in his desk drawer, opened it and punched the appropriate numbers. His hand began shaking, but he couldn't help it. Lester was always uneasy when

36

he made this call. The man he was about to talk to was as powerful as they came. Life was so much easier when you stayed on his good side. For that, you had to keep him informed. He just didn't appreciate being kept in the dark.

A female voice with a thick Hispanic accent came on. "ABC Messages, how shall I direct your call?"

"I'd like to speak with seven-seven-four-three."

"Who's calling?"

"This is two-six-zero."

"One moment…"

A series of clicks.

"You have something for me?" asked the low-pitched voice.

"We think someone might have tried making contact in Manville."

"How reliable is this intel?"

"Right now, it's speculation."

"When will you know for sure?"

"I presently have someone watching closely."

"Watching *what* closely?"

"Someone was seen following the woman on the street."

"Was contact made?"

"No."

"None at all?"

"No, sir…"

A pause. "It's not much."

"I agree, but it's something."

"Maybe someone just happened to be walking in the same direction. There are almost five thousand people living in that hick town, from what I understand…"

"Agreed, but we've got to make sure."

"And how long should this take?"

"Like I said, we should know pretty soon."

"We need to know *before* something else happens. I want to know the moment anyone approaches this woman and starts talking to her."

"I understand that, sir."

"Other women are out, so don't even worry about them. So is anyone local. We're looking for a male between the age of thirty and forty, probably well-dressed, and someone who doesn't look local. Anyone driving a rental car is probably a good guess."

That told him they could be on the right track in this case. "The man we're checking on right now could be driving a rented Challenger."

"Perfect. If this doesn't turn out, do you have any connections with rental agencies in the area?"

"I know a couple of people running agencies in the Wheeling area and a man who owns one in St. Clairsville. Someone coming from Orlando would probably rent something at the airport. I think we should check out this lead first. If it doesn't pan out, I'll try something else."

"Whatever. Remember--no one local. No women. No one in overalls. No one chewing tobacco, sporting a gray beard, or one of those baseball caps that advertises the local feed store. In other words, no good ol' boys. If it really is someone from down here, he'll probably look like someone who works in an office--get it?"

"Yes, sir."

"You'd better. A lot of money is riding on this."

"I've got some local kids looking around. I haven't told them much, so they won't ask questions."

"Kids?"

"Bouncers. Local punks who'll do anything for easy money."

"What were they told?"

"Very little. I figured you wouldn't want anyone else to know what this is all about."

"You figured right. Call when you know something." *Click.*

Lester removed the SIM card from the burner, tossed it in the trash and pressed a button on his intercom.

"Yes, sir?"

"Get me Johnny Favor. I need to speak with him immediately."

***

Rosellino's Men's Club had just opened for the day. Sonny Luponi, the club's barman, usually unlocked the front doors at eleven, and the bar customarily saw a respectable number of transactions by the time Dom Tortelli wheeled out the buffet entrees at eleven-thirty.

Johnny Fabborini, known as Johnny Favor to his friends and business associates, had been managing the popular Wheeling club since Benito "Uncle Benny" Rosellino, the club's owner for the last twenty-seven years, suffered his third heart attack and agreed to let Johnny, club promoter and manager for the last eleven years, take over.

About half an hour after the doors opened, Johnny came in. Four males and two females sat on barstools, quietly sipping drinks. All four wore business attire. One of the men spoke into a cell phone. The women carefully stirred their mixed drinks with their straws as they chatted. Sonny stood at the other end of the bar, wiping down a spill.

Johnny went down the hall, past the stairs and rest rooms, to his office in the rear of the eighty-year-old brick building. Amy was on the phone in her little cube when he came in. She didn't look up when he passed.

Johnny headed straight for the coffee station, grabbed his brown mug and poured a cup. He slipped into his office, sunk into the comfortable high-backed leather chair and sipped the strong, hot brew. He'd had two cups before leaving his apartment, but Amy always made better coffee than Brandi, his third and present wife. He set down the mug when his intercom buzzed. "What is it, babe?"

"It's Miles Lester, boss," Amy said. "He says it's important."

An easy grin took over Johnny's dark, pockmarked features. Lester was an important associate and an invaluable contact. He'd asked Johnny for his help several times in the past, and each occasion had brought in serious cash. Judging by their last talk a few days ago, Johnny suspected something big was going down in Orlando, Florida, and that Lester was going to need Johnny's assistance.

"Switch him over," he told Amy.

Click.

"Johnny?"

"How goes it, Mr. Lester?"

"Could be better."

"What's goin' down?"

"That Orlando matter we discussed coupla days ago."

Lester had been asked to do a favor for an important Orlando contact. Lester was to keep an eye out for some Manville woman who could be getting in touch with an out-of-towner on the outs with some big boys down there in sunny Central Florida.

"I remember," he told Lester.

"Well, it looks like I'm gonna need your help sooner than I thought."

"Any changes to this gig?"

"The very same deal."

Johnny sat back.

"You still in?"

"Yeah..."

"You sound...well, uncertain."

"Just wanna know what's goin' on."

"Nothing's changed, like I just said."

"And we're still talking the same amount?"

"Twenty-five K."

Twenty-five K just for keeping an eye on a middle-aged woman and her crippled daughter seemed like a lot of jack, but since Lester wouldn't go into much detail, Johnny knew how stupid it would be to cause problems. Johnny suspected some dangerous local characters could be involved in this. If he was right, the best thing he could do was keep quiet. Johnny had known about the Mob all his life and avoided getting close. He knew Lester could be directly involved but was careful to give the man his space and not ask too many questions. If those boys suspected that you'd opened your mouth to the wrong folks, you became dead real fast.

The only safe way of doing this was quietly and under the radar. If they were lucky, this might not be too much of a big deal. Pay his boys five grand each and pocket the rest. Johnny was the planner and wouldn't be doing any of the heavy lifting. When you were looking the big four-oh in the face, you started taking things easy. Besides, setting up something like this was the tricky part.

"Anything else on your mind?" Lester asked.

"No, sir."

"I'll keep in touch."

CHAPTER THREE

Earl couldn't stop wondering what the dude was doing in the church. Something about all this didn't make sense. Mob guys didn't go to church, did they? Especially in the middle of the day. This wasn't even Sunday, for Chrissakes...

What have I gotten myself into?

Mr. M had been pretty tight-lipped about all this. Everyone knew rich people never got rich by being honest or talking too much. It just didn't make sense that an honest man would approach a total stranger at a buffet restaurant and offer him quick money just to follow someone around. Why not pay someone he knew and trusted to do the job?

Like those TV shows and movies about con men and informers... You just didn't mess with the Mob. They took people they didn't like to deserted warehouses, hung them from meat hooks and beat them to death with baseball bats...

No reason to think about *that*, was there? Mr. M told him he didn't have anything to worry about--if he stayed hidden and didn't do anything stupid.

If... That didn't exactly give Earl a warm fuzzy. In fact, it sounded the same as: *We won't use your head for batting practice*--if *you tell us why you were snooping around that church...*

Earl closed his eyes, took some deep breaths and tried to clear his mind. When he thought all the bad stuff in his head had made tracks, he opened his eyes and reminded himself why he was here.

A simple tail job--remember?

Yeah. *That's* why he was here. But right now this felt a lot scarier than just driving around town and keeping an eye on two chicks.

You didn't butt heads with the big boys unless you knew what you were getting into. And you sure as hell didn't do it if you weren't a badass yourself.

What the fuck am I doing? I live in Bridgeport with my mother. I wash dishes and bus tables. I'm five-six and weigh one-thirty after a heavy meal. I've never been a badass and always run at the first sign of trouble.

Most of all, I don't like getting hurt.

His hands began to shake. He needed a cigarette to calm his nerves. He pulled the pack from his shirt pocket. It slipped through his fingers and dropped in his lap. Two smokes slid out and fell to the floor. He picked them up and put them right back. He knew he'd drop the lighter in his lap and end up setting his 'nads on fire. He rubbed his palms together and took another deep breath. The shaking stopped, but a strange tingling started up between his shoulder blades.

I'm scared shitless, and I don't wanna be here anymore.

He needed to split as soon as his relief showed. That's what Mr. M wanted him to do, anyway. He'd just sit here and wait for the next couple of minutes. It didn't matter who this dude was, what he'd done or who he'd done it to. It didn't even matter if he *hadn't* done anything--or if he was the parish priest dressed in civvies. All that mattered was keeping the Challenger in sight and waiting for the other guy to show.

As long as the Challenger's sitting there, everything's cool...

Once this job was finished, Earl wouldn't have to worry about this scary shit anymore. He'd drive back home and see what Mom had in the fridge. Then go to his room, lock the door, grab his porno DVD collection from its hiding place behind the loose board in the closet, shove Gia Paloma, Madison Young or Adrianna Nicole into the machine, turn on the TV, lie down and enjoy himself.

Yeah, this couldn't be simpler.

But the urge to split quickly grew unbearable. He began squirming in his seat as he stared at the rearview, waiting for his relief.

Nothing. The side mirrors. Nothing. The rearview again. Not a damned thing.

C'mon, c'mon... Get here, dammit...

What if the dude came outside right now, got back in the Challenger, and drove away?

Shit. I'll have to follow him again.

His hands shook even worse. *Damn, damn, damn. Why the fuck did I agree to do this?*

Maybe he didn't have to wait here after all. He could just drive away and hope the other guy Mr. M had sent would pass him on his way back to the Interstate. That sounded reasonable, didn't it? They knew where the church was; they didn't need him anymore.

It was time to get out of here, and if Mr. M didn't like it, Earl would give him back the money.

With trembling fingers, Earl reached for the ignition--

A harsh tap on his window.

A chill raced down his spine. He'd expected to see the face of the other guy Mr. M had sent. But in that same moment he remembered that he hadn't heard anything or seen anyone approaching.

Earl jerked his head around. He felt his body turn ice-cold as the dark figure with steel-gray eyes gestured for him to roll down the window.

* * *

Brad Jacobson, Special DEA Investigator for the Orlando Police Department, followed his partner Billy Osmond and twelve other DEA cops out of the conference room. The lunch hour was approaching and hall traffic was already heavy.

Jacobson's cell phone buzzed. He fished it out of his pocket and kept walking.

The display said, *Unknown Caller*. His pulse hammered. *Cool it. You can't let anyone know what's going on. Especially Billy.*

Only an idiot or a die-hard masochist would want to take this call. But he knew better. He glanced at Billy and forced a grin. "I have to take this."

"Talk later." Billy kept moving down the hall toward the elevators.

His arm suddenly felt like it weighed a ton, but Jacobson managed to lift the phone to his ear. "Jacobson," he whispered, turning away from the slow-moving knots of passing cops.

A click, followed by another click.

"You alone?" asked the low, abrupt voice.

"At the moment."

"I just talked with one of my associates. I may need some work done in Southeastern Ohio. Manville, to be more precise. It's a small hick town about twenty miles west of Wheeling, five miles south of Interstate 70."

Some work done. This man's terminology made Jacobson's skin crawl. It gave these arrogant dregs a sense of false security, letting them think they could talk freely without others suspecting what they were actually doing.

But the terminology wasn't what concerned him. An extremely unpleasant job would certainly follow once he'd arrived in Ohio. And if anyone discovered what he was doing, his career would be toast.

"You still there, cowboy?"

"Yeah." He used the stairs to return to his third floor office. He didn't want to bump into anyone and give them any indication that he was on the phone with a notorious criminal.

"Listen to me, cowboy, and listen good. You don't have to do this if you don't want to. I can get somebody younger and much smarter--someone who knows how to take orders better than an asshole like you. Just remember what happens if I'm forced to do some comparative shopping. I really don't like comparative shopping. It takes too much time out of my hectic schedule and often makes me cranky and unfulfilled. Understand?"

Jacobson understood only too well. He also knew that if he didn't jump some dangerous hoops for this bastard, he wouldn't see Jennifer or his ten-year-old twin daughters, Wendy and Amber, ever again. And his career with law enforcement would be over.

"Yeah."

"It's nice to know we're on the same page."

Fighting organized crime was extremely difficult and dangerous. It put a cop in contact with scum and forced him to dirty his hands. But in the process, it often dirtied them so badly that all the scrubbing in the world couldn't get them clean again.

Jacobson had been an investigator for nine years and was responsible for closing down dozens of escort services, drug drops, stash houses and countless other illegal operations. He'd been shot twice, stabbed three times, beaten up half a dozen times and threatened more than he cared to remember. But he always had the satisfaction of knowing that by the time he left the Station after a tough day and went home to his family, he'd made Orlando a little safer.

Jacobson wasn't about to let anyone ruin his life or career--least of all this dirtbag. He promised himself long ago that he'd find some way to break free from his slimy claws.

He opened the office door and slipped inside. The frantic clicking from keyboards filled the large area. His cube was the first one on the right, about ten feet behind the coffee station. Luckily, the next cube was empty. He went right in and collapsed in his chair.

"Still there, cowboy?"

"Yeah." He kept his voice low.

"You sound…well, tired."

"I'm just dandy."

"What's with the attitude? No offense, but yours sucks the big one, cowboy."

He wanted to toss the cell down the toilet and wash his hands. His gut burned as if he'd just swallowed a plate of red hot chili peppers. He always felt this way whenever he was forced to deal with this bastard. But he couldn't do anything about it--not right now. This man had his balls in a death grip, and a man could only move in one direction under those circumstances.

A quick glance at his wife's photo on his desk instantly doused the flames in his gut, and he began breathing normally again.

"Well, cowboy? Are we on the same page or what?"

"I really don't have much of a choice, do I?"

A chuckle. "I guess that'll have to do for now. What I might have mentioned to you before is in the works, and I'm going to need your professional services, understand?"

He hated the way this man continuously belittled him. Bad enough the bastard had stuck that stupid "cowboy" moniker on him. "Yeah."

"I'll need you to take off work for a day or so, say, in the next couple of days."

The Division Captain had been hinting that Brad take off a week this month anyway. However, this bastard didn't need to know that. "I'll try."

"Just do it. Don't plan anything meaningful or fun with the family for a while. Since I'm your Number One Guy right now, this means you'll probably have to sleep in the garage for the next couple of weeks--understand?" *Click.*

Yeah. His Number One Guy...

Jacobson snapped the cell shut and tossed it on his desk blotter. He leaned forward, his elbows resting on his thighs, and forced himself to relax. Then he stared at the trashcan and hoped he'd have enough time to yank it toward him if he felt the sudden urge to toss his breakfast.

***

Miles Lester shrugged into his dark-blue tailored Armani jacket and stepped into his private office bathroom to give himself a last-minute inspection before leaving for lunch. He gave his hair a quick smooth-over with the pick, careful to pull as many jet-black strands as he could find to cover the growing bald spot taking over at the crown, then darkening the works with a light dusting of *Toppik*, which he kept in his medicine cabinet for emergencies. After dabbing his cheeks with a generous splash of *Obsession for Men*, he winked in approval before going back out into the office.

His cell buzzed.

The display said #21. Johnny Favor had handed out several burn phones to his boys for this latest bit of business. #21 was assigned to Ralph, the musclehead Favor had chosen to relieve the busboy outside the Manville Catholic Church.

"I expected to hear from you earlier." Lester checked his Rolex. "How long does it take to drive ten miles on the Interstate?"

"About seven, eight minutes..."

"It's been half an hour since I called Favor about this. Didn't he get with you? Couldn't you find the church?"

"Found it right off, sir."

"The busboy should've been right there. I told him to stay put."

"He's gone, sir."

Lester froze. "Gone?"

"Yes, sir."

"He told me he was driving a beat-up blue '97 Ford pickup. And he was parked about half a block down from the church."

"No sign of anyone there, sir."

Lester took a breath. "Let's try this from a different perspective. Was there a gray Challenger parked in front of the church?"

"No one there. Just the priest and the clerk."

Goddammit... What the hell happened?

Lester went back to his desk and flipped the phone on speaker. He'd suddenly lost his appetite. He dropped into the chair, pulled his cigarettes out of his shirt pocket, found his gold lighter and fired up. Tendrils of gray smoke immediately drifted up toward the slow-moving ceiling fan.

He'd given a stupid kid two thousand bucks just to watch a middle-aged woman for a couple of days. It was such a simple job, any idiot could manage it. That was why he'd picked the busboy in the first place. A loser was needed for this. His old friend, Aaron Porter, the owner of the Buffet Garden, told him Hinkley lived with his mother, had no friends, didn't talk much and never had any money. And since the kid had had a brush or two with the law, no one would be surprised if something went wrong and the kid turned up dead.

"I gave that kid strict orders to stay put. Whatever would possess him to leave before you got there?"

"Maybe it wasn't his idea."

That was certainly possible. "But if he was spotted, why hasn't he called to tell me?"

"He could be hidin' somewhere. If he's scared, he's not thinkin' right."

Something was slightly off about this.

"He told me he couldn't be seen. Why would he just disappear?"

"The dude the kid was watchin'. Do you know anything about him?"

Lester thought about the kid's last call and felt his blood pressure rising again. "Well, since we don't know exactly who or what the kid actually saw, we have no idea what's actually going on."

"That makes it tough."

Lester felt guilty for not telling these boys anything else, but since he didn't know much himself, he saw no reason to make this more complicated. Besides, he hadn't met a kid yet who could keep his mouth shut for very long.

"He'd call if he saw the Challenger pullin' out, wouldn't he?" Ralph asked.

"The kid's stupid. We have no idea what he'd do."

"So whaddya want me to do now, sir?"

"I've got to make a call. In the meantime, I want you to retrace the boy's steps. Go back to the Corner Newsstand in Manville. That's where the kid first spotted the man in the gray Challenger. If you can't find any sign there, try the Buffet Garden in St. Clairsville. Who knows? Maybe the kid spooked and hauled ass back to familiar territory. If he isn't there, try his mom's Bridgeport apartment. Those will be the places to look."

"I'm on it, sir."

Lester clicked off. Before making his next call, he opened a desk drawer and snatched up the Dewar's bottle.

It was bound to be one long, agonizing day.

***

The half-naked blonde gyrated in perfect cadence to the agitated jungle beat thumping from the sound system on the credenza behind Johnny Favor's office chair.

He felt his blood pounding as he sat through the audition. This babe was sizzling hot, and he cursed himself for squirming in his seat like a stupid kid. Though barely twenty, she had him ready to burst the seams of his silk slacks. He'd been auditioning sexy babes every week for years. He should be used to this, for God's sakes. He was a grown man who ran a club oozing with hot babes. And he sure as hell shouldn't be acting like a punk kid with an angry hornet wandering around loose in his undershorts.

He had to grab this chick before the competition sniffed her out. He swiveled in his chair, reached for the control panel and killed the irritating beat. "I've seen enough. You'll do just fine."

"Thanks, Mr. Favor." Smiling brightly, she bent to pick up her street clothes from the chair in front of the window.

Favor just couldn't get over this babe. Her ass was perfect, and the fact that she didn't have many tatts added to her marketability. In his view, tatts were distracting and counterproductive for a stripper. They detracted from the overall package, shifted the customer's attention away from the good stuff. Besides, too many tatts made a chick look slutty. This babe wore a slim barbed wire encircling her left ankle, as well as a tiny blue Playboy bunny on her right hip. She also had a large heart-shaped black mole just above her tailbone that fascinated him. But the mole was natural.

She was just about as perfect as they came. But even so, he needed to find out something very important before hiring her on. "Take off your bra and panties."

She tilted her head. Her thick blond mane slid down her shoulder in heavy ringlets. Her big blue eyes stayed on him as she reached behind her back to unclasp the pink laced brassiere. It dropped quietly to the floor, and her tits stayed right there, staring at him. Without hesitation, she hooked her thumbs beneath the thin material at each hip and began easing them down.

No bullshit. Not even a second's pause. She was a natural.

"Good enough. You can put everything back on."

She pulled the panties back up and bent to recover the bra.

Favor couldn't take his eyes off those tits. They were perfect--not big, but perky enough and firm enough to keep the customers salivating.

When she was fully dressed, he said, "Stop by Nancy's office on your way out. Her office is on the right if you leave through the back. She'll offer you a contract. It'll prevent anyone else from grabbing you while you're working here. You wanna work here, right?"

"That's why I'm here."

"It's a standard contract, good for three months, and it's for your protection as well as the club's while you're working here. It'll guarantee you twelve full weeks of work. If you wanna leave after three months, there will be no hard feelings. If you wanna stay, you'll be asked to sign another contract."

"Sounds good." She picked up her bag, waved and left.

His cell buzzed.

He sat back and read the display. It said, simply, *ML Investments*. He glanced at his watch--a little early for Miles Lester to be calling. It hadn't been that long since Ralph had left the club.

Dammit. If that steroid freak fucked this up, there would be hell to pay.

"Yes, sir?"

"There's been a problem."

"Ralph didn't deliver?"

"My guy seems to have vanished."

"Vanished?"

"That idiot wasn't where he said he'd be. Ralph called me right off and did what he was supposed to. Right now I have him looking for this moron. We need to find out what happened before something else goes south."

Favor began breathing easier. At least he didn't have to ream Ralph a new one. "Any idea what happened?"

"I've got your boy retracing this idiot's steps. We've got to find him before we can proceed. If something went bad, we need to find out and hope it won't involve the cops. I'm calling to let you know I'm gonna need those other two in Manville as soon as possible. They need to find and keep an eye on the woman we're watching."

"They already have photos of her and her daughter. What's the story?"

"There could be some out-of-town talent showing up. If he's in the area, he'll go after her."

"Are you saying she's in danger? Or is this something else?"

"I wasn't told what's going on. I only know that I'm responsible for keeping watch on anyone trying to contact or take this woman out of the picture."

"How will you know if it's someone out of town after her?"

"We won't. We're to keep a close watch and report anything suspicious. The mother and daughter have a set routine and never seem to deviate from it. If a stranger shows up and spends time with them, we've got to know immediately. Your boys were told to use their cell phones to photograph anyone who goes near this woman or the daughter. They've got orders to send any and all photos immediately to me."

"And if someone does contact this woman?"

"I'm to use my discretion to decide what needs to be done. In the worst-case scenario, we're to gather up the woman and the man."

Favor took a breath. This was beginning to sound like something he might not want to be involved with. "What's this all about? I mean, is there a hit order on this woman?"

"Actually, I wasn't told specifics."

"If there *is* contact…just how do you want this handled?"

"I want her watched closely. If she and a male fitting the general description I provided your boys meet up somewhere, I want them waiting in the wings."

"And then you want these two picked up?"

"Undamaged."

"You realize how much harder this makes the job--especially since we won't know who this stranger is. For all we know, he could be a hitter. I really don't want my boys tangling with a professional hitter. They're bouncers, but they're no more than kids. They wrestle people to the ground and toss them out in the street. They're no match for a pro."

"The man I'm working for wants it done this way. To the letter."

Favor could feel his ulcer flaring up. He had an idea what might be going on but knew better than ask for details. When you knew too much, you tended to get burned. Favor was content knowing only what lay on his end. But this sounded like a major deal. "If they meet in a crowd, this could turn bad."

"Have your men wait until there are no witnesses before they go in."

"If my boys have to wait, this'll turn bad anyway…"

"If any communication is shared with this woman, some important people will be very angry."

"But you just said you wanted them picked up undamaged…"

"I did."

A minute ago, they were talking about surveillance work and a possible scuffle in the back of a van. Now Lester was talking about something else. Favor ran a nightclub and pedaled drinks. He'd been forced to dirty his hands a few times, but that came with the territory. Some unsavory characters were wandering around, and the only effective way of dealing with some of them was to pay someone to tune them up and dump them somewhere.

This was different. They weren't talking about crooks or perverts, or the occasional customer leaving the club without paying his tab. They were talking about a middle-aged woman with a grown daughter. "Listen… I didn't hire on to get involved with--"

"You hired on the moment you accepted the job," Lester said flatly.

Favor sighed. *Dammit...* He'd wandered a little too close to the fire this time.

"Do we understand one another?"

"Perfectly."

"Give me a progress report in one hour."

Favor ran a shaky hand through his professionally styled black hair and struggled to keep his cool. This didn't *have* to be as bad as it sounded, did it? But he had to get everything down right. He didn't want his boys trying to handle this without clear instructions.

"I'll need the woman's name and a few other details. I don't want those boys going in looking like shitheads. They're not exactly rocket scientists as it is. They gotta know exactly what they're supposed to do."

"Got a pen?"

***

Laura hadn't been able to concentrate on anything since she'd talked to Momma. It was twelve-thirty, but instead of logging out and getting ready for the short two-minute drive to the jewelry store, she continued staring blankly at the blue screen in front of her.

She couldn't stop worrying about how Momma sounded. She'd been so *distant...*

Momma hadn't been acting like herself the last couple of weeks. Laura couldn't help wondering if this had something to do with Dad. Laura didn't know what else could be bothering her. Although she and Momma had gone through the grieving process long ago, she believed Momma hadn't healed completely. The signs were obvious. The sadness in her mother's eyes showed at odd moments. There were also periods of silence, when Momma abruptly withdrew within herself and stared off into space.

Laura strongly suspected that the sadness, for whatever reason, had come back.

"Everything okay?" Maddie placed a small stack of receipts on the blotter next to Laura's elbow.

Laura didn't want to tell Maddie what was on her mind. This was a private matter. Besides, Laura wasn't one hundred percent certain anything was wrong. Momma could be coming down with the bug.

"I'm fine."

"I surely thought you'd have logged off by now. It's lunchtime and you're not even out the door."

Laura tried reading Maddie's expression. "Are you hinting at something?"

Maddie chuckled. "When have you *ever* known me to *hint* at anything? I usually just blurt out the first thing that pops into my head and apologize later, when I've realized what actually slipped out of my big mouth."

Laura just smiled.

"Kiddo, you've had your eye on that ring for months. It's on sale now, and I just think it's kind of strange that you aren't already over there, forcing them at gunpoint to hand it over."

"For a moment I thought you were suggesting something about my work habits."

"You're the best worker we've ever had, silly girl. Now get outa here and buy that ring."

Laura logged off. She sat there a moment, wondering if she should even waste her time. Her mind wouldn't stay focused. "I guess I'm just having doubts if I even want it."

"It isn't gonna be there very long, you know."

Laura shrugged.

Maddie's dark red brows knitted together. "*Is* there something you're not telling me? If there is, you know I've *got* to pull it out of you, right?"

"I'm fine, Maddie. Really."

"All right, then. Get out of here. And don't come back without that ring."

Laura squirmed into her jacket, left the office, and made her usual stop in the bathroom. Ten minutes later, she went out into the cool, sunny afternoon and shuffled over to the Honda, knowing full well that she wasn't going to the Mall. She had no intention of fighting the hectic lunch crowd--not when something much more important could be amiss.

What really mattered was making sure Momma was all right.

***

Miles Lester parked the silver Caddie in one of the six reserved spots in front of the popular Wheeling eatery and flicked off the engine. *Cusina Romana*, one of the best Italian restaurants in the tri-state area, awaited him just fifty feet away, at the end of the cobblestone walk. The place offered the best shrimp pasta in the city. He'd been thinking of nothing else since he'd left the office.

After that irritating business with the missing busboy, he intended to treat himself with some high-quality food, a small bottle of wine, and a little relaxation.

His cell buzzed. Groaning softly, he pulled it from his jacket pocket and flipped it open.

The display said #21. Hopefully, Ralph had located the busboy, and they could finally figure out what the hell was going on.

"I'm listening."

"Found 'im, sir," Ralph said flatly.

Lester sat back in the leather seat. This was good news. At least, it *should* be. However, Lester could sense the negative vibes coming through the line. Judging by his tone, Ralph was definitely not happy. This meant the busboy was probably dead.

"Where'd you find him?"

"At the Buffet Garden, sir."

Lester gasped. Why would anyone dump a body there? The stupid kid worked there; he'd be identified right off. The cops would be notified immediately, and the damned thing would hit the Wheeling and Pittsburgh stations before the dinner hour.

Whoever did this knew exactly what he was doing. Now Lester could understand why the busboy was lured to a church. They were obviously dealing with a professional hitter. A pro could spot a tail in his sleep. He'd lead the kid out of town, to some out-of-the-way place with no witnesses. Then he'd circle around and nail him from behind.

"Where'd you find the body?"

"Kid's alive, sir. He's in the dining room."

Had he heard him right? "Say that again."

"He's busing tables."

What the hell was going on?

"He's not dead?"

"No, sir."

"Did you talk to him?"

"No, sir. I wanted to talk to you first."

"And he appears to be all right? I mean physically? No marks on him? Bruises? He's not staggering around? Any sign that he might have been worked over or drugged?"

"He seems all right to me."

This just didn't make any sense. If the kid had been spotted, he most certainly would have been capped on the spot. The Mob had no qualms about capping anyone. No regrets. No guilt.

This was beginning to look less and less like a mob thing.

"Sir? What should I do now?"

Lester started up the ignition. Dammit. This was the second time today his lunch had been interrupted. He'd really had his taste buds set on that shrimp pasta, too.

But this was more important. He had to talk to that stupid kid and find out what went wrong. He sure as hell didn't want the Big Man nipping at his short curlies.

"Stay right there. Make sure the kid doesn't leave the building. I'll be there in twenty minutes."

CHAPTER FOUR

At quarter to one, Barbara Neilson logged out of her computer, got up from her desk and grabbed her jacket and handbag from the clothes tree. It was only a ten-minute walk to the Land Management Office on South Chestnut, so she didn't have to hurry. Sam had called just a few minutes ago, telling her to make sure Peter Foss paid particular attention to specific addendums on pages three, four, and five of the titled documents included in Sam's land proposal.

East Main tended to be hectic during the lunch hour but usually settled down shortly after one-thirty. Her nerves had been jumpy since her talk with Laura earlier and she needed something to calm her down. The Land Management Office was just half a block down from Rafferty's Bar & Grill. After she delivered the papers and talked with Peter for a few minutes, she could stop at Rafferty's on her way back. A glass of white wine would help her relax.

She slid the black leather satchel into her bag, pulled the thick strap over her shoulder, opened the door and went out into the main area.

Edna's desk was cluttered with papers and manila envelopes. Her reading glasses rested on the tip of her nose as she pored over her work. A pencil was clamped between her teeth.

Noticing Barbara, she straightened and pulled the pencil out of her mouth. "Going out again?"

"I'll be an hour or so. I'm stopping at Land Management first. Then I'll probably have a bite. I suggest you send out for your lunch. Unless, of course, you brought something…"

"I've got a tuna salad in the fridge, thanks."

Barbara went over to the door.

"Is everything all right?" Edna asked. "I mean, if Mr. Albright calls, should I tell him…"

"I've got my cell with me." She patted her bag. "See you then."

Barbara took the stairs down to the street level. Stepping outside, she pulled in some cool, exhaust-laden air. Her heart pounded as she hurried down the street, dodging shoppers and folks coming out of stores. A few familiar faces came into view but she merely smiled and kept moving, hoping they wouldn't expect her to stop and chat. She didn't want to come across as being snobbish; she just wasn't in a chatty mood. And in spite of her efforts to stay focused, she couldn't stop thinking about her dream.

It was only a dream. You've been having them all your life. What's so different?

She'd dreamed of Joe before. In fact, she'd dreamed of him practically every night for nearly two years after he left. Was this really any different?

Yes. It was different. She didn't know how, exactly. She only knew that it was.

She didn't think she was going crazy but you just never knew. She'd read somewhere that crazy people didn't know they were crazy, and thus never questioned their own actions.

Did this mean that if she questioned herself, she wasn't crazy?

Or was she just deceiving herself?

Or worse--making excuses?

She had to stop obsessing over this. There was nothing about her dreams that should cause her to worry about her mental state. She was just going through some weird phase in her life.

But no matter how hard she tried convincing herself that the dream about Joe didn't mean anything, she couldn't ignore the overwhelming feeling that something terrible had happened, or was about to.

Focus on your errand. Forget about the stupid dream. It meant nothing.

She approached the intersection of West Main and Chestnut when a sudden shout across the street yanked her back to harsh reality.

"*Momma!*"

***

As soon as the traffic had stopped at the red light, Laura hobbled across the street. As she drew closer, she clearly saw the tension on her mother's face.

Momma didn't move. Her face had become a taut mask. Her dark eyes were fixed on Laura. Laura tried to recall everything she'd done and said in the last few days but just couldn't focus. Her mother's cold expression had unnerved her, preventing her from thinking clearly.

This was ridiculous. She had to pull herself together.

This isn't some flesh-eating monster from a bad horror flick. I shouldn't be terrified of my own mother...

Trembling, she struggled to collect herself, but the fear and anxiety had made her legs rubbery. For one frightening moment she thought she'd stumble.

She knew she was being silly. She hadn't done anything to upset or infuriate Momma. It was the interruption, no doubt. The sound of Laura's voice had startled her.

Laura took another cautious step.

"Momma?" A lump formed in her throat. "Everything okay?"

"I'm busy right now, baby."

Laura stiffened at the negative energy oozing from her mother. She really shouldn't have come here. Momma had told her about her errand. She'd also said that they could go to the Mall tomorrow morning.

But this doesn't explain why Momma looks so angry...

"Have I...done something wrong, Momma?"

Momma blinked and took a deep breath. Her features relaxed, and a smile appeared. Laura began feeling a little better. Perhaps Momma *was* deep in thought after all.

"You surprised me, baby." Her voice had become softer, gentler. "I thought you'd be at the Mall, buying your ring..."

"Well, I *wanted* to, but..." It wouldn't be wise to tell Momma that she'd rushed right over because she was worried. Momma didn't like anyone changing their plans for her sake.

"But what, baby?"

67

Laura struggled to think of a good excuse, but her mind refused to cooperate. Now she felt even guiltier for coming here.

"You've wanted that ring a long time."

Laura wanted to disappear--or at least say something that wouldn't make her sound like an idiot. She should've just gone to the stupid Mall and bought the stupid ring. Momma was a grown woman; she certainly didn't need a babysitter. Laura shouldn't be so overprotective.

"Well, I just thought...we haven't had lunch together in so long..."

Momma didn't reply; she was staring at Laura's forehead.

"Momma?"

Momma still didn't reply.

"Momma? You all right?"

Momma shook herself. "I guess I'm just a little...light-headed..."

"You skipped breakfast again, didn't you?" Laura remembered the half-eaten piece of toast Momma had left on her plate that morning, before they'd left the house.

"I...can't remember..."

"C'mon." Laura grabbed her arm and coaxed her gently over to the curb. "Let's get you something to eat."

"But my errand..."

"You need something in your stomach. We can have coffee and a biscuit or something. You'll have plenty of time to do your errand."

***

The two young men in the light brown van followed the slow-moving line of traffic heading west, toward the red light at Main and Chestnut Street.

The passenger, Jack "Flex" Stillson, reached awkwardly into his pants pocket for his cell. His yard-wide shoulders and huge arms stretched the flimsy material of his black *GOLD'S GYM* tee shirt, preventing extreme movement in such confined space. The seat belt made things even more complicated. He grabbed the cell and flicked it on. Then he sat back and scratched the red-brown stubble peppering his jaw with his free hand. He'd been trying to grow a goatee for the last six months but wasn't having much luck. He was twenty-two but still couldn't grow a beard. The steroids didn't help. Lucky for him he didn't have to shave for his job. Everyone expected a bouncer to look rough.

He studied the images of the two chicks on his phone display. He and Stomper were being paid five thousand big ones just to follow them around and take pictures of anyone they talked to.

A good-looking older lady and a young babe with a limp weren't gonna be hard at all to watch. Especially since the babe with the gimpy leg couldn't move around very well. She was hot, if you liked gimps. Had a cute little bod, lots of hair-- even a nice face. The mother wasn't bad, either, if you didn't mind older stuff.

Their timing was perfect, it looked like. The chicks were going into the eatery on Main just as Stomper stopped at the light. All they had to do now was set up somewhere close and keep an eye on things. "That's them," he said, pointing.

Stomper just sat behind the wheel and watched. Stomper wasn't much of a talker. He kept quiet and stayed inside his head most of the time. Like Flex, Stomper was one of Johnny Favor's bouncers. At five-ten and one-eighty, Stomper didn't look much like a bouncer, but he'd learned some intense fighting moves during his Saudi stint a couple years earlier--Commando stuff, and even some of that nasty *Krav Maga* Israeli shit tossed in to make things even more intense. Stomper could beat the living shit out of dudes a hundred pounds heavier.

No one messed with Stomper.

Flex pocketed his cell and thought about that heavy-duty lat machine he'd had his eye on for the last couple of months. Sucker could support half a ton and didn't weigh much more than a hundred pounds. With the money from this gig, he could have the machine delivered in the next couple of weeks. In his head, he'd already cleared out the section in the garage where the old man kept those nasty-smelling stacks of old spare tires. Flex could put the lat machine right next to the Power Station. The old man would squawk about it, of course, but he'd shut up about it once Flex slipped him an extra fifty for rent.

The two chicks went inside the eatery.

Johnny had been real specific about what he wanted Flex and Stomper to do. "If a dude shows up and starts talkin' to them, you want us to bring him in?" he'd asked Johnny earlier. "Or just take pictures and send 'em to ya?"

"If you see him talking to the women, or if he takes them somewhere away from everyone, yeah, you're gonna have to bring him in."

"That shouldn't be too tough."

"It isn't that simple. You can't hurt him."

"Why not?"

"I don't know. I'd guess it's because someone important needs answers from him. Use the taser I gave you. And make sure you do it on the quiet. This is important. You can't have an audience. That's an order."

The light changed. Stomper made a right at the intersection and went a little ways up Chestnut. Then he turned into the parking lot behind the Manville National Bank. The lot was pretty full, but they found a space near the far end, facing Church Street.

Flex opened the console and pulled out the Taser C2, with its lithium-powered magazine. It sure was scary looking, but Johnny said it was safe to use, and it worked. Flex had seen Johnny use it on a customer who kept grabbing one of the hostesses and wouldn't leave the club. The gun was good up to fifteen feet, but the damned thing took nearly thirty seconds to put a guy down. Plenty of time for something to go wrong. And if the victim was drunk, it took longer.

Flex pulled up his shirt and slid the gun carefully under his belt, in the small of his back. It was a little uncomfortable back there, but it wouldn't be there long. The shirt hung loosely over his small, muscular waist and couldn't be seen.

Stomper pushed open the driver's door.

"We're not s'posed to do anything, remember? And we're s'posed to wait to hear from Ralph."

Stomper got out and winked.

Dammit. Stomper was definitely up to something. This wasn't good. Stomper loved kicking ass, said it made him feel warm inside. Flex didn't know what Stomper had done in Saudi, but he was pretty sure the dude had seen some intense killing. Flex had never seen him lose a fight.

Still, he didn't think Stomper should take so many chances. There were too many nut jobs out there. So far, Stomper had been lucky, getting the drop on them because they were drunk, and their reflexes were all messed up. Flex could bench four hundred pounds, but even he knew better than go up against some of those nutcases he'd seen wandering around the city.

"We're really not s'posed to get too close." Flex had to make sure Stomper was still thinking clearly. When Stomper zoned out, he just didn't notice anyone anymore.

Stomper slammed the driver's door. "I'm gonna watch things from the bank till Ralph shows."

Good. At least he was still listening.

Flex got out. "I'll be in the knickknack place on the other side of the eatery, then."

Stomper didn't respond as he headed briskly for the sidewalk.

***

Emma's Edibles offered an array of fresh salad dishes, with dozens of soups and appetizers to choose from. The menu included grilled burgers and submarine sandwiches made to order. Mixed aromas of charbroiled steak and cooked onions sizzling on the griddle filled the room as hungry customers devoured the tasty daily specials.

Barbara followed Laura over to one of the two available booths. As her daughter carefully slid into the booth, Barbara found that she wasn't the least bit hungry. She'd experienced some queasiness from skipping breakfast, but that had passed a few minutes ago. She hadn't really wanted to come here; she'd only done so because she knew her daughter wouldn't leave her alone if she suspected anything was wrong.

Barbara was determined not to mention her dream to her daughter. Like Barbara, Laura hurt very deeply from Joe's leaving. Telling Laura about the dream would most certainly bring back the pain.

"Momma? Aren't you gonna sit down?"

Only then did she realize she'd been standing there like an idiot. Embarrassed, she slid in beside her daughter. A quick bite and coffee wouldn't hurt anything. Fifteen minutes, tops, and she could drop off Sam's papers, enjoy a glass of wine and relax for a few minutes before returning to the office.

"Momma?" Laura's voice again.

"Yes, baby?"

"What would you like?"

Barbara suddenly realized they were no longer alone. Pad in hand, Emma's daughter Colleen had snuck over. Barbara wondered how long the poor girl had been standing there.

"Hi, Colleen. How's everything?"

"Fine, Miss Barbara. What'll it be today?"

"I think I'd love a cup of your French vanilla."

Colleen scribbled. "What else?"

"A croissant would be nice. You, baby?"

"I've already ordered, Momma."

"When?"

"Two minutes ago, when Colleen came over."

Barbara smiled sheepishly and glanced at her watch.

"Momma? Are you still feeling queasy?"

"I'm just a little rushed, baby. I told you--my errand."

"Yes, but I thought--"

"I'll be back with your coffees," Colleen said. "And your croissants." She whisked away.

"Momma?" Laura lowered her voice. "What's wrong?"

"What makes you think something's wrong?"

"You're so...tense. You keep checking your watch."

She immediately began drifting away again and no longer heard Laura's voice. She and Joe had come here dozens of times in the past and sat in this same booth. Joe always ordered a rare T-bone steak, seasoned fries and a bottle of dark beer. Barbara usually chose the garden salad, or a chicken sandwich. She'd worked part-time at the bank as a cashier back then. She usually put in twenty hours a week and frequently shared her lunch break with Joe, who, as an independent insurance agent, dictated his own hours.

She remembered the time he'd gone on about a car he'd seen in a magazine. It was a black Audi, and he'd spent the morning calculating how much it was going to cost him in monthly payments. He was really excited about it and told her he'd seen the exact model at one of the St. Clairsville dealerships. He'd wanted to take her to see it after lunch. When she asked him why it was so special, he said she really needed to get in it and experience the comfortable leather interior for herself. And then he told her that she really needed to see its color--

"Momma?"

"Silver." Barbara told him she preferred silver. Black looked all right, but you could see every speck of dirt, and you had to keep it washed and waxed all the time...

"Momma, where *are* you?" Laura shook her gently.

A warm wave shimmered up her back. She blinked. Joe disappeared, and suddenly Laura was there beside her.

Panic tugged at her. She sensed that she'd wandered into some strange sphere. *What's happening to me? Is this all because of that silly dream?*

"Momma? Where'd you go?"

"I'm right here..." *My God... My voice sounds so far away...*

"You seemed a million miles away. And when I said your name, you acted like you were about to come out of your skin. *Please* tell me what's going on..."

She couldn't stay here. Laura would eventually figure it out. She already knew something was wrong. Barbara couldn't possibly tell her that she'd somehow got caught in some weird time-loop, or that she might actually be going crazy.

She opened her bag, pulled a ten-spot from her wallet and dropped the bill on the counter. Then she closed her bag. "I hate to do this, baby, but I really must scoot. My errand..."

"What about your coffee and croissant?"

"Sam wants me to get these papers over to the Land Office. We can do this again some other time..."

"There's something wrong--I *know* there is. *Please* tell me what it is..."

"There's nothing wrong, I just have to--"

"Momma, I'm not gonna let you leave until you tell me what's wrong!"

"Baby, work with me here, okay?"

"I don't like what I see in your eyes, Momma."

Barbara blinked. "What...do you see?"

Laura swallowed. "Dad..."

***

At one-fifteen, the St. Clairsville Buffet Garden continued struggling with heavy lunch traffic. Diners flocked the salad bar and dessert stations while a long line targeted the meat cutter, who stood diligently at his post, carefully slicing paper-thin strips of roast beef and ham and sliding them onto awaiting plates. The three busboys, their shirts and aprons soaked with sweat, grease and

76

gravy, scrambled to keep up, dropping dirty dishes and silverware into gray plastic tubs and stacking them onto the three-tiered metal cart.

Hands on hips, Miles Lester stood in the foyer of the large open area, his gaze on the Hinkley kid. This made no sense whatsoever. Without a word of explanation, the kid left the church, drove here and went right back to work. Apparently the little bastard preferred working his tail off for minimum wage rather than sitting in a truck with a pair of binoculars for a thousand bucks a day.

"See there, boss?" Ralph stepped closer. "The kid looks okay to me."

Lester's neck had grown hot and splotchy. High blood pressure ran in his family. Being forty pounds overweight didn't help. Neither did the heavy smoking, or his penchant for fifty-year-old Scotch and twenty-ounce, blood-rare steaks.

"Something's wrong." Lester loosened his tie. It eased the pressure and made him feel slightly better, but did nothing for the knot in his gut. "The kid was paid off. Nothing else makes sense."

"Maybe the guy he was watching scared 'im off."

"Whoever made the kid haul ass here did *some*thing weird."

"How will ya know for sure?"

That was the thing. Lester *wouldn't* know for sure. He only knew what his gut told him. Big Al hadn't really shared anything with him. All Lester knew was that whoever came from Florida to see the Neilson woman had to be stopped before he had time to do any damage.

Something about all this made no sense. Someone who'd come all this way to do a specific task wouldn't waste his time scaring off a kid. He'd do what he came to do and get out while the going was good.

There had to be a lot more was going on than what Lester had been led to believe. But he knew better than tell these kids his suspicions. Ralph and his two buds would no doubt want to impress him by doing something stupid to show off without considering the consequences. Lester didn't need the clueless actions of three clowns getting him on Big Al's bad side. And since he had no idea who they were dealing with, he didn't want to be held responsible for the deaths of three young men.

"I *won't* know for sure," he told Ralph. "I don't know much more about this than you do."

"Johnny didn't seem to know, either."

The anger trickled back. If word got around that he was involved in something he knew nothing about, he'd be laughed at. He had to get Big Al to open up and give him something. But anyone who'd ever dealt with Big Al knew that getting anything out of him was like squeezing blood from a rock. "It's got to be done," he muttered to himself.

"Howzat, boss?"

"Look at us, for Christ's sake. We're standing here like shitheads, trying to figure out what the hell's going on. I feel like this is some crazy bastard's idea of a sick joke."

"So what do we do?"

"The only thing we *can* do. We question the kid."

"And then?"

"We'll figure that out after we get some answers." Lester turned. "Bring him outside. I'll be waiting in the car."

"What if he doesn't wanna leave?"

"Pick him up and carry him outside. Pretend he's a dumbbell or something. That shouldn't be difficult."

Two minutes later, Ralph, gripping the kid's skinny arm, brought him outside, pulled him around the front of the Caddie and opened the passenger door. He let go of the boy's arm and stood close, dwarfing him. "Get in."

Without a word of protest, the boy got in.

Ralph slammed the door shut and stood fairly close, his arms crossed over his massive chest.

Sitting behind the wheel of the Caddie, Lester smoked the last of his cigarette. He'd wanted a sip of Dewar's from the flask in the console but decided to wait. He needed to stay angry--to hang on to his edge. Besides, he had more driving to do and didn't want to risk getting pulled over on his trip back to Wheeling.

He flicked the spent butt through the open window and sent a thick plume of smoke out with it. Then he turned and carefully studied the boy on the seat beside him.

The kid's face was wet with sweat. There were sweat stains on the front of his shirt and large dark circles under his arms. He was also giving off a strong odor. Nothing odd about that--the kid had been busting his hump since he'd left the church.

That wasn't what concerned Lester.

The kid's face showed no expression. No fear. No tension. He wasn't even shaking. He'd abandoned a simple job that paid him good money. Now he faced his irritated employer. But instead of shitting his drawers, he just sat there.

"Remember me?"

"Yes, sir."

"Like to tell me what happened?"

"Sir?"

Lester examined the boy's eyes. He could tell the kid wasn't trying to hide anything. Whoever he'd met up with might have done something to his head. Sneaking up on a stupid, naive kid would not be much of a problem to a professional hitter, or mob guy. A blow to the skull could cause amnesia or dizziness that might lead to temporary memory loss. But as far as Lester could tell, there was no sign of a blow—at least, not from the front.

"Turn your head."

"Sir?"

"Turn around and look at the big guy standing outside."

The kid turned slowly to his right.

"Now look up. I wanna see the top of your head."

The kid obeyed the order.

There were nicks, scars and tiny bald spots on the boy's damp, darkly shaved skull, but no sign of a blow, gash, or lump.

"All right. Now look at me."

Again, the boy complied.

"I want you to tell me what happened at the church."

The boy stared blankly at him.

Lester blinked. This wasn't exactly a good time for this punk to start acting stupid. "The church, remember? It's got a steeple, a cross, a bunch of pews and a parking lot. Statues, holy water--get it? You said you followed some man there. He was driving a gray Challenger."

"Yes, sir. I remember."

"So why're you here?"

"Huh?"

Lester wanted to slap some sense into the kid but suspected that would do more harm than good. "I wanna know why you're *here*, when I specifically told you to stay put and wait for Ralph to meet you outside the church."

"Ralph?"

"He's that big guy standing behind you. You were just looking at him. He just brought you outside."

The kid swallowed. "I *had* to come here, sir."

"What?"

"I had this feeling…I think."

I think. That was a start, anyway.

"The man you followed. Did he come out of the church and approach you?" He focused on the kid's eyes. "He didn't say anything to you?"

"Everything's kind of a blur."

The boy's eyes were clear, but that didn't mean anything these days. Kids were so goddamned messed up, it took serious study to find one who wasn't smoking, snorting, shooting up, or just plain crazy. "You weren't smoking anything, were you?"

"No, sir."

"But you don't remember anyone talking to you?"

"Like I said, sir, I had this feeling."

"You had a feeling that you needed to come here?"

"I felt like I shouldn't be there...that I should be workin' here."

Weird. What he'd just said wasn't something a dumbass like him would likely say.

"You *wanted* to come back to work? That's about it in a nutshell?"

The boy nodded.

"You *like* working here?"

"It's what I do, sir."

"I get it. It's your calling. You live for it. You don't want anything else. And when someone offers you more cash than you'd normally make here in three months just to drive around for a couple of days, you'd rather be sweating your balls off picking up other people's garbage. Is that what you're telling me?"

"I felt funny, spying."

"You were *paid* to spy."

"I know, sir. But it made me feel, well--"

"Funny?"

"Yes, sir..."

Lester was beginning to suspect that the kid had been frightened--or coerced, somehow.

"What else happened?"

"Nothin', sir."

"You just came here?"

"I don't actually *remember*. I know I must have, because here I am."

"Your truck's parked over there. You don't remember driving here at all?"

"I really don't remember gettin' out of the truck. And whenever I try to remember anything, I keep wonderin' if it was all just a dream."

A dream. Now it was beginning to make sense.

But there was no sign of drug use, or evidence of a concussion. Not that he could see, anyway...

"A dream," he said, more to himself than to the kid.

Who--or what--were they dealing with?

"Sir?"

"What?"

"You want your money back?"

That was the least of their problems. Lester didn't want to deal with this kid anymore. "Keep it."

"You're sure? I have most of it right here in my pocket..."

"I said keep it, dammit."

"Can I...go back to work now?"

"Get the hell out of here."

The kid opened the door, got out, veered around Ralph and sprinted back to the building.

Lester watched him. Why was that kid in such a damned hurry to get back to busting his hump in a crowded restaurant? What the hell had frightened him so badly at that church?

This was way the hell more than weird.

"Sir?" Ralph was standing beside the opened door, looking down at him. "What do we do now?"

"As I told you before, we have to find out what the hell happened."

"I thought you just did."

"Did you hear any of that shit?"

"Pretty much."

"Did any of it make sense to you?"

Ralph shook his head.

"Well, it made even less sense to me." Lester started up the ignition. "Drive back to Manville and get with your two buds. We'll continue this just as if nothing happened."

"You want us reportin' to you, boss? Or should we call Johnny and let 'im know what's goin' on?"

"You three answer to me. And make sure that from now on, you tell me everything that happens. I don't care how insignificant or silly it sounds, I want to know. And be extremely careful. If you see anyone, don't be stupid. And whatever you do, don't try to be a hero. I'll give you a call in an hour or so. And I'll let your boss know the new setup."

He pulled away and hurried toward the main road. As he drove, he took the burn phone out of his side pocket.

It was time to put in a call to Orlando and tell Big Al that something seriously strange was happening up here. Something strange and much more dangerous than they'd expected.

CHAPTER FIVE

The thickset, middle-aged man in the dark-blue custom-fitted Baroni suit slipped outside his Disney Village office building for a breath of fresh air. As always, he felt infinitely better the moment he took in the sweet scents of honeysuckle and looked out at the palmettos, palms and manicured gardens of the Village Oasis Resort, his most successful investment property in the Disney Village area.

His cell buzzed. He pulled it out of his jacket pocket and checked the display. It said simply: *#747*. His broad forehead immediately wrinkled, and his small dark-brown eyes grew intense. He flicked it on. "Start talking."

"It's done."

His face showed no reaction, but relief immediately shimmered down his back. *It's done*. Two words he'd been longing to hear for the last week and a half. The man had come through for him. But that should be no great surprise. When you'd forked out two hundred K to eliminate an exuberant news jerk bent on exposing fraud in one of your enterprises, you expected great results.

"Any problems?"

"None."

"Will there be any word of this on any of the local stations?"

"Not without evidence."

This was even better. With no body, there was no crime.

"I'm pleased. The balance of the wire transfer will be sent to your offshore account."

Click.

He removed the SIM card from the cell, dropped it and ground it into the pavement with the heel of his imported casual. Then he tossed what was left into the trashcan and continued his stroll down the walk to enjoy the beautiful sunny day.

That call had been just what he'd needed. It had even helped take the edge off the last hour, which he'd been spent trying to reason with a bunch of pampered idiots. The stress had been so severe, in fact, that without a word of explanation, he'd left his large, air-conditioned office in the middle of the last conference call.

Those imbeciles working at the City Commission Office were an obnoxious, unpleasant bunch, and impossible to deal with. Zoning issues, business loopholes and tax write-offs were becoming more expensive to acquire and maintain. Filling the right pockets had been getting increasingly trickier. Florida politicians were as corrupt as anyone else, but their insolence had grown unbearable in recent years. In their eyes, the cash crammed into their pockets for certain favors barely justified their valuable time.

His second burner phone buzzed.

The display read: *ML WV*.

The irritation showed clearly on the man's grim, heavy-featured face. That idiot Miles Lester calling from Wheeling again. This had better be good news. Otherwise, he might as well just go back inside and resume fighting with those idiots.

He lifted the phone to his ear. "This better be worth my while."

"Sir, there's been a...new development," Lester said uneasily.

Dammit. That meant more problems. "Explain."

"I really don't know how to begin..."

"Just talk, goddammit. I'm damned busy. I had a rough morning and this afternoon isn't looking much better."

"Something weird's going on. Something just happened to one of my men."

"What the hell are you talking about?"

"It's kind of hard to explain..."

He wasn't in the mood for this. He hadn't wanted to deal with Lester in the first place, but it was necessary. Lester was an important figure in the Valley and knew a lot of people. When you needed to cut corners, you frequently had to make certain concessions.

"I'm in the middle of a conference meeting. Needless to say, I'm not having a good day. I don't want to go back to the meeting pissed. In case I'm not making myself clear, let me put it this way. For the last hour, I've been dealing with a bunch of idiots whose favorite hobby seems to be tossing large amounts of bullshit at me, and in just a few minutes, I have to go right back and sit there while they toss even more of it in my direction. The only things that aren't driving me into a psychotic episode are my comfortable chair, my view of the gardens, and the a/c. In other words, I really don't need anything else adding wrinkles to my mad face right now. So tell me what the hell's going on. Did someone show up or what?"

"We don't know. Not yet, anyway."

"What the hell is *that* supposed to mean?"

"We thought we *might* have spotted someone, but--"

"But what?"

"The man I hired to watch the Neilson woman… He's…not talking about it."

"Is he dead?"

"No…"

"Then why the hell isn't he talking?"

"He seems to be…well, he's not right."

"You're not making any sense. Worse, you're beginning to sound just as stupid and as dense as my last three ex-wives. Did he or did he not see someone?"

"Like I said, he's not right. We don't know what happened--not exactly."

"Did you ask him?"

"I sure did."

"What did he say?"

"It was all gibberish."

"Did you find out if he actually saw someone in the first place?"

"Personally, I think so. I just don't know what happened."

"This man you hired…is he reliable? Or did you just toss a few twenties to the first flake you came across on the street?"

"I gave him more than that. And yes, I thought he was reliable…"

"But you have no idea what happened?"

"Like I said, we're not sure. I suspect he was frightened off, and he disappeared. We eventually found him, but…"

"Why do you think he was frightened off?"

"Nothing else makes any sense. At first I thought he hit his head, or was given something that scrambled his brain."

"Are we talking about drugs? Hypnosis? Or did someone take him aside and tune him up? What the hell are we dealing with?"

"I didn't see a mark on him, but we won't know what happened for sure unless we take him to a hospital or have a

doctor brought in…"

"That's all we need right now--a fucking hospital report on record. Ever heard of a paper trail? Records? Files? Texts? Emails? It puts everyone in the limelight. Limelight is for movie stars, athletes, and politicians. Limelight is something I don't want. I've *never* had my name or picture in the paper, and I intend to keep it that way. Is that clear?"

"Yes, sir…"

"I should have thought someone like you would have realized that." He sat down on the park bench in front of the building. Just twenty feet away, his classic white Bentley gleamed from one of the four reserved spaces facing the palmettos. Something fishy was going on up there. Lester had obviously picked the wrong idiot for this. Now he was trying to cover his pitiful ass.

Lester was typical for a West Virginia backwoods hick. He owned a decent suit or two and half a dozen business interests, but he was still a hick, and anyone with business sense knew hicks lacked normal brain activity.

But the problem remained. Whoever had gone up there to hook up with Barbara Neilson needed to be found and taken out of the picture immediately.

"What should we do, sir?" Lester asked softly.

"Stick to the game plan." Best keep Lester in the dark. If he was told anything else, his lame brain would malfunction, and he'd melt down. "In the meantime, I'll be sending one of my top men up there to take over."

***

Barbara stared at her daughter's troubled face and wondered what in heaven's name was going on.

Was I so obvious? Can Laura actually see what's going on in my head?

Hopefully Laura was just guessing. She might have even been thinking about her father right then. Barbara had no idea how often her daughter thought about him these days. They'd both discovered some time ago that depression stayed at arm's length if such unpleasant memories weren't openly discussed.

This could be the result of their last phone conversation. Laura was excited about her horseshoe ring and wanted her mother with her when she bought it. When Barbara begged off, Laura thought something was wrong and decided to drive to town to see things for herself. Her anxiety grew when she surprised Barbara on the street. Barbara's dizzy spell had made things even worse.

She could understand Laura's confusion. But what she couldn't grasp was why Laura automatically thought of Joe...

"Are you saying you can actually see your father in my eyes, baby?"

Laura sat stiffly in her seat, staring at the table. "I don't know, Momma. I think I might have just sensed something..."

Barbara shifted her attention to the table. Could an inanimate object capture certain memories? Could these memories remain trapped within it for all these years? Could they actually be *felt* by someone?

Surely there was something very wrong with this theory. Barbara could hardly imagine how many others had occupied this same table in one week's time, let alone several years...

But the fact remained: Laura had obviously sensed *some*thing.

"You actually *sensed* your father?"

"I'm not really sure. Maybe I'm just picking up something I see in your eyes. It's something I saw right after Dad left. Back then, I used to see it almost every day. I don't know why I just saw it a moment ago. It could be my stupid imagination. When I'm upset, my brain gets sort of crazy..."

"What exactly did you see, baby?"

"You looked like you'd...gone back..."

"Gone back where?"

Laura shrugged. "To happier times?"

Barbara didn't reply. Her daughter's sensitivity was often terrifying.

"I hope I didn't say anything wrong, Momma. I'm just worried."

"I know, baby. And there's nothing to worry about. I'm just a little rushed and need to get my act together."

At that moment, a tall, broad-shouldered young man came inside and lumbered over to a small table next to one of the windows facing the street. He was around Laura's age and obviously worked out at a gym. He was well over six feet tall and probably weighed two hundred and fifty pounds, with an enormous chest and huge muscular arms.

Barbara turned back to Laura. "Baby, I really hate to leave you, but..." She glanced at her watch.

"You haven't even had your coffee..."

"It can't be helped. I've got to get these papers in before Peter leaves for the day. Sam said he usually takes off early on Fridays, so..."

"I understand, but I really wish you'd tell me what's going on."

"Whatever do you mean?"

"You seemed angry when you first saw me, Momma. I honestly thought you didn't want me around you..."

"Why on earth would you think something like that?"

"You didn't seem to want to talk to me when I called."

"Baby, I just don't have the time to spend with you right now. I'll make it up to you. I promise."

"Then you won't mind if I tag along for a little while, will you?"

"If you really want to." There was no sense arguing. Laura could be stubborn. "But I really do have to get moving." She grabbed her handbag. Just as she straightened, another wave of dizziness swept over her. She sat back down and dropped her handbag on the table.

"Momma?" Laura grabbed her arm. "Are you all right?"

"Just a little light-headed." She patted Laura's hand and waited for it to pass. *You haven't eaten since breakfast. You've had six cups of coffee in the last two hours. Now you want to rush out of here, drop off these papers and dash off to Rafferty's for a glass of wine. What's happened to your common sense?*

The waitress hurried over. "Is everything okay?"

"I'm fine, Colleen. I'm just a little stressed today."

"Can I get you an aspirin?"

"No, I'm okay. Really."

"You'll let us know if you need anything, then?"

"Of course."

Colleen stood there a few moments, nervously watching Barbara. Then she smiled awkwardly and hurried back to the kitchen.

"We really need to go," Barbara said, a little less urgently. She'd better pass on the wine.

"You're sure you don't want to sit here and rest for a little while?"

93

"I'm sure." She got up again, this time easing carefully out of the booth and using the table for leverage.

The dizziness didn't return. She was good to go.

They crossed the room. As she and Laura reached the front door, Barbara noticed that the muscular young man was hunched forward in his chair and whispering into a cell phone.

***

Special Agent Brad Jacobson left the OPD building and went out to the back lot, where his cruiser awaited him amongst the dozens of other vehicles glistening beneath the bright Florida sun. Billy Osmond was supposed to join him in just a few minutes. Then they'd head on over to Church Street Station and hook up with Ronald "Arjay" Johns, Jacobson's most reliable Confidential Informant.

Arjay had recently learned about a large shipment of AR-15's stashed in the trunk of a rental van that would soon be stolen, taken somewhere to the St. Cloud area and stolen again before it could be recovered and taken to Impound. By the time the theft was reported, the shipment would already be on its way to I-95, transferred to another vehicle and taken to Miami, to be distributed to a local street gang.

Although this had happened twice before in the last few months, no one had any idea who was behind it. Arjay had learned that a transplanted Cuban gang specialized in such schemes. He'd also discovered that two members of this group had taken over a couple of West Orlando gangs. This hijacked shipment of assault weapons would prove essential in establishing them as a significant threat in Central Florida.

Jacobson slid behind the wheel and rolled down his windows. He pulled out his cell and placed it on the console. Then he thought about the plan while hoping that the man who'd been destroying his life for the last several months wouldn't bother him again.

But he knew better. The man's shady dealings had lately undergone a bump in the road. Apparently a business associate had been responsible for the death of one of their bookkeepers. Originally considered a simple alcohol-induced highway accident, further investigation raised one or two disturbing questions. The victim's employment records placed him in a business office suspected by Orlando Law Enforcement of criminal activity. But since the dead man had a clean record, his prints didn't show up in any criminal database.

Jacobson knew what this could mean. For one thing, it happened on the big man's watch. Everyone knew the importance of a bookkeeper-- especially in a large business with ties to organized crime.

Whoever had done in the bookkeeper would have access to extremely damaging information. This would raise suspicion and draw attention to the entire organization. Once clients and associates learned what happened, chaos would result. People would want blood. The man in charge would need to resolve the matter immediately.

Even if such information hadn't been stolen or misappropriated, this was still very bad. Operating under such suspicion would be certain disaster for the man in charge. To his associates, he'd look incompetent. To the opposition, he'd look like a clown. A successful business leader has to know how to pick his people. When an employee brought unwanted attention to the organization, it made it appear that the leader no longer had full control. Also, he was obviously unable to instill the fear required in his position.

The big man's associates would begin looking elsewhere for their future business dealings. They might even conspire to have him eliminated. The fact that the big man was highly connected would complicate matters but wouldn't make a hit impossible. Even if he wasn't eliminated, he would lose respect--and along with it, profits, contacts and future ventures. No businessman, legitimate or otherwise, could tolerate such a setback. This was why such a high-priced crook sought out valuable people and blackmailed them into getting him out of tight jams.

Jacobson's military stint in Saudi twenty years earlier had proven both a blessing and a curse. It had earned him recognition when he came back home and embarked on a career in law enforcement, but also exposed him to dangerous criminals. Such men had climbed so far up the food chain that it was impossible to deal with reputable local businessmen without mixing with the vermin.

And since this was the direction in which the world had been moving, it was apparent that it would not only remain this way but get progressively worse.

His cell buzzed. The display said: ***Jennifer***

As always, every negative thought vanished from his head like tendrils of smoke in a blast of wind. However, the grave nature of this latest development had dimmed Jen's bright image, making him realize that his days with his wonderful family could be approaching a dismal end.

But now was not the time to cave in. Jen would sense trouble and ask what was bothering him. Keeping the scum away from his family had proven difficult. He'd promised himself long ago that he'd never bring these bastards into his private life.

"Hi, babe," he said, forcing brightness into his voice. "What's going on?"

"I'm not interrupting anything, am I?"

"Just sitting here, thinking of you. And the kids, of course. But mostly you."

"You're sweet."

"You really know how to bring out that quality."

"You make it easy."

"I'm certainly glad of that." He glanced at his watch. 1:38. *So far, so good. If there is a God, I'll be back in this gorgeous woman's arms in five hours.*

"Honey, I was just wondering if you could maybe stop by the store on your way home and grab me a pack of--"

His phone beeped, alerting him of another incoming call. *Dammit.* His pulse hastened. "One second, babe." He checked the display. Hopefully, it was Arjay calling, or maybe Billy.

Unknown name, Unknown caller. His temples pounded. *Dammit!*

He took a deep breath. *Calm...* Another deep breath and he clicked Jen back on. "Honey, I'll get back with you, okay? It's…the Station."

"Call me when you get a chance. Love you."

"Love you, too." As always, he experienced a deep throbbing emptiness when he hung up on Jen. In this case, the emptiness had become a cold, bottomless chasm. He sat back and took more deep breaths. *Keep the heart rate under control. It's the only way you'll be able to get through this.*

"Jacobson," he said softly, staring at the palmettos swaying in the warm afternoon breeze. Gentle. Soft. Quiet. *That's it...*

"Catch you at a bad time, cowboy?"

The bastard's voice grated into his flesh like shards of glass.

Any time is bad whenever you call, you slime ball.

Telling this crook something like that would only make this worse. The man loved getting off on other people's misery. Best use the opposite approach. The man hated it when he invoked little or no reaction. "I'm fine. Just wonderful."

"Glad to hear. It makes things much more pleasant."

"I'm happy for you." Jacobson forced himself to focus on the palmettos. It helped a *little...*

"That bit of business we talked about earlier. Seems it's happening much quicker than I'd hoped. But it's right up your alley. In fact, you're the first asshole I thought of when it first came up."

"I'm touched." Jacobson winced at the sharp pain in his left hand. He'd been gripping the phone so hard that it had dug into the soft flesh of his palm. He took a deep breath and eased his grip a little. "Just tell me what you want me to do."

"How quick can you grab a flight to Pittsburgh?"

He forced his attention away from the palmettos. "I can be there in the next day or so. Is this your way of asking me to fly there?"

"It's my way of *telling* you, cowboy. Be there by five o'clock."

"Five o'clock?" He couldn't be serious. "You mean *today*?"

"That's pretty much what I meant. In fact, that's *exactly* what I meant."

He had to be totally insane. There was no way anyone could book a flight and fly up there that quickly.

"That's not even *four hours*!"

"Actually, it's just a tad more than three, if you wanna be technical."

"How the hell can I possibly get a ticket and--"

"Don't have a heart attack on me, cowboy. Not yet, anyway. Take a breath and listen. Your ticket's waiting for you at Orlando International. Flight 471. Takes off, let's see...one hour and twelve minutes from now. Better hurry. I hear they don't wait--not even for cowboys."

"You're all heart."

"That's what they keep telling me. Give me a call on that protected line the moment you land. I'll give you your instructions from there. It's now one-forty-three. Make sure you make the call no later than five. Get it?"

Click.

Jacobson dropped the phone on the seat next to him. For the next few minutes he sat quietly, trying to convince himself not to pull his piece out of its holster and shove a .45 slug into his lame brain.

That wouldn't solve his problem. And it would only make life worse for Jen, Wendy and Amber.

He had to find some way of getting this bastard behind bars.

But first, he had to find out who this bastard was...

***

The two women came out of Emma's Edibles.

Flex felt his pulse skip a beat while watching from the storefront window of Manville's Knicks & Knacks. His hand shook as he pressed Stomper's number on speed dial. "Stomp, they're on the move."

"Looks like they're headin' over to the corner."

"Anyone behind 'em?"

"Not that I can see... You saw Ralph follow 'em in, right?"

"He just called and said they were leavin' and that we should be ready."

"I'm out the door."

"I'll be right behind you. Remember…we're not s'posed to get too close, and we move in only when the coast is clear."

The line went dead.

Flex pushed his nose against the window and frowned. Stomper had already crept up to the small crowd at the light, stopping just a few feet behind the two women.

Shit. He's already too close.

Two dudes stood off to the side, about five feet from the women. Neither glanced in their direction, but Flex knew this could be trouble.

He shoved his cell down the pocket of his jeans and gently patted his lower back, where the taser rested. He scrambled down the aisle, nearly bumping into a shelf covered with fragile Hallmark ornaments.

He made it out into the street without incident. Once his heart had settled down, he shuffled up the walk, keeping behind a small crowd heading for the bank at the corner. Just as he reached Emma's, Ralph stepped outside and came right over. "He's gonna fuck this up," he whispered, frowning at the crowd gathered at the corner.

"We can't just walk over there. There are two dudes standin' right there. What if neither of 'em cares about the women? This could make us look like dickheads."

"What if one of them *is* the dude we're lookin' for?" Ralph asked.

"Then we'd better stay back. We can't get Stomper's attention without makin' noise."

Ralph scratched his ear. "Maybe it ain't as bad as we think. The ladies don't even know anyone's lookin' for 'em. If one of those dudes is our guy, he probably thinks he's safe, so we're pretty much in the clear. He won't know about us."

"I kinda think he oughta be paranoid."

Ralph tilted his head. "You know somethin' the rest of us don't?"

Flex shrugged. "I'm just thinkin' about who we're workin' for. Johnny deals with some scary dudes."

"It don't change anything. No one but us knows about our plan. Even if that dude does suspect something, he can't possibly know there are three of us. We'd have to be pretty stupid to fuck this up."

Flex pulled out his cell. "We gotta send pictures over to Johnny."

"Yeah, but we gotta take 'em without anyone gettin' suspicious."

"Any idea how we do it?"

"I think we need to wait, see what happens."

The light changed. The crowd began crossing. Stomper stayed with the flow, keeping about five feet behind the daughter, who hobbled along beside her mother. Directly beside them, the two dudes kept up the pace.

"Stomper needs to pull back," Ralph whispered. "Otherwise, this could turn bad real fast."

"That boy's tough," Flex said. "A lot younger than either of those two dudes. Stronger, too."

"Stomper needs to be back in Iraq, killin' Musballs. He keeps forgettin' he's home."

Flex did a quick study of the two men. Both were well into their forties and neatly dressed. The one on the right was around six-two, his companion half a head shorter. The tall one was balding; the other wore his reddish hair short. "Either of those two fit the profile?" he asked Ralph.

"Nope."

"Even so, this could go south quick. All they gotta do is catch Stomper starin' at 'em. If one of 'em says anything, Stomper will deck both of 'em. The ladies'll freak. And what if the *real* guy is around here somewhere? He'll see everything, get a good look at us, and that's all she wrote..."

Ralph nodded. "We have to pull him back before he blows this wide open."

They hurried over to the corner and jogged across the street an instant before the *WALK* signal turned red.

The crowd ahead of them turned left at the corner and proceeded east on Main while the women continued south on Chestnut. The two dudes turned right and went west.

"Well, at least we won't have to peel Stomper off of two harmless dudes now." Ralph sighed.

"But what do we do?" Flex asked. "Stomper's still followin' the women."

"I'll stay back and keep an eye on things. Less activity here. Both you and Stomp have keys to the van?"

"Sure do."

"Go get it, bring it down Chestnut and find a place to park. I'll buzz Stomp and get him away from them. Then we'll all sit in the van and keep an eye out."

***

Barbara suddenly felt something was very wrong. By the time she and Laura reached the curb and stepped up onto the sidewalk, she suspected someone was watching them. She glanced at Laura to see if her daughter showed any signs of stress. She saw only concern, most likely from Barbara's dizzy spell back at Emma's.

Gripping Laura's arm, Barbara led the way down the street. She could tell someone was walking behind them. Normally, this wouldn't have bothered her, but right now she couldn't shake the feeling that it might be a legitimate concern.

Just turn around and make sure.

What if she was right? What if someone *was* actually following them?

Even if she saw someone behind them, it didn't mean they were being followed, did it? After all, it was the lunch hour--a very busy time of day. There would be dozens of others out and about, tending to their own business.

This sudden paranoia had no doubt been brought on by the dream and her recent dizzy spell. There was no need to think someone was following them.

You need to snap out of this!

A few yards later, as they passed the hardware store at the corner, Barbara turned to Laura. "You can go now, baby. I'll be fine."

"Are you sure, Momma? I don't think I should--"

"I'm fine now. Just go back to work, okay? Tomorrow, we'll get up early and buy that ring. I'm sure it'll still be there."

"Momma, I'm really worried. You almost fainted back there..."

"I just need something in my stomach. I'll grab a bite on the way back to the office--I promise." The feeling of danger persisted. As they continued down the street, it grew stronger.

"Let's get you something at the burger place down the--"

"I said I'm *fine*..." Despite her efforts, a flare of panic stabbed her. Barbara stopped walking. So did Laura.

A quick glance to her right made Barbara realize she'd been right in her fears.

Someone walking closely behind them also stopped and nearly bumped into her. Instead of swerving around them, as an innocent stranger would have done, a young man stood just a few feet away, his gaze fixed on Barbara. Something frightening showed in his cold dark eyes.

"May I...help you?" Flustered, Barbara brought up her arm to push some hair away from her face.

The young man said nothing; his gaze was a mixture of anger and surprise. The instant she'd brought up her arm, he reached out for it with lightning speed.

Oh my God!

The young man's cold right hand closed around her wrist. She caught a glimpse of something poking out from beneath the sleeve of his shirt. It was a tattoo--some sort of tentacle...

I need to protect Laura!

Her thoughts reeling, Barbara sidestepped and tried pulling away. Hopefully, Laura would have time to slip past them and grab her cell to get help.

In the next instant, another man appeared from behind one of the cars parked along the street. He was fairly tall and fit-looking, with short black hair. He moved silently and gracefully, like a stalking cat, lunging for the young man.

Time slowed down, as in a dream. Everything in the background blurred and turned fuzzy—Laura, the two men, the vehicles parked along the street—then immediately dimmed.

Just seconds later, time returned to normal, and the young man was lying on the concrete at their feet.

Before Barbara could process what happened, another young man lumbered toward them from East Main, fists up and ready. He was the muscular boy she'd seen in Emma's.

As the boy charged down the walk, the dark-haired man moved to his right and touched the front of the boy's neck with his left hand. It was hardly more than a tap, but apparently forceful enough to knock him off-balance. The boy was jerked off his feet and pulled backward. His back arched, he slammed to the hard pavement with a loud thump. Groaning, he rolled over to the curb and lay still.

"Momma?"

Laura's voice snapped Barbara out of it. Adrenaline shot violently through her. She grabbed Laura's hand and pulled. Stumbling, Laura gasped in agony. Barbara could feel her daughter's pain but continued pulling her away. She didn't ease up until they were both huddled behind the two vehicles parked in front of the used bookstore. Then, deciding they were reasonably safe, she groped for her bag.

A squad car moved steadily up Chestnut, toward Main. The car stopped where the second guy lay sprawled near the curb. The driver, Deputy Neil Blankenship, spoke into his radio while applying the brake.

Laura smiled through her pain and squeezed Barbara's arm. "We'll be okay now, Momma."

Barbara turned to where the dark-haired man had been standing.

He'd disappeared.

***

The police cruiser stopped on Chestnut about a block south of Main. The door flung open and the big cop got out.

Swerving out of the way, Flex eased the van south, slowing down just a little for a quick peek. He put on his bored-to-tears expression in case the cop was watching. Just some dude passing by, checking out the action.

However, the sight jarred Flex so much that he nearly lost control of the van.

Stomper lay on the walk behind an old pickup, his head rolling from side to side. Ralph sprawled on the ground about ten feet down, rubbing the back of his head. As the cop walked over, Ralph struggled to sit up. The two women huddled between pickups parked in front of Oscar's Used Books, both obviously shaken up.

There was no sign of anyone else.

What the fuck happened here?

Flex inched the van farther down the street. This area would be crawling with cops in no time at all. Cops didn't handle things solo anymore--too many nutcases running around. Nowadays they called for backup for most everything. Something like this--two dudes beaten up, two women standing off to the side, freaking out—was a big deal in this piss-ass little town. Every cop in Manville would be here in fifteen minutes.

Flex couldn't possibly get Stomper and Ralph out of here with that cop right there and more bound to show. But he had to do *some*thing.

Mr. M was the one in charge. *He* was the one who had to know what was going on.

Flex drove another hundred yards or so and pulled into the Family Dollar Store about a block and a half down from the action. He parked in a space facing Chestnut and whipped out his cell.

Mr. M answered on the first ring. "What's going on?"

"Big trouble, boss." Flex's pulse raced. He hoped he'd be able to give the man the details without sounding like a dickhead. Mr. M might get the wrong idea and decide he was responsible for this.

"Hold on." There were a couple of clicks as Mr. M did his thing to scramble the line. "What sort of trouble?"

"Ralph and Stomper, they've been roughed up, and--"

"Roughed up?"

"I dunno what happened. I was--"

"You're there with them, aren't you?"

"They're across the street, and I gotta stay here, or I'll get hauled in…"

"What the hell is going on over there?"

Flex swallowed audibly, his pulse racing even worse. The man was getting antsy. *This isn't your fault, so stop sounding guilty.* "Ralph told me to fetch the van. He and Stomper were followin' the two women. Like I said, I dunno what happened, but they're both lyin' on the ground, and--"

"*Who's* lying on the ground?"

"Stomper and Ralph. They're all messed up, and this cop just showed up, and he's gonna take them in--"

"Cop?" Mr. M groaned. "You mean the *cops* are there?"

"I couldn't stick around, so I just drove on by--"

"Who else is there?"

"I didn't see no one else, boss."

"What the hell are you talking about? *Some*thing happened to those two. You *sure* you didn't see anyone else?"

Whoever did all this just disappeared, he wanted to say. But he knew better. "Nobody, boss."

"So what the hell happened to your friends? They just got into it and dropped each other to the ground?"

"I don't think they did it to themselves, boss…"

"Didn't you just say you don't see anyone else in the area?"

"I don't see anyone but the two ladies, Stomper and Ralph, and the cop. If someone else did this, they sure did it quick. Stomper and Ralph are tough dudes. They were most likely suckered. I was only gone two minutes."

"Where'd you go?"

"Ralph told me to get the van."

"Why?"

Flex hesitated. *Tell him. Otherwise, you'll end up taking the rap for this.* "Stomper was followin' the women. Ralph didn't want him gettin' too close, so he told me to get the van. He was gonna get Stomper's attention and we were gonna watch the women from inside the van once I found a good place to park."

"And you didn't see anyone else before you went to get the van?"

"No, sir."

"Tell me what happened when you left them."

"We were parked on the other side of the bank. It only took me a minute to drive back down to Chestnut, where this was all goin' down. I even got the green light, but by the time I got there, Stomper and Ralph were already down."

"So what's happening right now?"

"The cop's talkin' on his radio."

"What about the women?"

"They're right there. I don't know if they were the ones that called it in, but--"

"Get out of there."

"Boss?"

"Those two idiots are about to be hauled in. That means I've got to call in a favor to make this right. If you don't get out right now, they'll drag *your* ass into it and I'll have to call in a *bigger* favor. I don't like dealing with cops. I have to suck down half a bottle of good Scotch every time I'm forced to deal with the morons."

"But what about Ralph and Stomper?"

"Don't worry about them."

"But it looks like they're about to be taken in--"

"Get the hell *out* of there. I'll take care of this." *Click.*

Flex shook his head. *Get out of there.* Easy for *him* to say. He wasn't sitting there helplessly like a schmuck. Right now the cop was cuffing Stomper and checking his pockets.

Flex put the cell on the console. There had to be something he could do about this...

He grabbed the gearshift and froze.

Lights flashing, two more cop cars rushed down from Main and pulled in front of the first cruiser.

CHAPTER SIX

Sheriff Bill Kloss lumbered back into his office carrying two Styrofoam cups of steaming coffee. He placed them carefully on the edge of the table, just a few feet from where the ladies sat facing him. Neither acknowledged his efforts.

He couldn't blame them much. They were all done-in and needed a good lie-down. Poor Miss Barbara just sat there, looking down at her lap. A damn shame, a fine-looking, proper lady like her going through something like this. She hadn't had an easy time of it the last few years.

The daughter had it even worse, some damn idiot nearly doing her in on the Interstate just a couple years ago. No one should have to go through something like that.

Laura held her momma's hand, squirming a little in her seat every now and then. He could tell she was hurting.

Kloss circled the desk and lowered his fleshy butt onto the padded cushion of his swivel chair. "Coffee's fresh and strong." He picked up his own mug. It was still hot even though it had been sitting there the last fifteen minutes. "Hits the spot, too." Alice made the best java, always had a fresh pot going, bless her heart.

He set his mug down, pulled out a fresh sheet from the stack in his top drawer and laid it on the desk in front of him. Found a pen from the bunch in the plastic cup. Darned thing worked on the first try, too.

Kloss jotted down the time and date.

The mother kept staring at her lap. The daughter gazed in his direction, but he didn't think she was looking at him. She could've been daydreaming, wanting to be somewhere else. Home, maybe--or at the coffee shop, where she worked. Any place but here, no doubt. Police stations were like hospitals--no one wanted to go near them, let alone spend time in them.

"Neil told me you said someone else was involved in this." Since Miss Barbara had obviously zoned out, he concentrated on working with the daughter. "*You* told him that, didn'tcha, young lady?"

"Yes," she said softly.

Good start. "I take it you know this man who helped ya?"

She shrugged.

Hmmm... That made no sense. These women had been living here all their lives. They should know everyone in town. Were they saying a *stranger* had shown up and helped them? "You sure about that?"

"I didn't get a good look at him." Miss Barbara decided to rejoin the real world.

"Me neither," Laura said.

Kloss scribbled carefully onto the sheet. "Any idea why some stranger would risk his own neck helpin' out the two of you, then skedaddle when Neil showed up?"

"No idea," Laura said.

The negative vibes coming from her made him curious. Her big green eyes had grown larger. "In other words, neither of you has any idea why this

113

stranger just popped up from out of nowhere, beat up two scumbags dead-set on robbin' you, then left the scene just before my deputies arrived?"

Laura shook her head.

"It sounds strange, doesn't it?" Miss Barbara said.

Kloss was getting a strong sense that something else was going on. A fella only disappeared like that when he didn't want anyone to know he was there in the first place.

But he had no idea where this was going. Criminals weren't exactly known for being so helpful...

"Where were ya before this all happened?"

"Emma's," Laura said.

"For lunch?"

A nod.

"And you were just walkin' along when those two jumped ya?"

Laura nodded again.

"I had papers to deliver to the Land Office." Miss Barbara glanced at her watch and frowned.

Kloss could tell these two weren't going to volunteer anything unless he asked them the right questions. That method could really drag this out, but he knew better than bully them. For one thing, he never bullied females--especially proper ladies who'd done nothing wrong. For another, they'd been through enough for one day.

He might as well try reading their expressions and body language. He was generally good at that.

"This stranger... Tell me what happened--what he did."

"He put them both down." Laura stared at him dead-steady.

"At the same time?"

"The smaller guy came at us first."

"That would be Pellinger." Kloss consulted Neil's report. "Ted Pellinger. He's a bouncer at Rosellino's in Wheeling."

"He didn't tell us his name or how he makes his living," Laura said flatly. "He was following us, and when we stopped walking, he also stopped. When Momma turned around and asked what he wanted, he grabbed her arm. That's when this other man showed up and put him down. The big, muscular guy came running down the street a few seconds later--probably to help his partner."

"His name's Lupo. Ralph Lupo. He's also a bouncer at Rosellino's." Kloss knew a little about Rosellino's. It had been a popular spot for more years than he could remember and had the best dancers in the city. It was run by a man calling himself Johnny Favor. Favor was a small-time hood who kept a low profile and was not known to be involved in criminal activity.

But this surely smelled suspicious...

"Whatever his name is, he went down just as fast," Laura said.

"How?"

Laura squirmed a little, probably to ease some of the pressure in her back. "It happened too fast. By the time I blinked, the first guy was already on the ground. When I turned around, the second guy was rolling over to the curb. I didn't see the stranger hit him or anything. I didn't even hear any blows or slaps. But whatever he did really worked. They both went down and stayed down."

Kloss scratched his chin. Quick. Silent. Efficient. It sounded like martial arts. "This fella that helped ya--think he used Karate? Kung fu? Aikido? Somethin' like that?"

"I don't know. Like I said, by the time I turned around, it was all over."

"Can ya describe him?"

Both ladies shrugged.

"You don't remember anything?"

"It happened too fast," Laura said.

"Much too fast," Miss Barbara added.

"What about his age?"

"No idea," Miss Barbara said.

"I take it he's fit? He'd have to be, to do all that."

"He moved like a cat," Laura said. "He jumped out from behind one of the parked cars on Chestnut and was just a few feet away before we realized it."

This sounded like the man had been waiting for something like this to happen. Kloss wondered if the stranger could have been some sort of plant.

Best get into that later.

"I'll put down athletic." He wrote it down and scribbled "*ex-military?*" in tiny letters just above it. There weren't all that many guys in Manville who'd seen military action the last ten years or so. He could only think of three at the moment, but one of them had moved out of town and the others worked in St. Clairsville. Besides, all three had been wounded, so none of them could have done the sort of damage these women were talking about.

They could be looking for an ex-Navy SEAL, for all they knew. Or ex-Green Beret. Or maybe even one of those Ninja fellas he'd seen in movies.

Kloss could only wonder what someone like that was doing in Manville.

But that wasn't the only thing bothering him.

Kloss had been out in the reception area when Neil Blankenship and Mike Pugh brought the boys in. Lupo was as big as a gorilla and could probably haul around a small pickup on his shoulders all day long without breaking a sweat. Pellinger was much smaller, but since he worked as a bouncer, he could obviously take care of himself as well. Except for the nasty bump on the back of Lupo's head from hitting the pavement, neither boy was bleeding. And aside from a few cuts and scrapes on their hands and elbows from falling, neither showed signs of being in a fight.

"What happened after the second guy went down?" he asked.

Laura glanced briefly at her mom. "The deputy pulled up."

"And you didn't see where this other fella went?"

"He disappeared. He must've snuck into the alley next to the bookstore."

Kloss rubbed his eyes. Where had this mystery man gone? How in heck did he disappear so quickly? Neither Neil nor Mike had seen anyone in the area when they showed up.

"What else can you tell me about him?"

117

Laura shrugged.

The ringing of the phone made them jump.

Dang it. Kloss hated interruptions--especially when he was working on a case. He snatched up the phone. "Yeah, Alice?"

"It's the Mayor, Chief."

"Switch him on."

"He wants to see you."

"Listen, I'm right in the middle of--"

"He knows."

"And it looks like this case is--"

"He knows that, too."

Jeez... "Anything the Mayor *don't* know?"

"He was very insistent, Bill. More so than usual. You know he wouldn't interrupt unless it was important."

Alice was right. For a politician, Ernie was pretty laid-back. In fact, he was the only politician Kloss could actually talk to. The others made him want to pull his piece and shoot the bastards in their thick skulls.

But he still wasn't wild about this interruption. Ernie understood police business and stayed out of it, for the most part. Why the hell would the Mayor do anything that might compromise an investigation?

"'Kay." Hopefully he'd be back in ten minutes to finish up. "Tell him to give me two min--"

"He says now, Chief," Alice said softly.

"You mean he wants me--"

"Yep. Right there, right now."

He sat there a moment, staring at Miss Barbara and her daughter. He hated leaving them like this, but it was unavoidable. Whatever the hell the Mayor wanted, it had better be damn urgent.

"I guess I'm on my way."

***

Once the sound of Sheriff Kloss's heavy footsteps diminished into silence, Barbara lowered her eyes to her daughter's hands, which grasped hers tightly. Laura was apparently still frightened.

"Momma, *please* tell me what happened back there..."

"I wish I knew, baby." She couldn't help feeling a sense of guilt the moment she'd said it. Though she hadn't clearly seen the man who'd come to their aid, she'd somehow sensed Joe's presence. She couldn't explain any of this and wondered if it had something to do with her dream.

"Why do I have this feeling that you're keeping something from me?"

She's seeing it in my eyes again...or feeling it in my hands.

"Baby, why would you think such a thing?"

"I think you know *some*thing..."

"Even if I did, why would I keep it from you?"

"I don't know, Momma. You've been acting strange all morning, and now something like this happens. What am I supposed to think?"

"This happened to *both* of us. I'm just as surprised about it as you are."

Laura began staring at the desk in front of them. "Momma...when was the last time we heard about a mugging in downtown Manville? Especially in the middle of the day?"

"It's been a very long time."

"I can't stop thinking that what happened to us wasn't actually a mugging."

That was strange. Barbara had thought the very same thing. "What do you think happened, then?"

"I don't know. I wish I did. The whole thing was so...confusing. I don't even know why that man helped us. Shouldn't he have stuck around a little while? He could have at least answered some questions. I still don't remember when he actually disappeared. It was really strange..."

"For all we know, baby, he could be a war hero. We keep hearing about those Navy SEALS who live under the radar because they don't want their identity known."

"I guess he could be one of them. But what's he doing in Manville?"

"Maybe he's just passing through."

"You really think so?"

"If he is, I sure wouldn't want to show him our thanks by helping the police look for him."

"You're right, Momma. We've told them enough already. If he is just passing through, he should be able to leave without being detained by our Police Department."

This convinced Barbara that they shouldn't stay here. "Baby, I don't think we should answer any more questions."

"But...the Sheriff should be back any minute now."

"What can we do?"

"We're in a Police Station. We're not leaving until they've finished asking questions."

Barbara glanced at the door. "The Sheriff left. He's busy with the Mayor right now. I could be wrong, but they might be talking a little longer than just a minute or so."

"I'm right there with you, Momma...but I'm sure the lady out there at the desk won't let us leave."

"I'll call Sam and tell him where we are. He has friends who are top-notch attorneys. If we tell him what's happened and that we don't want to answer any more questions, he'll make a call and get us off the hook. I'm surprised he hasn't found out what's happened already."

"Don't you think it's weird that he hasn't called by now?"

Laura was right. It wasn't like Sam not to call. It wasn't like Edna not to call, either. It was nearly three-thirty--the lunch hour had ended hours ago.

"Call him now, Momma. Maybe he's been busy."

Barbara took her cell out of her bag.

Just then, the door eased open.

A man dressed in a plain dark-blue suit and drab gray tie stood in the doorway. He was about six feet tall, with small chestnut eyes and brown hair shaved almost down to the skull. His expression was grim.

"Barbara and Laura Neilson?" His voice was soft and low-pitched.

"Yes?" Barbara said uneasily.

"I'm Detective Arnold Weiss of the FBI." The flash of his badge took less time than the blinking of an eye. "I've come to escort you both out of the Station."

***

Mayor Ernie Tillborough looked all done in. His skin was pale, his eyes glossy and blood-shot. He sat slumped behind his desk, his fists resting on the blotter, his bald head lowered. He looked like he might've drifted off, or just had a snootful. Kloss knew better. The Mayor didn't take naps during office hours. He drank Scotch, but never at the office. But right now he looked like he'd just gone through some kind of hell.

"Close the door, Bill. And sit down."

Kloss eased the door shut, crossed the room, and sat in the chair facing the man's desk. He wanted to get this over with and honestly didn't care what the Mayor had on his plate right now. He needed to head back and wrap this up. He sure didn't like two innocent ladies getting roughed up in his town. "Listen, Mayor, I gotta case right now--"

"I know."

Alice had said the man knew what was going on. That sounded reasonable. After all, it was the Mayor's job to know about stuff like this. Kloss began thinking that whatever this was, it most likely involved their new case.

"What's goin' on, Mayor?"

"Nothing that concerns us."

The Mayor's face didn't reveal much, but Kloss had heard the man talk like that before. When his boss said something like that, it never meant anything good. But the Mayor wouldn't call

122

him up here in the middle of a case to tell him nothing was going on.

"What was that, Mayor? Sounded like ya said--"

"You heard what I said, Bill. Whatever just came in no longer concerns us."

"Talk plain, Mayor. What you're gettin' at isn't makin' much sense."

The Mayor clasped his hands together on the blotter. Then he cleared his throat and looked Kloss right in the eye. "I'm telling you it doesn't matter, Bill. None of this matters."

Kloss shifted in the chair. That last statement wasn't exactly what he wanted to hear. If this had anything to do with what just happened on Chestnut, Kloss needed to find out about it and didn't care who liked it. "What doesn't matter, Mayor?"

"The case that just came in. We have to drop it."

"By droppin' it, you mean--"

"I mean just that. Drop it. Forget it. Thank the women for their cooperation and tell them they're free to go. Then release the two perps. After you've done all that, you can bring everything you've got on this case straight to me and put it right here on my desk."

"Then what?"

The Mayor shrugged. "Get back to work and forget all this happened."

***

Barbara got up from her seat and cautiously approached the man blocking the doorway. "What exactly is going on?"

"As I just said, I've come to escort you two out of the Station."

"You said you're from the FBI?" Laura pushed herself up and joined her mother.

"Yes."

"I didn't realize the FBI even knew about this place."

Laura's boldness somehow helped Barbara focus. She began looking at this more objectively. Was this about the mugging? Why would the FBI care? How would they even know about it? And where was this man from? Manville had been getting by with two police officers until just a few years ago, when they hired on three more deputies. Barbara didn't even know the FBI had offices in the Ohio Valley. Most likely, the closest branch would be in Columbus, or Wheeling.

"I'm working out of Columbus," he said.

"That's a hundred miles from here," Laura said.

"I'm aware of that," he said flatly. "I just made the trip."

"Why would the FBI be interested in us?" Barbara asked.

Before he could reply, Laura said, "Does this have anything to do with those guys who tried to mug us?"

"Ladies, as I just said, I don't have the time to explain. We have to leave."

The vibes emanating from this man had caused her uneasiness to return. Barbara forced herself to stay firm. "Before we go anywhere with you, could we please see your badge again? You flashed it a little too quickly."

He reached into his jacket pocket and flashed it half a second longer. It then disappeared inside his pocket as before.

Laura sighed. "Would you mind trying that one last time? All I saw was something gold and shiny, with a vulture sitting on top of it."

He pulled it out again. This time, he held it out for them to examine closely. "The *vulture* happens to be the American eagle, miss."

Barbara and Laura studied it carefully. It showed the eagle and the blindfolded lady holding the scales of justice in the center. DEPARTMENT OF JUSTICE was stamped in bold letters beneath it.

Legit or not, Barbara still couldn't ignore the sense of wrongness permeating the air.

Agent Weiss pocketed the badge. "We have to leave."

"Where?" Barbara asked. "And where's the Sheriff? He was supposed to come right back…"

"He's with the Mayor. We've been working with the Manville Police Department the last couple of days. The Mayor and the task force I've been assigned to work with has given me specific instructions…"

"A couple of *days*?" Barbara's fears increased. "What's this *really* about?"

"Ma'am, I'm under strict orders to escort you ladies from this building and take you somewhere safe."

"We're not going anywhere with you," Laura said, "until you tell us what's going on…"

"I can only tell you that the man you encountered today could be the subject of a criminal case."

"What man?" Laura asked.

"I'm sure you both know who I'm talking about."

"Are you referring to that mugging on Chestnut?" Barbara asked.

"Why would the FBI be interested in a *mugging*?" Laura asked.

"The man we're investigating is a dangerous fugitive, and our latest intel has placed him in the Belmont Country area."

Barbara stared dumbly at the man. "Are you joking?"

"Ma'am, if you'll just come with me…"

"Where are you taking us?" Laura asked softly.

"A safe place, as I said."

"But--"

"We've got very little time."

Barbara gawked at Laura, who'd paled instantly.

"Momma? What should we do?"

Barbara could tell by this man's steady gaze that they should comply with his orders. She wanted to stall, to wait until Sheriff Kloss returned, but knew this man wouldn't tolerate a delay. He was obviously armed—which made her feel even more intimidated.

"Momma?"

Barbara decided right then that she shouldn't do or say anything that would antagonize this man or worsen this situation. In the event of a scuffle, Laura would get involved and suffer further injury.

She took a breath and hoped she was making the right decision. "I think we'd better go with him, baby."

Laura gawked at her—searching for reassurance. Barbara sent her back a smile. Laura smiled back and nodded.

Taking Laura's arm, Detective Weiss led them out of the room.

***

Bill Kloss couldn't understand what was happening with the Mayor. Hopefully, he hadn't heard him right. It wasn't something a body heard every day. And it surely wasn't anything a hard-working small-town sheriff wanted to hear from his boss. "Are you serious about that, Mayor?"

"You heard me, Bill."

This obviously wasn't a simple mugging. But since the Mayor had just told him to forget about it, Kloss wouldn't be able to find out what the hell it actually was. Only one thing was certain: such instructions clearly suggested others were involved.

Ol' Ern sat there, scowling. The Mayor was basically a good guy, but he was also a politician. He owed a bunch of folks, big-time. Everyone knew how these characters played their games. Sometimes favors involved money; other times, things only bad men with no conscience did. In his experience, Bill Kloss found that most of these favors were things that would turn the best of men surly in no time.

But that wasn't the issue. If something really bad was going on, they had to get right to the heart of it. Despite his orders, Bill Kloss would not stand by and let innocent folks get hurt.

"What ain'tcha tellin' me, Mayor?"

"All you need to know is that this case is closed."

Kloss had been in this business much too long to care about what was good and what was bad. Because of politics, everything good and bad got all tangled up, like bobwire when you tried pulling it free from a big roll. After a while, you couldn't tell what the hell was going on. The only thing that seemed to matter nowadays was that big money always had the final say.

"So you can't tell me any more about it?"

"You've got your orders."

"Awful hard when it involves doin' nothin'."

The Mayor shot a quick glance at his phone. "A lot of things about this are hard, Bill."

Kloss figured the Mayor had received one of those mysterious calls he got from time to time. The Mayor had friends and acquaintances all over the Valley. Whoever had called no doubt had firsthand knowledge of what was going on and didn't want it spread around, for whatever reason.

Kloss hated backing off. What if a killer was walking around? Or a rapist? Or child molester? Hard, sitting around on your ass and exposing your friends and relatives to danger just because the Mayor had gotten one of his phone calls from someone who wanted him to look the other way.

"I can tell you've got questions," his boss said.

"You've gotta see this from my point of view, Mayor. I don't give a rat's behind about politics. All I care about is the folks we're tryin' to protect. And if there's somethin' about to happen that'll hurt anyone in this town--"

"No need to worry about that, Bill."

Kloss could tell by his tone that the Mayor was serious, but it still wasn't enough. "Mayor, I swore to protect the good citizens of Manville, but I can't do my job when you tell me to back off in the middle of a case that involves two nice, law-bidin' ladies that did nothin' wrong."

"One last time, Bill. Go back downstairs and let the women go. Thank them for their cooperation, apologize for any inconvenience we've put them through, and open the door for them as they leave."

"You don't think they might be slightly irritated for what we put 'em through?"

"We didn't put them through anything. We showed up after they'd just been through a terrible experience, brought them here in a comfortable squad car and treated them very cordially. We even arrested the assailants responsible. The women have no reason to be angry at us."

Kloss had to hand it to the Mayor. The man had finesse to burn. That was one big reason why he was so damn good in politics. But it still didn't wipe the slate clean here. "Tell me somethin', Mayor."

"If I can…"

"The man that stopped that mugging?"

"What about him?"

"You weren't told by any chance that he might be the reason for all this hush-hush crap, were ya?"

Ol' Ern shifted in his chair. "As I told you before, Bill, bring me everything you've got just as soon as the women are released."

***

Parked one block down from the Manville Police Station, Desmond Roth watched the two women being escorted out of the building by a man in a dark-blue suit. The man led them down the front walk and to the right side of the building, where a dark sedan was parked between two police cruisers. The man stayed close behind them. When they reached the sedan, he opened the back door and helped Laura get in. Once Barbara slid in beside her daughter, he closed the door. Before opening the driver's door, he gave the parking lot and the street a quick scan.

The car backed out of its spot rather quickly. The driver scanned the area one last time before forcing the sedan down the street, to the turnoff.

Roth fired up the Challenger. He waited until the sedan was out of sight before taking off in the same direction. He had an idea where the man was taking them. He also had an idea who the man was and who he worked for.

His grim features tightened as he pulled away from the curb.

130

The women faced serious danger.

***

"Dang it, Alice, you've gotta be kiddin'!" A cold feeling washed through Kloss as he gawked at his empty office.

"I wish I was, Bill..." Trembling, Alice stood behind her chair, her skinny arms at her sides, her long, slender fingers playing with the material of her jeans. Anyone could see that the poor thing was barely holding it together.

Kloss just couldn't believe this. He'd only been gone fifteen minutes. How could something as weird as this happen?

But something weird *had* happened--there was no doubt about it. And whatever it was, it had done a number on Alice. He hadn't seen her so upset in a long time.

But she wasn't the only one who needed a good lie-down. After his meeting with the Mayor, Bill Kloss wanted to grind his teeth into powder.

But this *really* topped it off.

"A man with a badge." Kloss watched Alice closely, hoping for some other spark of memory. "No name? No other info?"

Alice ran an impatient hand through her dyed black hair. "Fella just came in, showed me a badge and said there would be some special briefing in just a few minutes."

"What were his exact words?"

"Ma'am, this is a Federal matter, and everyone has to gather immediately in the Conference Room for official information."

"Anything else?"

"He said you and the Mayor would be down shortly for the briefing, as well."

Kloss scratched the back of his neck. It sounded official, all right. That is, it *would* have, had he actually been told by the Mayor that someone from Columbus was on his way over. The Mayor would certainly have told him something like that. But since it hadn't been mentioned, Kloss knew something was off. And the fact that the Neilson women had disappeared during all this made the matter even more peculiar.

"And he managed to clear out the danged floor just by tellin' ya that?"

"No one else was around but Neil when this guy showed up. Everyone else was either down the hall or in the lunchroom."

Incredible. It was upsetting to discover how easily this had been done. True, there were only a dozen folks working here, usually no more than eight or nine in the building at any one time, but it still made him suspicious. Paranoid, too.

"And you *believed* this guy?"

"Like I said, he showed me a badge…"

"And just because you saw a danged badge, you thought--"

"I thought I should do what I was told," she said rather frostily. "It felt legit, Bill. He fit the picture--cheap suit, drab tie, bad aftershave. Even his haircut was awful. Strictly Jack Webb style. I didn't think I had a choice."

"It didn't seem odd that a stranger would come in off the street and tell ya to leave your post?"

"It surely did."

"But you did it anyway?"

"Like I just said--"

"I know, I know." Kloss rubbed his temples. Alice only did what she thought was right. And the more he thought of it, the more he realized she *had* done the right thing. She'd obeyed a Federal agent. And since Kloss had just been ordered off a case not ten minutes earlier, this seemed even more conceivable. The Mayor had no doubt spoken with Alice before Kloss went up to see him. Since she'd already been told to keep quiet, she probably figured this was even more secretive stuff and that she had no other option.

This could actually *be* Federal business, for all they knew. And any interference meant trouble.

But that didn't explain how a stranger could just come right on in, clear the floor, and take two victims away. Alice hadn't actually seen them leave, but Kloss knew it was just too coincidental for the women to disappear at this same time.

"What's this all about, Bill?"

"I wish I knew." It made him feel like an idiot, but he couldn't tell her what he didn't know.

"Was that man really a Fed?"

"I wish I knew that, too."

"If he was, what did he want with Barbara and Laura Neilson?"

"Alice, you're askin' me some danged good questions."

"Are ya trying to tell me you don't have any answers?"

"That's exactly what I'm sayin'." Piecing this all together was going to be tough. Anyone could buy a badge on the Internet, a cheap suit and tie anywhere. They sold cheap aftershave in every store in the country. And any barbershop would gladly buzz your scalp for just a few bucks.

This obviously happened the moment Kloss went upstairs to talk with the Mayor. That took planning. It also took organization and clout.

This mess might be Federal after all.

"I've known you a long time. Bill. It's not like you to have no answers at all..."

He knew better than tell her his suspicions. Alice was a good worker, but like most women, she suffered from flapping gum syndrome. "All I know is, whoever did this has some serious resources."

"It doesn't explain why it was done, though."

"Nope. It doesn't." He snatched up her phone. "But I'm danged sure gonna find out what's goin' on around here..."

CHAPTER SEVEN

Huddled together in the back seat of the sedan, Laura and Momma held on tightly to one another. The spasms rippling through Laura's lower back had subsided, making her discomfort slightly more tolerable. Even so, she couldn't let go of Momma's hand and noticed the full extent of her anxiety only when Momma winced from the pressure.

"Sorry, Momma," she whispered, relaxing her grip.

"It's all right, baby."

The FBI man drove east on Belmont County Road out of Manville. He drove rather quickly. Although she couldn't see the speedometer from her position, she guessed he was doing close to twenty miles over the posted limit. At this rate, they'd reach the Interstate in just a few minutes.

A shiver sliced through her. This felt very wrong. Laura couldn't help thinking that she and Momma had been kidnapped. It seemed only logical, considering the strange circumstances. When they were first brought into the Station, half a dozen people sat at their desks, working. The black-haired lady named Alice sat at the center desk, taking phone calls. Everything seemed normal--a strong sense of business as usual. But when this man led Laura and Momma back out into the reception area, it was deserted. Everyone had disappeared.

Laura began studying Agent Weiss in hopes of committing his image to memory. His hair was a dirty brown and cut extremely short. His small chestnut eyes barely blinked. His face showed no expression. There were no scars, moles, pockmarks or wrinkles. His clothes looked cheap. His aftershave probably went for two bucks a gallon.

Laura wanted the Sheriff and everyone else to know about this man. She didn't want him to get away with this. No one--not even a federal agent--should be able to walk into a Sheriff's office and take someone away without a word of explanation.

He didn't even want them making any personal calls. He'd said it would compromise the investigation.

She didn't believe a word he said and could tell by Momma's expression that she felt the same way.

Laura thought it odd that Maddie hadn't called. She knew Laura would never take this much time for lunch. But there was no word, and Laura wondered if this man was responsible. She'd heard that the FBI liked to control things, keep everyone in the dark. She wouldn't be at all surprised if Maddie had been notified and told that Laura and her mother were involved in some legal matter and were not to be contacted.

What would Weiss do if her phone buzzed? Would he let her answer it? Or pull over and take it away? *Sorry, Ma'am, we can't take the chance, but don't worry, the phones will be returned to you once the investigation is over...*

These people had to obey the law, too, didn't they? They couldn't kidnap innocent people and take them wherever they wanted. That wasn't what this country was all about.

The panic flared once again, turning her limbs ice-cold. *Stop this.* This man was *not* a criminal. He was a government man. The FBI, no less. He'd even shown them his badge, and it looked legit. He wasn't kidnapping them, just getting them out of harm's way.

Was this really about those two who'd attacked them on Chestnut?

Or was it about the man who'd saved them?

Why would the FBI be on his trail? Was he a wanted criminal? He'd *have* to be, wouldn't he? Why else would the FBI be interested in him?

No matter how this looked, it felt very wrong. Momma sensed it, too. During the last few miles, Momma hadn't taken her eyes off Weiss. Her hands had become so *cold...*

Laura's anger stormed back. Her fears quickly vanished. She could tolerate the fear and the terror of being taken from the Police Station. She could also handle being shoved into the back seat of a strange car and driven out of town...

But when you upset Momma, you'd ventured into dangerous waters. Momma didn't deserve this. She hadn't deserved what happened on Chestnut, either. But this was much worse.

"I demand you tell us where we're going." She was surprised her voice was so calm and steady.

He didn't reply.

His silence made her even angrier. "In case you didn't hear me the first time, I asked you a question."

"As I told you both back at the Station--a safe place."

137

"We were in a *Police Station*. That's just about as safe as it gets, wouldn't you say?"

"Ladies, I've come all the way from Columbus because of an official report that a dangerous fugitive was seen in this area."

"You shoved us into this car. Now you're driving us out of town. You won't tell us where you're taking us. This might be hard for someone like you to understand, but we're more than just a little frightened and confused right now."

"As I've already told you, I'm not at liberty to say--"

"Just what *are* you at liberty to say?" Momma sat up and glared. Laura could tell her mother's hackles were up. This made Laura feel much better. "You can start by telling us why you've taken us--against our will, I might add--from a Police Station!"

"Ma'am..."

"And while you're explaining *that*," Laura added, "you might also tell us why you've discouraged us from making calls to people who might actually be concerned about our whereabouts."

"Orders."

"What sort of orders?"

"As I said before, you'll both be told very soon."

"We want to be told *now*!" Sizzling pain raced up Laura's back. She cringed. It was only then that she realized she'd arched her back the same moment Momma had sat up.

"Baby?" Momma grabbed her forearm.

"I'm all right..." She ignored the pain and focused on the back of the man's head. For an instant, she fought off the urge to swat him. It would have made her feel fantastic--temporarily, anyway. She really didn't want to die--especially in another traffic accident. And she certainly didn't want to endanger Momma. She forced herself to relax in the seat. The pain lingered for about thirty seconds and then slowly ebbed. "If you don't soon tell us something, I'm gonna call the Police Station and tell them exactly what happened to us."

"That sounds good, baby." Momma opened her bag. "I strongly suggest you start cooperating with us, Agent Weiss."

"Ladies," he said tiredly, "I was ordered to take you out of town for a very important reason."

"Go on," Laura said.

"I've recently received information indicating someone in the Manville Police Station has been compromising this investigation."

"What exactly does that mean?"

"We believe someone with the Manville Police is somehow involved with organized crime in the Wheeling area."

"And?"

"This person could be an employer of the dangerous fugitive we've been trying to track down."

Laura turned to Momma, who'd paled. No. This *couldn't* be. "What exactly are you trying to say?"

"Someone in the Police Department is working closely with the fugitive we're looking for."

"This fugitive. Who *is* this man?"

"We think he could be the man who fought off your attackers."

Laura gawked at Momma. She found that she could not speak.

Momma cleared her throat. "Are you…absolutely sure?"

"We believe this man has been hired to kill you, Mrs. Neilson."

***

"Mayor, somethin' weird just happened down here." Bill Kloss' voice sounded even raspier than usual.

Ernie Tillborough sat back in his chair and tried to ignore the frustration building up steadily inside him. Typical of them to work so quickly, cleaning up, covering their tracks. He shouldn't be at all surprised.

"I have a pretty good idea what happened, Bill."

"Mayor, someone came in here and took two ladies right out of the Station!"

"It's out of our hands, Bill."

"This isn't right, Mayor."

"I don't like it, either."

"Then just give me some idea--"

"Drop it."

"I wish you'd just give me a hint about what the heck's goin' on--"

"That's an order!" The Mayor killed the line and sat back. He had another shot of Scotch. When he thought once more about the call that came in

140

thirty minutes earlier, he began getting angry all over again.

The caller refused to state his name. Being a busy man, Tillborough's first instinct was to hang up. He hadn't the patience for crank calls. Bad enough the call had come through his private line, bypassing the switchboard completely.

He picked up his pen and was about to jot down a reminder on his memo pad to talk to his people about this breach in security when the caller quickly mentioned a name from Tillborough's past.

Startled, Tillborough dropped the pen on the blotter. Knowing how things were, he realized how much better things would have been if this had actually been a crank call.

The caller immediately mentioned more names. Tillborough recognized them as those directly responsible for illegal contributions that had helped launch his political career.

He waited tensely for the caller to finish. There was no need for someone to phone him out of the blue and remind him of past sins. There was, however, an urgent need to find out the purpose of this call.

"Just what is this all about?"

"The Governor has asked me to inquire about your health, Mayor."

Had he heard correctly? Or was this a subtle ruse to steer him toward forbidden territory?

Politics was a vicious game, its players nothing more than well-dressed street thugs with money and connections. Tillborough had accepted this long ago but told himself that it didn't matter. He wanted to fulfill his ultimate dream and was prepared to take the bad with the good. Like everyone else trying to build a career in this foul-smelling cesspool, he'd suffered his share of wounds and scars but had been fortunate enough to overcome them. As his reward, he was given his post as Mayor of Manville, enjoying both consecutive terms without too much irritation or reminders of past indiscretions.

He found it strange that this call had come at the beginning of a new case, and quite upsetting that it had come only minutes after the call from Wheeling just minutes earlier.

"Did you just ask about…my health?" he asked softly.

"Word has just come down concerning a matter of major concern in your jurisdiction…"

His instincts were right; this was bad. He realized right then that he should have taken that Wheeling call much more seriously.

Miles Lester had called ten minutes earlier to tell him that something serious was going down in the Belmont County area. Lester had been extremely tight-lipped, saying only that this matter would be handled by the people directly involved, and that Manville should stay out of it completely.

"Still there, Mayor?"

"Of *course* I'm still here." Tillborough fought to keep his voice from cracking. "And my health is just fine."

"We're all pleased to hear that."

"So now you can tell the person who is so worried about my health--"

"It's the Governor, actually."

Tillborough sagged in his chair. This was getting worse. "And how's the man doing?"

"He could be better."

"What seems to be the problem?"

"The Governor's friends and associates have expressed concerns."

"Concerns?"

"The current state of affairs in Manville, of course."

Tillborough's heart thrashed. It was never a good thing for people in the political arena to be discussing your post. It almost always meant dissatisfaction, and with dissatisfaction came immediate change. And change, in politics, was never pleasant.

"It was mentioned how awkward it would be for so many if a certain matter wasn't handled properly."

This *had* to be what Lester had just warned him about. Nothing else made sense. "Does this involve a mugging case I was informed about less than an hour ago?"

A sudden *click* made him jump. The line was being switched over--or whatever nonsense they called it--to make sure the call couldn't be monitored. This happened quite often. Tillborough was doubly concerned about it this time.

"All you need to know is that this matter must be resolved immediately, and the less who know about it, the better."

"I think I have the right to know--"

"Certain individuals have been sent to your jurisdiction to correct this problem. See that you don't get in their way."

"But--"

Another *click*.

"It's been nice talking with you, Mayor. I will send your former associates and constituents your best wishes."

"I think I--"

The line went dead.

"Understand," he finished. Then he sat there with the receiver mashed hotly against his ear.

Once his brain finally began working again, he replaced the receiver, sat back and for the next few moments stared at the insides of his eyelids.

There was nothing else that could be done. Too much was at stake. If he opened up this wound, a lot of people would suffer. And the man who'd suffer most would be Ernie Tillborough himself-- that same humble, God-fearing man who hadn't a prayer of surviving in the political arena until he'd made nice with the appropriate individuals.

It had been a wonderful arrangement. It enabled him to be his own boss, and without too many people peering over his shoulder. Re-election had been no problem. His third term was just a year away and he'd already been assured he wouldn't have to worry about facing a formidable opponent.

But as with all debts, the time had come to pay up. He'd just suck it up and do what was necessary. He'd done it before and would have no problem doing it again.

What bothered him was that others were involved. His friends and associates. People he'd grown to rely on. People who relied on him--who answered to him, worked for him, looked up to him. Bill Kloss was an honest, hard-working man who lived to right wrongs, make the public safe and put the criminals away. He'd served in the Merchant Marines, displayed the American flag proudly in his front yard and made it known that he'd gladly give his life for his country.

With a deep sigh, Tillborough poured more Scotch and tried very hard not to despise himself so much.

**

Hired to kill you...

Suddenly light-headed, Barbara lowered her head, closed her eyes and tried very hard not to panic. Every image in her brain had become dark and hazy. All she could hear was that horrible phrase...

Kill you...

She wondered if it was true. Did someone actually want her dead?

Kill you... The voice in her head persisted, but she knew right then that it was mistaken. She wouldn't believe it. Couldn't. Refused to accept it. It made no sense.

What would be the reason? The purpose? Why would anyone want her dead?

Like everyone else, she had faults--dozens of them. No one was perfect. But did that mean someone wanted her killed? Did it mean someone had actually hired a professional killer to come to town and murder her?

Her thoughts automatically scurried back to her past, searching for things she'd done, things she hadn't been proud of. There were two or three soured romances, a few unresolved promises, some hurt feelings...things she'd said in anger to Joe during those last few months...

But surely nothing that would justify a contract on her life.

Weiss merged onto I-70 and headed east, toward Wheeling.

Her heart sputtered. They were getting farther and farther from home. Where on earth was he taking them?

A safe place, Weiss had said. But he hadn't been specific. He'd mentioned only that someone bad was working at the Police Station.

And, of course, someone who'd been hired to kill her.

This struck her as odd. He hadn't told them anything else--why would he break his silence and tell them this single horrible detail? It would be a breach of security, wouldn't it? And it certainly wouldn't make her *or* Laura feel better about this.

Was it sympathy that had prompted him to tell them? Hardly. Weiss was a government agent. Everyone knew these individuals had ice water running through their veins and could care less about the public's feelings.

Why else would he do it? Embarrassment? Fear? Had he panicked when Barbara and Laura tried bullying him?

Once again, it seemed unlikely. Weiss was hardly the type to be intimidated very easily.

Sam had to know about this. It was still fairly early--he might have returned to Wheeling by now.

She found it very strange that he hadn't already called. After all, she'd been out of the office for nearly three hours, and it was rapidly approaching the dinner hour. But anything was possible, especially when it involved business. She forced herself not to jump to conclusions. A simple call would fix everything. Then she could call Sheriff Kloss and tell him where they were.

She was convinced more than ever that Weiss wasn't really an FBI agent. Worst of all, she had the horrifying feeling that he wasn't taking them to a safe place at all.

"Momma?" Laura whispered.

"Yes, baby?"

"You don't believe what he said, do you? You don't believe that a hired killer would come to town to...*kill* you?"

"It can't be true, baby. No one would want me dead, would they?"

"Of course not, Momma."

Once again her brain went wild, rummaging through her memory banks for past mistakes.

Enough of this. Right now, it was important to let someone know what was going on. She carefully slid her hand inside the leather pocket of her handbag.

Laura leaned closer. "What's up?"

The car jarred to the right as Weiss suddenly switched lanes in the heavy traffic. The cold smoothness of the cell phone slid into her palm, reassuring her. She moved closer to Laura and whispered, "Sam."

"I'll call nine-one-one." Laura reached for her jacket pocket.

Barbara flipped open the cell and pressed Sam's personal number. Luckily for them, traffic was hectic enough to keep Weiss occupied.

Barbara stared numbly at her cell. The display light didn't come on.

"Something wrong, Momma?"

A gush of coldness filled her gut. "It's...not working..."

Laura dropped her eyes to her lap. "Oh my God..."

Barbara swallowed a lump in her throat. "Yours, too?"

Laura's eyes had grown enormous. Her nod was shaky.

Barbara's heart crawled sluggishly up her throat. The realization made her want to scream.

Both phones. Jammed.

"We're...in trouble, aren't we, Momma?"

Barbara could manage only a slight nod.

***

After getting off I-70 in Bridgeport and taking Route 40, Arnold Weiss took the sedan up the narrow one-lane road and coasted down the street. Then he made another turn, went straight for about half a mile and pulled up to the curb in front of the drab two-story frame house.

No signs of life on the street or in any of the other houses. This was how things had been since the last of the homeowners took their money and moved out.

Weiss saw no movement behind the dark, smudged windows of the house at the end of the sloped walk. He glanced at his watch. 4:48. Even with the rush hour, he'd made good time. No problem: if the boss wasn't already inside, he'd be here shortly.

"Why are we here?" The daughter was looking around nervously.

Weiss struggled once again to hold his temper. Hopefully this bitch would shut her trap and stop fussing so damned much. He'd roughed up females before, but never a cripple. It would be like kicking a sick dog. But if she pissed him off, he'd have to do *some*thing to keep her in line...

"As I've been telling you, you'll be safe here."

"I don't *feel* safe. It's so...isolated."

His patience was wearing thin. If she kept this up, he'd definitely have to slap her around a little. He'd been ordered not to resort to any rough stuff, but sometimes females just didn't respond to anything else. "That's why it's safe. Nobody's around."

"We've been here before, baby." The mother patted her daughter's hand. "Your cousin lives just a couple of miles down the road. We came here for a visit just a few months before your accident, remember?"

"I remember, Momma. I also remember coming here when I was little. I'd just like to know why we had to come *here*. Why not the Holiday Inn? It's just a few minutes from the Mall, but it's secluded. People go there all the time." She frowned at the house. "It's clean there, too. And probably a *lot* more comfortable."

You're really asking for it, bitch...

Weiss was suddenly aware that his hand had unconsciously slipped inside his jacket pocket and clutched the chloroform packet he'd brought along for insurance. "It's safe here. No one will look for you."

"You mean that hired killer?"

"I'm not allowed--"

"Yeah, everything's a secret. But you told us about this guy anyway. I guess it's not much of a secret if you told us, is it?"

He knew that had been a mistake the moment he'd told them, but they'd been getting on his nerves and he had to tell them something to shut them up. He hoped he wouldn't have to face a ration of shit for that. "I shouldn't have told you."

"Why did you?"

"Baby..." The mother patted the girl's hand. "You're not helping."

Weiss liked the mother. She was the classy kind of chick a guy could talk to. He really didn't want to get rid of her. He always felt bad when he was ordered to snuff classy ladies. But a job was a job, and he'd never been one to piss off the guy carrying around the paychecks.

Besides, a conscience was something he really never cared much about. The killing business paid entirely too damned much for a guy to complicate things with unnecessary feelings.

"I'm not *trying* to be difficult, Momma." She glared at him. "I demand that you let us call someone."

He wanted to smile. The daughter had serious balls for a chick. "Go ahead, I won't stop you."

"You know our phones aren't working."

Milan and Levinson had followed him on the way over. Levinson was a techno geek; jamming a couple of cell phones wasn't a problem. Hopefully they'd be here in a few minutes as well. They were probably coming back a different way to make sure they hadn't been followed by the guy from Orlando everyone seemed to be afraid of.

"Maybe they need a recharge."

"How stupid do you think we are?"

"Baby, *please...*"

He glanced at the house and snuck another peek at his watch. *Boss, where the hell* are *you?*

"Can we please use your phone?" the mother asked.

He needed to pacify them somehow. "There's a phone in the house. You can use it when we're inside."

"That would be fine," the mother said. "We'd appreciate it."

The daughter said, "While you're being so *nice*, I guess you wouldn't mind telling us how long we have to stay here, would you?"

"Baby, let's not make this more difficult, okay? Once we're inside, we can make some calls and let everyone know we're all right."

151

"Momma, aren't you worried? This neighborhood looks like something out a horror flick, where everyone was taken away by aliens..."

"Baby, please stop imagining things. We'll be all right."

Weiss got out. It wouldn't hurt to take them inside and get them situated. It wouldn't be much longer before the boss showed.

He reached for the rear door and pulled it open.

The sharp clicking of footsteps on the concrete walk behind him caused him to turn sharply.

Weiss sighed in relief. Let the boss take it from here.

The mother had already gotten out. Hearing the footsteps, she peered around Weiss. Her eyes grew; her face lit up. "*Sam?*"

CHAPTER EIGHT

Nervous and light-headed, Brad Jacobson got off the plane at Pittsburgh International and moved stiffly through the heavy, slow-moving crowds. The huge open area smelled strongly of colognes, perfumes and sweat, as well as tangy scents of flavored coffee, grilled subs and burgers oozing from the food court. He discovered that he was much too upset to be hungry. The mixed aromas nauseated him.

The terminal clocks said it was 5:03. Just three minutes late, but he strongly suspected he was about to face serious consequences.

Jacobson was in no mood for a lecture. He'd been running full throttle since that last phone call in Orlando. Lying to the Chief about a family emergency and then to Jen about a work assignment that just came up, rushing to the locker room, changing into the sport jacket and slacks he kept there for emergencies, then finally getting a cab to the airport...it had all been murder on his nerves.

But he'd made it. With any luck, this errand wouldn't take long, and he could fly back to Orlando and be with Jen and the kids sometime tonight.

He knew he was deceiving himself, but he couldn't help it. Depression would set in if he assessed this more objectively. He couldn't screw this up by letting the paranoia take over.

Doing a job for any criminal was never a good thing. This would be no exception. He was reasonably certain that this involved the murder of the bookkeeper, and that whoever was responsible had fled to the Ohio Valley. He'd personally seen intel linking organized crime in Orlando to mob activities in this area. This job could be as simple as finding the hitter and bringing him back to Orlando.

Jacobson knew that his association with these criminals would eventually lead to his demise. Once he'd brought the traitor safely back to Orlando, his part in all this would forever seal his doom. His career would be shitcanned. So would his marriage, pension, and reputation. Jen loved him dearly but wouldn't be able to live with this. Wendy and Amber would be forced to face the horrible fact that their father had turned his back on the law and human decency.

Enough self-pity. Get this over with.

Breaking away from the crowd, he found a vacant corner a few yards down from the restrooms. Settling in amongst a group of potted plants, he sighed deeply and dialed the number. His pulse thumped wildly while he listened to the silence.

Maybe he won't answer. Maybe he's at a meeting and can't get to his phone. Maybe--

The dreaded voice answered on the second ring. "You're ten minutes late."

"The clocks here say--"

"I don't give a shit *what* the clocks say. Late is late."

"The plane encountered some turbulence along the way..."

"Excuses don't matter, cowboy. I told you what I wanted. You know better than fuck with me."

He wanted to toss the cell and just walk away. His only prayer right now was to somehow get this bastard to forget about the time and focus on the job at hand.

"I'm here, okay? Whenever you've finished your stupid chest-thumping, you can tell me what you want me to do."

"Easy, cowboy." The man's tone quickly changed. "Didn't we talk about your attitude earlier?"

"*You* talked about it. Anyway, I'm here. What do you want me to do?"

"Get a cab. Wait for instructions."

"That's it?"

"That's it. And cowboy?"

"The name's *Jacobson*. I'm a *cop*--not a cowboy."

"Just make sure you find the right cab."

Click.

***

"Sam?" Barbara couldn't believe her own eyes. "Is that really *you*?"

"It's me." He took hold of Laura's left arm to help her out of the back seat.

Barbara's mind began spinning. What was Sam doing here? How did he know Agent Weiss? Had he heard about the mugging? Why were they *here*, of all places?

"Barbara?"

She struggled to focus. Sam Albright, her employer for the last five years, had mysteriously popped up in the middle of this nightmare. He was standing less than three feet away, watching her, and he looked worried.

"Barbara, are you all right?"

I really need to snap out of this...

"I think so..."

"Let's go inside." He gestured.

Totally bewildered, Barbara took Laura's hand and followed Sam down the uneven front walk, to the weathered wooden stairs leading to the front porch. While she helped Laura up the five wobbly steps, Sam hurried on ahead and opened the front door. Barbara turned around. Weiss had already slipped behind the wheel of the sedan and was talking on his cell.

Sam nudged her arm, startling her.

She followed Laura inside. Sam closed the door behind them.

The modest-sized living room smelled of Lemon Pledge and mustiness. There was no carpeting to hide the scuffed, well-worn wooden floor. A beat-up armchair, faded loveseat, and a couple of scratched end tables served as the only furniture in the room.

The house had probably been earmarked for a flip, or demolition. Working for Sam, she'd seen enough places on the market to recognize a cheap investment. A couple of years ago, he'd acquired a block of old buildings in this area to be renovated. That could explain why he was here and why there were no signs of life on the block.

But it didn't explain why she and Laura had been brought here by an FBI agent.

"You two must be exhausted." He gestured to the loveseat.

Barbara and Laura crossed the room and sat. The cushions were kind of hard. Sam appeared more edgy than usual. The blue vein over his right temple stuck out prominently--clear evidence of stress.

"I thought you were still in Pittsburgh," she said.

"I was."

This didn't make sense. Sam usually called the office whenever he'd finished his business and was back on the road. He should've called while she and Laura were at Emma's. If Sam had been in Wheeling since then, he would've definitely called her by now.

"Why haven't you called to ask where I've been?"

"I've been up to my neck in conferences. You know how unpredictable those damned things tend to be."

"So you drove to Wheeling and have been in conference since then?"

"That just about covers it."

She'd hoped for a better explanation. When he didn't elaborate, she told herself not to get upset. Since Sam had shown up, things didn't seem quite so bleak. Hopefully they'd be going back home soon.

But she still needed a few details cleared up.

"That doesn't explain why you're here," she said.

"An associate of mine called and told me you were in some trouble. I called the Police Department to find out more."

"You just said you were busy in conference."

"I got the call about an hour and a half ago. My priorities changed, so I canceled my last appointment. Mayor Tillborough told me the matter had gone Federal and that you and Laura were escorted out of town for your own safety. I asked where you were taken, but he had no idea. I knew I wouldn't be able to get more out of him, so I used up a favor from one of my contacts in Columbus. He made a couple of quick calls, got back with me and told me you were about to be sent to a safe house."

"We don't feel very safe, if you wanna know the truth," Laura said.

"The FBI actually *told* you we were being taken to a safe house?" Barbara asked.

"I have a contact or two with them, and since I'd served as a consultant with them once before on a case, they provided me with some intel. They were discreet, of course. They told me they were initially going to take you to one of their spots in Wheeling. That would've been even farther away."

"Why are we here, then?" Laura asked.

"I didn't think Wheeling would be safe. Since I also know a couple of Federal people in the Pittsburgh area, I told them I personally know the location of two of their safe houses--which told them right off that their security had been breached.

They asked how I knew, but I told them I couldn't reveal my sources. As proof, I gave them an address. This was on a protected line, of course. It convinced them I knew what I was talking about. I suggested one of my investment properties as an alternative." He shrugged. "Now here you are."

It sounded too pat. Barbara's suspicions grew.

"So how long do we have to stay here?" Laura asked.

"As long as the threat remains."

"The threat?" Barbara asked.

"Apparently there's someone in Manville looking for you. From what I understand, he came very close to apprehending you."

Barbara found that she was growing even more uneasy. She realized Sam knew a lot of people, but this was a little much, even by his standards. "What else do you know?"

"The man looking for you is very dangerous, and as long as no one knows his whereabouts, the two of you have to stay hidden."

"Here?" Laura asked.

"It's the safest place at the moment. Don't worry. The authorities are combing the Tristate area--as well as Belmont County--for this man. It shouldn't be long before they find him. I'll wager he'll be found and arrested in just a few hours."

"This place is awful," Laura said. "It's so depressing and has a really bad smell. Is there even a kitchen?"

Sam grinned. "I'll have food brought in. I imagine the two of you are probably starving by now."

Laura shook her head. "I'm too upset to eat."

"Me, too." Barbara unbuttoned her coat. "I would *love* a cup of coffee, though."

"I'll have a fresh pot made." Sam pulled his cell phone out of his pocket.

"Sam...what else do you know about this man who's looking for me?"

He was silent for a moment. She hoped he was trying to remember--not just thinking up something else to pacify them. "I was told that he's very dangerous and good at his job."

"Anything else?"

"I don't think I really should say anything else..."

"*Please* tell us..."

"I've been told that he's been sent here to kill you."

She'd hoped he would have said something that would make her feel less frightened. His statement only made her more suspicious. It sounded like something he'd been told to say.

"That's what that FBI agent told us," she said.

Sam blinked. "Weiss...*told* you?"

"We dragged it out of him," Laura said.

"He wasn't supposed to tell you that. But at least now you know. Listen. Try and make yourselves comfortable for now. I'll start up that pot of coffee." He turned and crossed the room.

"Sam, how do you know what he was supposed to tell us?"

He stood there for a few moments, watching her. She noticed the darkness in his eyes, the tension in his jaw.

160

Just then, he shrugged. "Well, it doesn't sound like something a federal agent should be telling someone he's supposed to protect, does it?"

That made sense, but it didn't kill her suspicions. She found it very difficult to look into his eyes. They appeared so *cold*...

"What's wrong?" he asked. "Don't you believe me?"

"I'm just trying to understand how you came into this. How you seem to know everything that's going on. The safe house. The FBI. The man who wants to kill me. How you managed to get them to bring us here..."

"Barbara, I've lived here all my life. It's my business to know what's going on in this area."

She knew she should have expected such a reply. But like everything else he'd said, it had made her extremely wary.

"It helps to know things, right? Find the right circles? Develop valuable contacts, friendships?" When she didn't answer, he added, "It sure did come in handy for you and Laura, didn't it?"

She suddenly wanted him out of her space. She needed fresh air. He was sucking it out of the room.

"Well? Didn't it?"

"Yes." Her throat had become hot and raspy.

"Is something else bothering you?"

She forced herself to look into the unfathomable darkness of his eyes. "I guess I didn't realize you had Federal connections."

He said nothing. Had she blindsided him? Unlikely. The man was sharp. He was probably the quickest thinker she'd ever known.

Sure enough, she was proven right. "As I just said, it helps to develop valuable contacts." Then he disappeared through the archway.

Barbara sat stock-still and waited for her pulse to settle down. A few deep breaths did wonders, yet she still couldn't shake the horrible thought that Sam had lied to her about all this. She had no idea why. But she no longer felt safe.

"Momma?"

"Yes, baby?"

"Is everything okay?"

She knew better than lie to her daughter. But she didn't want to voice her fears. "I'm not sure, dear."

Laura gently stroked her hand. "I'm scared too, Momma..."

***

Seven taxis sat at the curb outside the terminal at Pittsburgh International Airport.

Jacobson slipped through the heavy glass doors leading to the sidewalk and froze.

Make sure you find the right cab...

His mind raced. *What the hell?*

Seven of them were sitting there. Not one, but seven.

Just how the hell am I supposed to know which one is the right cab?

His pulse hammered as the crowd veered around him. He found that he was suddenly afraid to move. Moving would take him out of his comfort zone and bring reality thundering back. As long as he stood here, reality remained in the background. The instant he took one step, he

162

became fair game, with reality the predator. With it came indecision, confusion, and the fear that he'd make a terrible mistake.

The cold fact remained: Seven cabs sat there. There were no signs, no red flags--nothing that would give him any indication of which one to pick.

A middle-aged couple hurried over to the cab in front, opened the rear door and climbed in. It pulled away and joined the busy flow. Seconds later, a well-dressed woman carrying a tan briefcase slid into the back seat of the third cab. It pulled away as well.

Five left. He wondered if he should just wait and hope for the best.

What if he waited five seconds too long? Or ten? What if some other fare took the cab intended for him?

That would be abysmal. Calls would be made. The Chief would be notified. Jacobson's career would be destroyed.

Maybe I'm supposed to make the first move...

What *was* the first move? Walk over and hope the right cabby gave him a signal? Would the driver know what was going on? What were his instructions? Pick up someone from Orlando? Was Jacobson the only visitor from Orlando?

Am I supposed to say anything? Ask questions? Mention Orlando?

Had the cabby been given my description?

He knew he wouldn't accomplish anything if he stayed here and continued being a statue.

I need to pull myself together and stop acting like a frightened kid...

Wrenching himself out of his numbness, he took two, then three awkward steps toward the curb.

The driver's door of the cab in the rear swung open. The cabby got out and stood in front of the open door, watching him.

Jacobson's heart did a tap dance. Could this be his red flag?

Still uneasy, he assessed the immediate area. There was no one to his left. To his right, three people scurried outside and rushed over to the other cabs.

The cabby raised his right arm.

Jacobson found that he was still afraid to make a move. Was this cabby simply looking for a fare?

Cabbies didn't get out of their cabs to flag down fares. There were just too many people looking for a ride. In a busy place like this, the average cabby didn't have to wait much longer than two or three minutes for a fare.

The cabby was about forty, short and wiry, and built like a jockey. He wore his cap low on his forehead, and sunglasses with large lenses and thick black frames. He gestured again, this time with his thumb.

His senses alert, Jacobson waited for a break in traffic and began crossing the street. No one else was in the cab; the meter wasn't even running.

"Orlando, Florida?" The cabby's high-pitched voice penetrated the flow of traffic.

"Yes..."

164

"No bags?"

"No..."

The cabby opened the rear door. Jacobson got in back and the cabby pushed the door shut. The photo ID on the visor didn't match the face of the man getting behind the wheel.

Jacobson's neck grew warm. "Where's the other guy? The one in the photo?"

"He's off today."

"I guess you just forgot to switch photos."

"Guess I did."

"Someone else might get nervous about that."

"Mebbe."

They merged into the heavy flow.

Jacobson squirmed in his seat to get more comfortable. He'd never been in this part of the country before and had no idea where he was going or what the driver had been told. But he knew this man had obviously been told *something*...

He stared at the reddish-brown stubble on the back of the cabby's slender neck and decided that a couple of well-placed questions might be all he needed to clear this up. Just two guys shooting the breeze--nothing out of the ordinary about that, was there?

"I don't know where I'm supposed to tell you to take me..."

"No problem."

"If you've already been told about this, I wouldn't mind if you'd let me in on what's going on--"

"Not necessary."

Jacobson kept staring at the driver and wondered how he could phrase his next question. *If he knows where he's taking me, he might also know what's going on. He really doesn't have to tell me much...*

"I'd appreciate it if you could just give me a little hint--"

"No questions."

"All I want to know is what's going on. You don't have to say anything else."

The cabby didn't avert his eyes from the traffic in front of them. "I'm s'posed to drive ya. I ain't s'posed to get chummy. Got it?"

"Loud and clear." So much for well-placed questions...

Jacobson sat back and forced himself to relax. *Take it easy and forget about everything else. In the meantime, enjoy yourself. It's the only revenge you'll get.*

The rage returned; he grew tense once again. He'd come here to do a nasty errand for a major criminal in Central Florida. How in hell could he possibly enjoy himself?

***

Momma's face was pale as she huddled close to Laura on the loveseat. She hadn't taken her eyes off the front door since Sam had left the room.

"Momma? Are you okay?"

"I'm...all right, baby."

Laura could tell Momma was trying to be strong. It was so typical of her to act like nothing was wrong. She was always more concerned about Laura than she was about herself. But this wasn't

166

the right time for them to keep things from one another.

"You're so *pale*..." She placed her hand over her mother's hands. They were ice-cold.

"It's all right, dear." Momma forced a smile. "Just nerves."

"Momma, why is Sam really here? I heard what he said, but I don't believe him. He's a developer. He buys and sells buildings and real estate. Sure, he knows a lot of people, but how could he possibly know about something like this? He couldn't have known we were coming here."

"He said--"

"He said a lot of things, Momma."

"I know, baby."

Laura tried looking at this a little differently. Sam was confident and outgoing--two qualities necessary in big business. He was the type of guy who knew everyone and always knew what to say at the right time. To thrive in his field, he had to maintain a pleasant relationship with as many people as possible.

But that wasn't the issue here. Normally, Sam would have patted Momma on the shoulder, squeezed her arm and flashed one of his gleaming grins. But he'd been cold and detached ever since he'd met them outside. He'd been considerate to both Laura and Momma during the short walk to the house, but there were no friendly displays.

Sam's presence should have made them feel better. Instead, it had made this more frightening. If she and Momma were to believe what he'd just told them, Sam had *told* the FBI to bring them here.

167

That notion defied both logic and belief. Laura suspected it was all one big fat lie.

How would Sam know Wheeling wasn't safe? How would he know the location of an FBI safe house? As far as she and Momma knew, Sam had nothing to do with the FBI. Even if he did know people in the Bureau, who would give him the authority to discuss a federal case with them, as well as change its venue?

Had he been working for the FBI all these years without anyone knowing?

Momma got up from the loveseat and crept over to the small oval window in the center of the front door. She watched for about half a minute, came right back and sat back down beside Laura. Her face remained pale, her features tense.

"What's happening out there, Momma?"

"There's no one out there. Just the sedan and a big black SUV on the other side of the street in front of that abandoned garage."

"Is Weiss still sitting in the sedan?"

"I think so, dear."

"What about the SUV?"

"I can't tell. Part of it's hidden by the sedan."

Something occurred to Laura. "Didn't you tell me Sam bought up some property out this way?"

"That could explain why there's no activity out there."

"He probably bought everyone out so he could clear the buildings for demolition or refurbishing."

The strong smell of fresh coffee drifted lazily into the area. Laura heard the murmur of voices and what sounded like a hard object placed on a counter, or table.

"He's handling a major project out here that's scheduled to begin breaking ground later on this summer--" Momma stopped talking. She and Laura turned sharply toward the archway.

Sam came in carrying two Styrofoam cups of hot coffee, which he placed on the end table at Barbara's left elbow. "Sugar and cream," he said. "Just as you like it, Barbara."

"Thank you." Momma continued staring at the front door.

"Cream and sugar for you, too, Laura." He straightened. "I wasn't sure. I just guessed."

Barbara. Laura. Sam had always referred to them as "Barb" and "Laurie." Two more signs that something was amiss.

"Thanks."

He smiled briefly. "I've got to take care of something. I'll be back in a few minutes." He disappeared through the archway.

Laura shivered in her seat. She was more convinced than ever that she and Momma were in grave danger.

***

Across the street, Leonard "Gorilla" Crowley sat behind the wheel of the black utility van, playing Solitaire on his iPad. No one had called lately to tell him anything new, and he was getting damned impatient. He'd been sitting here for nearly an hour and had already been cramping up. If he didn't get out and stretch shortly, he'd be miserable. The leather seat was comfortable, but these long periods of immobility kicked his ass. He'd been a soldier most of his adult life, but when a man passed forty, his old wounds fussed much louder and more frequently than they used to.

He was about to take a break from the iPad when something cracked sharply against the passenger window.

Crowley jerked in his seat. With shaky fingers he dropped the iPad on the console beside him. Using his other hand, he snatched the Glock from the pancake holster clipped to his belt beneath his jacket. His gaze on the abandoned garage thirty feet to his right, he pulled his cell from the cup tray on the dash and flicked it on.

Josh Milan's voice came on immediately. "'Sup?"

"Somethin' just hit my window."

"Bird?"

"It was more like a rock. Or a chunk of gravel."

"Some asshole hidin' in the woods, playin' games?"

"Might be. It happens again, I'll call back."

He pocketed the cell and kept his eye on the sloping hill extending next to the garage. Since Sam Albright owned most of the block, no one should be nosing around. The area was deserted, and their instructions were pretty clear.

Miles Lester, whom Crowley had worked for many times in the last few years, said that someone big in Florida might have paid a hitter to come to the Valley and dust Sam Albright. Crowley knew that could be highly possible. Albright had made a lot of enemies. A competitor would pay a lot of money to take him out of the picture.

Lester was paying Crowley, Weiss, Milan, Devlin, and Levinson good money to keep Albright safe, and had offered a bonus of twenty K to anyone who found this hitter and brought him down. A really great incentive package indeed. Crowley hoped this was true. Otherwise, the bonus could be just bullshit to keep everyone in line.

His eyes still on the building, Crowley rolled down a window and listened. After five minutes of intense silence, he closed the window and sat back. His nerves, no doubt. Milan might be right-- probably was a fucking bird after all. This gig was getting to all of them.

Albright shouldn't have brought along those two females. One of them was a cripple, so Crowley didn't think it was a sex thing. Weiss said the older one worked for Albright and the younger one was her daughter. If the mother worked for Albright, she probably knew things she shouldn't, and could be a liability.

Crowley hoped Albright wasn't using them as bait. Or, even more likely, a shield if things blew up. Rich jerks like Albright weren't usually heroes.

Whatever the reason, Crowley hoped this wasn't some complicated kidnapping scheme. He'd done some bad things for money before but wanted no part of it when it came to snatching folks. A double kidnapping would earn you the needle if things went bad and the women turned up dead.

The silence continued. Crowley settled back in his seat and tried to relax.

About a minute later, another sharp *crack*! made his ears ring as something ricocheted off the glass.

What the fuck? Ducking down, he whacked his beefy shoulder on the console. His three-hundred-and-fifty-pound frame prevented extreme movement, even with the seat pulled way back. But at least now he knew it wasn't his imagination. Someone was tossing pebbles at his window.

No reason to call anyone. If the hitter was out there, Crowley saw no need to share that bonus.

He got out. Crouching, he kept his six-foot-six-inch frame below the level of the SUV's windows. A quick glance told him Weiss was watching him from the sedan across the street.

Weiss rolled down his window. "Everything okay?"

"Just checkin' somethin'."

"Lemme know if you need backup."

"Right." *In a pig's eye, asshole...* Crowley would never ask Weiss for help. The bastard was as crooked as they came. You didn't want him eyeing your back.

Keeping low, Crowley peered around the rear end of the SUV and caught a blur of movement at the bottom of the hill, behind the abandoned garage. It looked like something had shifted on the ground.

Staying close to the block wall, he crept across the slope, past the overgrown brush hugging the corner of the building. His gun was out. His senses alert, he kept a steady watch on the area directly in front of him. It had been twenty years since he'd

172

worn his Green Beret uniform, but that kind of training stayed with a guy.

He finally made it to the rear of the building.

The crumbling pavement was a mess. Stacks of old tires, food wrappings, car husks on blocks, food scraps, beer cans, shattered bottles and piles of cigarette butts covered the large area.

A Belly Buster cup lay on its side, rolling around in a small circle. It might have been what he'd seen moving before.

But *some*thing had whacked his passenger window--not once, but twice. A Belly Buster cup couldn't have done that.

Tossing rocks was a crude but effective way of setting up an ambush. An experienced hitter would go after them one at a time. Weiss would be next, then Milan and Levinson. With Albright and Devlin the only two left, suckering Devlin would be the final step. Devlin wouldn't go down easy, but once he was out of commission, Albright would be a sitting duck.

This definitely smelled like a trap. But with the element of surprise gone, the enemy had lost its advantage.

Time for a little distraction of his own...

Crowley reached into his pants pocket, grabbed a handful of change and tossed the coins high in the air. They came back down, hopping on the cracked, uneven pavement twenty feet away and then rolling in several different directions.

Crowley waited a full minute but heard nothing. Then, his gun held straight out, he took two quick steps and pivoted around the corner.

No one was standing there.

Crowley kept his arm steady as he aimed the Glock at the dark open area straight ahead. He knew he should start shooting but found that he didn't want to pull the trigger. Was it because he didn't see anyone or hear anything? Or because he didn't want to give his position away?

He also didn't want Weiss knowing what he was up to. If Weiss heard a gunshot, he'd be here in a flash. Then he'd try horning in on the bounty money even though Crowley was the one who'd sniffed out the hitter...

But he had to do *some*thing. He didn't want to stand here all day. It wasn't the wind that had tossed those pebbles at the SUV...

The killer could be hiding in the darkness, waiting for Crowley to make a move. Twenty thousand bucks could buy a ton of steak dinners, a case or two of Italian wine--even a couple of custom-tailored imported suits. With the hitter out of the way, Sam Albright would be extremely grateful...

But something didn't add up. If a hitter *was* hiding in the garage, why hadn't he used his gun? He wouldn't be too concerned about making noise; pros almost always used silencers. So what was the story here? Crowley surely couldn't see him. But Crowley was outside, and in plain sight. An easy target.

"Anyone in there?"

Silence. Time to try a bluff.

"Listen...I know you're in there. There's no other place you can be. C'mon out."

Dead silence.

He squinted, trying to see into the darkness beyond the collapsed doors. He wanted to rub his eyes but soon found that he needed both hands to steady the gun.

Why do I suddenly need both hands to hold onto a Glock 19? Damn thing doesn't even weigh two pounds...

A shadow began moving slowly toward him. Once it emerged from the darkness, it became a tall, fit-looking man with short dark hair and clear gray eyes.

Crowley suddenly found that he was no longer afraid.

The man continued approaching. He had no gun. His hands were empty.

Just then, his left hand came up and rested on Crowley's shoulder.

A shimmer of warmth rushed down his body. Crowley felt as if he'd just been revitalized. He felt no cramping whatsoever from sitting in the SUV for so long. He looked at his hands again. They were empty. His gun lay on the pavement at his feet. He couldn't remember dropping it, nor could he remember hearing it clatter...

What mattered was that he knew he'd never use it again. This was good because he didn't *want* to use it again. He didn't even want to *look* at the damned thing again. It brought back *way* too many bad memories.

You need to turn your life around...

The voice was soft and soothing, and sounded like it was in his head.

The man's hand left Crowley's shoulder, and Crowley found himself thinking about the church at the bottom of the hill, just off the main road. It had been a long time since he'd been in a church--a long time indeed.

Crowley closed his eyes. He thought of his father, his mother, his sisters and his brothers. It had been years since he'd thought of them. Back then, when he was growing up in the Bronx, he played stickball in the street with his brothers and friends. He'd skipped school all the time and did bad things that brought shame to the family.

But that happened a long time ago, and many of the things he'd done were long forgotten. Momma and Dad were dead. Leonard was a grown man, and things were going to be different.

He pulled in some fresh air and opened his eyes.

Feeling warm and happy for the first time in ages, Leonard Crowley began walking down the hill that would take him to the church.

***

Sam came back into the living room and stopped cold. He stared at the coffee cups on the end table. "You haven't touched your coffee."

Coffee was the last thing on Barbara's mind. Her feelings of isolation had intensified during the last few minutes. She couldn't stop thinking that she and Laura had somehow become involved with some very bad people and that Sam was one of them. "I'm all right. I'll have some later."

"It might relax you, make you feel better."

He actually sounded concerned. Or was he putting on an act for some ulterior reason?

She was being silly. She'd known Sam for five years. He was her boss and good friend. She'd met him for the first time at the Ohio Valley Mall one bright Saturday afternoon. Joe's departure a few weeks earlier had prompted her to do a complete makeover of her bedroom. She hadn't been able to sleep very well since Joe had left and was convinced it was because so much of him lingered in the room.

After discussing it with Laura, Barbara decided to redo the room. This required painting the walls and changing the bedclothes and curtains. All family photos, except those showing him with Laura, were dropped in a shoebox, taped shut and tossed in the attic.

Sam bumped into them at the Food Mart, where they'd stopped for lattes. He timidly approached their table and handed her a twenty-dollar-bill he'd seen drop from her handbag.

Barbara had been skeptical at first. Since Laura had paid for their lunch that day, Barbara hadn't even remembered opening her bag. But she knew she hadn't been thinking clearly since Joe had left and conceded that she might have dropped the bill without even being aware of it.

Who else but an honest man would have done such a thing?

You're being ridiculous. This is Sam, for heaven's sake. You know he's not going to hurt you, so stop acting so suspicious!

177

But although that made perfect sense, she still found the last few hours difficult to process. The mugging. The mysterious man appearing from out of nowhere to save them. Weiss taking them from the Police Station, bringing them here. Sam's explanation of what was going on.

Most of all, someone wanting her dead.

Have you ever considered the fact that Sam might have told you the truth?

"Barbara?"

"Yes?"

He held out the cup.

She took it. Sam was only trying to help. He knew how much she loved her coffee. He'd gone to the trouble of making a pot just for her and Laura; it would be rude not to drink at least some of it.

"I'm sorry. I know I'm not acting like myself--"

"You have every right to be upset. I would be, too, under these same circumstances."

She took a sip; it was strong and a tad bitter. Like most men, Sam seldom took the time to clean out the pot. But at least it was hot. "You don't think I'm being too…paranoid?"

"You've had quite a shock. You were attacked in broad daylight then told that a man has come here to kill you, and possibly Laura as well."

"Why would anyone want to kill *me*?" Laura pushed herself up. "*I* haven't done anything!"

"If you're with your mom when he finds her, he'll have no choice."

"My God!" Laura turned pale.

He handed Laura her cup but she shook her head. He put it back on the table. "We don't know who hired this man. That's the one thing that'll explain all this. You won't know what's going on until you find out who his employer is."

"But it makes no sense," Barbara said. "I haven't done anything to deserve any of this."

"As I said, we don't know who hired him. For all we know, your ex-husband might be involved."

That made no sense, either. "Joe was an insurance agent. He couldn't have been mixed up in anything like this. Besides, we haven't seen or heard from him in five years."

"You don't actually know what he got into when he left, do you?"

Barbara felt her skin heating up. She didn't like the insinuation. As much as she hated Joe for leaving, she couldn't believe he'd be involved in anything criminal. "Joe was the type who stopped at stop signs even when no one else was around. He wouldn't even toss a gum wrapper from a moving car. He'd *never* be involved in anything illegal or dangerous."

"I'm just grasping at straws. He left you, moved to Florida and you never heard from him again. Now, five years later, a hired killer shows up, and the word is that he's looking for you. Someone might think your ex-husband may have communicated with you recently."

"He left me, Sam. I waited a full two years before I filed for divorce on grounds of desertion. I don't know how my attorney got with his...if he went through the Florida legal system to find him…but apparently everything went through. Joe signed the papers. So why would he need me for anything?"

"I don't know, Barbara. Maybe he got into something really deep and found himself backed into a corner. Maybe you were the only one he thought he could trust. He might have taken something from the wrong person. It might have been an accident or a fluke, and by the time he realized what he'd done, it was too late for him to return what he'd taken. He may have heard people were looking for him. It might have scared him, sent him into a panic. Maybe you were the only one he could trust. Maybe the owner of the stolen merchandise also thought of that and hired someone to come here to find you, retrieve what your ex-husband took, and bring it back."

She suddenly felt warm. Everything was taking its toll on her nerves. And she was fairly certain the coffee hadn't set well with her. "Sam, I haven't seen or heard from Joe since the day he left."

"He never called?"

"You know he didn't."

"He phoned Laura, didn't he?"

"At the hospital," Laura said. "That's what they tell me, anyway. It's kind of tricky to talk on the phone when you're unconscious."

Barbara opened her collar. The room was getting even warmer. The excitement, no doubt. Some fresh air would be wonderful…

"You sure you didn't talk to him?" Sam asked.

Sam's grim expression frightened her. Once again she sensed that he didn't believe her. "Yes,

Sam. I'm sure. The only thing I'm not really sure about--"

A tall, broad-shouldered man with long dark hair tied in a thick ponytail, dark eyes and a handsome young face slipped quietly into the room. Barbara hadn't even realized he was in the room until he was just a few feet from Sam. He stepped closer and whispered something to him. Sam straightened abruptly and the other man turned back around and left the room--just as quietly.

Sam gave them a quick nod. "I'll be right back. Enjoy your coffee." Then he hurried through the archway.

"Momma?"

Barbara gazed at the archway. She barely heard anything, just an occasional murmur. She wondered what the other man had said to Sam. She'd seen genuine alarm on Sam's face just before he'd left the room.

She found herself growing suspicious again. Angry, as well. Sam had never doubted her word before.

This room had become uncomfortably warm and musty. She needed some fresh air. If only she hadn't suddenly become so *tired...*

She rubbed her eyes. *Force yourself up, cross the room, open the door and step outside. You'll get all the fresh air you need. Fight the dizziness, the overwhelming desire to lie down...*

Why were her eyes so tired? Why were her eyelids so heavy? Why did her arms feel so *rubbery*?

"Momma? You all right?"

181

Laura's voice sounded so far away...

PART 2 - *Predator*

CHAPTER NINE

While Devlin kept watch on the women, Sam Albright opened the back door, stepped out onto the tiny porch, and pulled the cell from his pocket. He pressed the appropriate number and waited nervously for the familiar voice to come on.

"Why'd it take you two minutes to call me back?" Big Al sounded angrier than usual.

"I was...questioning the women." Albright loosened his collar so he could breathe easier. Talking to this man was always stressful.

"Any progress?"

"I just started a couple of minutes ago, but they're not telling me anything. Not what we need to know, anyway."

"Maybe you're not asking the right questions. Or maybe you're just not asking them the right way. How hard are you doing this?"

He regarded the shadow in the kitchen archway and felt a chill sliding down his back. As much as he dreaded all this, he knew the time would come when Devlin would have to be called in.

Hopefully, this would be their last resort. Devlin tended to get overenthusiastic very quickly about his work and frequently turned deaf when asked to stop his interrogations. Devlin was young, but he'd been killing and torturing folks for years and enjoyed it. He did it quite well and didn't seem to mind when someone died before giving him the information he'd wanted.

Albright was a businessman. Violence--especially during a business transaction--made his ulcers act up. This had to be handled delicately. The two victims involved were female, and one of them was crippled.

"I think I should go easy for a little while," he said.

Big Al groaned. "We don't *have* a little while, dammit. We're running out of time, and I'm not getting the cooperation I've been paying good money for. Some idiot flew up there to blow this wide open, and no one up there seems to be having any luck finding him. What's really ticking me off is that he's making a mess of everything that's being done on your end."

"We've got people looking for him all over the County."

"They haven't found him yet, have they?"

"Well, no, but--"

"Any chance that he might get to the women before we find what we're looking for?"

"No chance, sir. I've got them hidden in a good place. And I've got four good men watching the property. No one can get close enough to pose a threat."

"Well, at least you did *some*thing right."

Albright sighed. "I'm sure that I'll only need another half-hour or so before Barbara Neilson will tell me--"

"Let me put it this way: If you're not up to this, you'll need someone else to step in--someone who does this sort of thing for a living. I've used Devlin before. He can get a cadaver to talk in five minutes if given half the chance."

That statement made Albright nauseous. "I'm up to it..."

"You'd better not be blowing smoke up my ass."

"I can do this."

"Just reminding you what the stakes are. We're talking a minimum of eight figures for this project, but only if it takes off when it's supposed to."

"I don't need a reminder. As I just said, I can do this--and without reverting to any of...*that*..."

"Then *do* it, goddammit. We don't have all fucking day."

Click.

Another chill rolled down his back as he pocketed the cell. He pulled in some fresh air and went back inside.

"Need me to step in?" Devlin stood in the center of the kitchen, his dark eyes glittering. He looked like a drug dog anxious to search a vehicle.

Albright scowled. It irritated him that this man enjoyed such nasty work so much. But sadists weren't wired like normal people.

"Not yet." Albright went over to the archway and froze.

Laura had apparently hobbled across the living room and was in the process of opening the front door.

***

185

A hand came from out of nowhere, encircling Laura's upper arm in a viselike grip. She wrenched free, slamming her shoulder into the wall. A giant knot of blinding pain exploded in her lower back. Gasping, she clenched her jaw, closed her eyes and stood perfectly still, waiting tensely for the flames to ebb. When she opened her eyes, the man with the thick ponytail faced her. He stood just inches away. His dark eyes glistened; a tense smile appeared on his face. His eyes stayed focused on her neck for long, terrifying moments before drifting down to her breasts, then returning to her neck...

Oh my God... He's actually enjoying this...but it doesn't feel like a sex thing, it's something else... He wants to do horrible things to me...

She tried to move, to look away, but found herself trapped in his gaze. Drool trickled from the corners of his mouth, gathering on his chin. His hands were open and moved steadily toward her neck.

Her heart thrashed wildly. Dizziness turned everything gray. She hoped she'd pass out before his hands reached her neck...

"You need to go back in the kitchen..." Sam's voice sounded far away. *"Now!"*

The man blinked, snapping out of it. His smile vanished immediately. His hands lowered to his sides.

Laura felt as if she'd just been released from his grasp. The pain in her back returned, slicing through her. She gasped and leaned against the wall.

186

When her vision cleared, she saw that the psycho had already disappeared.

"Sorry, Laura. That shouldn't have happened. I hope you're not--"

"I'm fine..." The words burned as they squeezed out of her throat. The fire in her spine roared. "Just *fine*."

She glanced toward the archway. There was no sign of him. But that didn't reassure her. He was somewhere in the next room, just seconds away.

Sam seemed genuinely concerned. "If there's anything I can do..."

"I said *I'm fine!*" The pain climbing up her spine had diminished. She staggered back to the loveseat, where Momma sprawled, the back of her head on the padded arm. She hadn't stirred at all during the commotion.

This told Laura she'd been right: something definitely *was* wrong.

"Where were you going?" Sam asked softly.

"It's not important now, is it?" Laura struggled to keep her anger in check.

"There's a dangerous man out there, and if he finds out where you two are, he'll...well, it would be disastrous for you to be out in plain view right now."

She collapsed in the seat beside Momma. Her back still ached. Ignoring her own discomfort, she covered Momma's stiff, warm hands with her own. "Momma?"

No response.

This wasn't just exhaustion or stress. Momma had never passed out like this before...

Sam frowned. "Laura, I've been looking out for both of you since--"

"You're not looking out for us. You're keeping us here against our will!"

"Whatever would make you think *that*?"

Laura gawked at him. "Weren't you paying attention to what just happened?"

"Let me apologize once more for that. As I've said before, there's a killer out there, and we can't afford to let him know where you and your mother are... "

"I don't want to debate that right now. Right now, I'm more concerned about my mother. She's sick, and something tells me you know why."

"She's not sick, Laura."

"Look at her. She's totally zoned out, and she has a fever."

"She's not sick." He approached the loveseat. "Laura, I don't know why you're suddenly so suspicious..."

"I've been suspicious ever since we were hauled out of the Police Station. Nothing makes sense, but that no longer concerns me. All I care about is getting Momma to a doctor."

"There's nothing wrong with your mother. She's exhausted--no doubt from all this running around."

"It's more than that and you know it."

"She's sleeping. This incident has obviously taken its toll. I'm sure that when she's in her own bed, she'll be back to her old self."

"And when will that be?"

"When the killer is caught, I'll take you both home and we can forget all about this."

"I'm sick and tired of hearing about some killer that no one seems to know anything about!"

"Why all this suspicion? Why would you think I'd do anything that would hurt you or your mother?"

"Look at her. And look at me. Momma's practically comatose, and I'm a bundle of nerves!"

"You're not yourself. It's understandable. People react in extreme ways during a crisis. Everything is frightening, strange, and confusing."

"Yes. I know. We're all safe and sound right now. All tucked away and hidden from some dangerous killer who came all this way just to murder my mother. And according to you, he'll do me in, too, if I happen to be within earshot of Momma when he kills her. I know all that. There's only one thing that bugs me about all this."

"What's that?"

"It doesn't make any sense--especially the part about the FBI handing us over to you. C'mon, Sam. Do you honestly expect us to believe any of that?"

"It's the truth, Laura. I know how it must sound, but--"

"There's really no killer, is there?"

"Of course there's a killer. Whatever would make you think otherwise?"

"I've been wondering about this ever since we were brought here. I don't personally know any professional killers, but it seems to me that if one *was* sent here, he would've done the deed long before anyone would have even found out what was going on. Killers have to know how to blend into the shadows. Otherwise, they'll be caught and put in prison, or executed. But Momma and I are still alive, and this tells me that if he's here, it's for some other reason. And since you're involved, I think you know what that reason is."

"And just how would I know that?"

"As you keep telling everyone, you know everything that's going on around here. Isn't that right?"

The tension on Sam's face increased, but he merely smiled. It frightened her, convinced her once again that he was concealing something.

But in spite of her fears, her suspicions, the only thing that mattered was getting help for Momma.

"Will you *please* get a doctor here to look after my mother?"

"Laura, she doesn't need medical help."

"What if you're wrong?"

He took a few steps closer, bent and smiled at Momma. "Barbara? Can you hear me?"

Momma stirred. "Yes, Sam," she whispered hoarsely.

Momma's sing-songy tone frightened Laura.

"Momma?" She rubbed her mother's wrists. "Can we get you anything?"

"You don't need anything, do you, Barbara?" Sam asked gently.

"No, Sam. I really don't..."

"All you need is a little rest, and you'll be fine."

"Yes, Sam... I'll be...just fine..."

Laura gawked at her. This felt very, very wrong. Momma acted like she'd been wakened from a deep sleep. Just ten minutes ago, she'd been fine.

They had to get out of here as quickly as possible. The pain in her back had returned. She needed fresh air, a shower. This building had become a tomb. Everything was closing in, growing darker. Momma lay there, so lifeless. The back of her head rested on the arm of the loveseat, just inches from the end table, where the coffee cup sat…

The coffee cup. Sing-songy voice. Blood-shot eyes. Exhausted. Sleepy.

Everything was fine before Momma had sipped the coffee.

My God. What did Sam put in the coffee?

Laura straightened; her spine protested strongly. She needed her meds but didn't want to hunt for them with Sam standing there…

His cell buzzed. He snatched it from his jacket pocket, turned around and whispered into it. Then he turned back around. "I've got to run an errand. It's unavoidable, I'm afraid. But I won't be very long."

Laura shivered.

Sam noted her reaction. "Don't worry. When I return, we'll continue our little talk. Your mother will be feeling much better shortly. I've got a few questions I need to ask her, and I'm sure she'll feel more like herself after her nap. You should relax and have some coffee, too. It'll do you a world of good." He turned and slipped through the archway.

191

Laura closed her eyes and struggled to keep the panic away.

***

"I've got to leave right now." Albright led Devlin out through the kitchen, to the rear porch.

Devlin eased the door shut. "The big man?"

"I'll probably be at least an hour. Watch them, but whatever you do, don't get physical. And don't pull that same stupid stunt. That could've turned disastrous."

Devlin looked like a child whose favorite toy had just been taken away. "She tried to *leave*..."

"As you've no doubt noticed, she can't move around very well, and she can't run at all. There was really no need to get physical. You could have *killed* her, dammit. And with the daughter dead, the mother would prove totally useless."

"But she was opening the door..."

"She's worried about her mother."

"That makes her dangerous." Devlin's eyes had grown more animated. "We don't want her to leave, right?"

"To repeat what I just said—*don't touch her.*" Albright sincerely hoped his message sunk in. Like all sadists, Devlin let his own savage animal instincts dictate his movements. With him, violence was a strong biological urge, much like sex in normal people. And when something twanged the right nerve, Devlin zoned out and immediately slipped into his own dark world. Albright didn't want to come back to find two corpses.

"We need answers from them," he said. "We can't get the answers we want if they're hurt. As

192

you well know, when you're in pain, you focus on the pain."

Devlin smiled coldly. "I know how to get answers, and sometimes the only way to get them is to--"

"I know all about your work, believe me."

"It's why I was sent here, isn't it?"

"The project needs someone with your skills. But my reputation is on the line, so this has to be done my way. When I get back, we'll have to work a little harder to get the answers we're looking for."

Devlin's eyes sparkled. "You'd be surprised how effective a broken finger or two can be at the right time…"

"You heard me. None of that unless the drugs don't work. But we need to give them a little time. I could work on the mother if I didn't have to leave right now. I'll call you the first chance I get. You'd better not tell me you've done anything to them. Understand?"

No reply.

"I said, understand?"

A nod.

"Just keep an eye on them. The mother will probably sleep until I bring her back around."

"How do I handle the daughter if I'm not supposed to do anything physical?"

"She's all fired up right now, but as I just said, she can't run. Even if she could, she won't leave her mother. As long as they think there's a killer out there looking for them, they'll stick around. If you want to do something constructive, get her to drink some coffee. Then she'll zone out like the mother and probably sleep until I get back."

Albright left the porch and headed for the garage at the end of the walk. He got out his cell and pressed Levinson's number. "Where are you?"

"About half a block north. I'm watchin' things from the front porch of the beat-up two-story. Haven't seen anything."

"We need to be at the Mall."

"What's goin' on?"

"We just got a call. Apparently one of our contacts saw a familiar face at the Mall."

"Why there?"

"The daughter works at the coffeehouse out there. We've been watching the Neilson house for the last two weeks. If this man really is who we've all been looking for, he'll know the house is being watched. His next logical move would be to look up the daughter."

"But why the Mall?"

"He might've gone there first to see if anyone followed him. He could shake a tail a lot easier in a crowd. Then he'll probably slip back out through some other exit and check out the coffeehouse on his way out."

"He doesn't know any of us, does he?"

"We have to assume he knows everything that's going on. We've got to get there, spread out, and find him before he disappears again."

"We have a description?"

"Weiss apparently does."

"Can't Josh and Weiss handle this?"

"In this case, four people can find one man in a crowd a lot faster than just two. We're running out of time and we've got to speed things up. Anyway, I'm leaving Devlin with the women, so we won't have to worry about them. I'd like Crowley there, too, so I'm going to text him as soon as we leave."

"Milan called me a while ago, said the big guy was checkin' somethin' out behind the abandoned garage."

"Damn. He really needs to know what's going on. But we can't wait. I'll call him before we get there."

"Sounds good."

***

Peering around the corner of the vacant house next door, Desmond Roth watched Albright marching briskly toward the two-car garage at the end of the drive between the buildings.

Roth hadn't liked what he'd just seen. He'd heard all about Leon Devlin years ago and had seen his work. People with big money contacted Devlin whenever they faced problems that needed fixed quickly and didn't care who was killed in the process. Devlin was barely thirty, but apparently had killed more than sixty people. He'd been a bodyguard and wet boy for one of the Colombian cartels at the tender age of eighteen--a distinction that would demand respect from the most vicious, cold-blooded killer.

Roth knew not to underestimate a professional killer. Devlin had to be brought down fast and hard. And since Albright was leaving the premises, this left Devlin alone with the women.

The problem, of course, was how to bring Devlin down without endangering the women. You just didn't go up against a psycho like Devlin and expect to walk away without anyone getting hurt.

***

Laura cringed the moment she heard the muffled moan of a vehicle hurrying down the drive past the house. A moment later, the floor creaked lightly a few feet on her right. The guy with the ponytail and the scary eyes appeared through the archway and stood there, his big-knuckled hands clasped together in front of him as he watched her.

Despite the cold fear growing within her, Laura forced herself to stay strong--not only for herself, but especially for Momma, who lay slumped beside her.

Why would Sam leave us here with this monster?

I won't be very long...

My God...five minutes alone with him was enough to make her want to scream!

She had to fight the fear. She somehow had to convince him that she wasn't as weak or as fragile as she appeared. Her back throbbed, but it didn't matter. She mustn't show weakness. She could tell that he was the sort who fed on it.

I'll protect you, Momma, she thought, grasping her mother's forearm. *I won't let him do anything to either of us.*

Momma moaned softly and moved her head a couple of inches in Laura's direction.

"I'm right here, Momma."

"I feel...so weak..."

196

"I know."

"I'm so...thirsty..." The tip of Momma's tongue came out, sliding across her parted lips. "I need...water..."

The simple request fired her up. Laura shot him an unflinching look. "My mother needs water." Thank God her voice sounded strong enough. It might convince him she wouldn't be intimidated.

He didn't budge.

"I said--"

"I heard you." His voice was a mere whisper. But he still didn't move.

"Then why aren't you getting her water?"

His eyes didn't flinch. "She hasn't finished her coffee."

"She wants *water*..."

Silence.

"We won't try anything."

He almost smiled.

Laura understood right then. He *wanted* her to try something. His nostrils had flared, opening and closing rapidly. He was obviously getting excited. She remembered his expression when she'd tried opening the front door. He'd resembled a wolf hungrily eyeing its prey.

Stay strong... Crumbling would only feed this man's hunger.

"My mother's thirsty. She doesn't feel well. But you probably already know that."

No response. His nostrils continued to flare.

He wants me to beg... It'll be another turn-on...

"I won't try to escape, I promise. I'll get her the water if you don't want to. I'll even use her coffee cup."

He still didn't move.

Laura felt the back of her neck growing warmer. She wanted to leap from the loveseat and claw his face.

He watched Momma for a few moments. Then he glanced at Laura, turned around and disappeared through the archway.

Laura stared at the empty archway in disbelief. She listened but heard nothing. She hoped he wasn't just standing around in there, waiting for her to grow impatient and do something stupid...

I'll wait him out if I have to.

But she knew she couldn't wait very long. She had to think of Momma.

"Don't worry, Momma, I'll make sure you have some water..."

She suddenly wondered what would happen if Sam's story about the killer was actually true. What if the killer had found out where they were? What if he'd been watching the house and was waiting for Sam to leave?

She tilted her head, listening. She heard nothing, but couldn't shake the feeling that someone could be out there, waiting to sneak in.

She began wondering about the vehicle she'd heard driving past the house just a few minutes earlier. Was that Sam? Weiss? How many of them were there?

Momma stirred. "Baby? Everything...all right?"

No need to worry Momma in her present state. "Momma, just lie there and relax. I'm just a little worried right now…"

"It's okay. We'll manage. Somehow…"

Laura closed her eyes and suddenly sensed someone outside.

It finally happened; she'd gone stark-raving mad. But it was no wonder. Given their situation, she should already be pulling her hair out.

But what if she was right? What if a killer *was* waiting for the right moment to sneak in? What should she do? What *could* she do?

She didn't have many options. She couldn't tell Sam's psycho friend. He'd suspect her of trying to pull something. Besides, she was more afraid of him than anyone else. That made no sense, but she couldn't help the way she felt.

A moment later, he came through the archway carrying a Styrofoam cup. He crossed the room and stopped just a couple of feet from the loveseat. His cold, dark eyes slithered over her as he held out the cup.

Avoiding the man's eyes, Laura kept her gaze fixed firmly on the cup as she took it. "Thank you."

"You should drink some, too," he said.

Had she heard him right? Was he really concerned about her after all?

No. It wasn't concern--it was something else…

Once again she thought she imagined a faceless shadow lurking out back. She felt unsteady and began shaking.

He's coming in and he's going to shoot all of us.

But why would a hired killer want to kill her and Momma?

The answer was simple: He wouldn't. Neither Laura nor Momma had done anything to deserve this. If a hired killer *was* coming in, he wasn't coming for her and Momma.

"Baby...the water...please?"

She realized only then that she'd been holding the cup out in front of her like an idiot. "Sorry, Momma..." Still shaking, she turned toward Momma.

"You have some first," he said.

"That's all right. Momma needs it more than I do."

"Drink some of it... *Now*..."

She stared at the cup and wondered what he'd put in it. *I can't drink this...I really can't... If I do, both Momma and I will be at this man's mercy--*

"Drink it!" His voice sounded like a bark.

Trembling, she caught a quick peek at this man's cold dark eyes and knew in that one instant that she couldn't possibly do as he'd said.

But how could she avoid it?

Everyone expects you to be a klutz, so act the part.

Yes. She was crippled, and much less coordinated than most others. Losing most of the strength in your back and legs almost always made a person clumsy and awkward.

She shifted her weight a little too quickly in Momma's direction. The movement, as expected, upset her balance. The cup leaped from her hand, splashing the man's trousers and shoes.

Ignoring the hot, razor-sharp pain slicing through her lower back, she gave him her most pathetic look. "I'm so *sorry*! So terribly *clumsy*!"

She bent painfully toward the cup. Before she could even get to it, she glanced up at him.

A savage-looking fillet knife was pointed at her face.

***

Hearing the panic in Laura's voice, Barbara forced her eyes open. She felt very weak, and her eyes just didn't want to cooperate. Everything was blurry and dark. She squinted. A dark figure was standing before them.   Then her vision cleared.

A gleaming knife protruded from the figure's right hand.

It was pointed at Laura's face.

Oh my God... What on earth is happening?

She struggled to sit up but discovered she was much too weak. Just as the panic took over, she caught a blur coming from the direction of the archway on their right.

Another dark figure, a man, had slipped silently into the room. He crept up to the other figure and stopped close behind him. The second figure flinched but didn't move.

"Drop the knife," the first man said.

The other man didn't budge. The first man nudged him. The second man spun around. There was a grunt. Something thumped loudly to the wooden floor.

Barbara's heart sputtered. In her panic, she was finally able to see everything. The man with the knife tried to strike the other man. Blocking the blow, the other man reached out with his free hand and touched the first man's neck. The first man immediately slipped quietly to the floor.

The man's knife lay on the floor beside him, just a few feet from a cell phone.

"You ladies all right?"

Barbara tried once again to sit up. She wanted to ask what was going on, but the inside of her mouth felt as if it was stuffed with cotton. Her head fell back. Then the man spoke again.

"What's wrong with your mother?"

"She's very weak. We've got to get her to a hospital. I think she's--"

"No time for that." He picked up the knife and cell phone. Pocketing them, he approached the loveseat.

Barbara watched him. Her thoughts were dark and hazy, but she could reason. This could not possibly be the killer Sam had told them about. She didn't know who he was but was convinced he was no killer. And as soon as he bent over her, she thought of Joe again.

"Wh-What are you doing?" Laura whispered.

He began gently rubbing her wrists. Barbara immediately felt a flood of warmth rushing up her arms. The warmth exploded the moment it reached her shoulders. The darkness smothering her disappeared. The sluggishness was gone as well. She felt alive again.

She sat up, totally alert.

"Feeling better?"

"Very much. Thank you."

"Momma? What...did he *do*?"

202

"He made me better, baby."

"How?"

"I don't know…"

He straightened and gently pulled her into a standing position. She felt some weakness in her knees and nearly collapsed, but he held her until she could support her own weight. "We've got to get out of here," he said.

Laura remained on the loveseat.

"You coming?" he asked Laura.

She raised her eyes and stared at him.

Barbara could tell Laura was confused. Barbara was confused as well.

What just happened? What did this man do to me? Why do I suddenly feel alive again?

She decided it didn't matter. She felt wonderful and suddenly realized that they might be able to get away from this place. But she also knew it would be dangerous to tempt fate. "C'mon, baby. Let's go." She wouldn't feel safe until they were miles away from here.

Laura reluctantly took her eyes off the man lying on the floor and raised them. "Are you here…to kill us?" she asked the man standing beside Barbara.

"Do you honestly think I came here just so I can take you somewhere else and kill you?"

Laura sighed. "I don't know… I'm so *confused…*"

He sighed. "You've got two choices. You can come with us or stay here and wait for him to come to. He should only be out for twenty minutes or so.

A word of caution: when he comes out of it, he won't be in a very forgiving mood."

Laura turned back to the man on the floor and trembled.

"C'mon, baby. It'll be all right."

Laura pushed herself into a standing position.

The three of them left the house without another word.

CHAPTER TEN

Once the cabby reached the downtown Wheeling area, he kept west on Main and stayed in the solid stream of rush-hour traffic.

Facing the rear window, Brad Jacobson took in every detail of his surroundings. He couldn't stop worrying about where he was being taken. He reminded himself that he'd been brought here for a specific reason. If he'd been targeted for elimination, a round-trip ticket wouldn't have been necessary; someone would have already done the deed in Orlando.

The cabby turned off the main drag a couple of miles outside the city limits, went two blocks and entered a business district. He drove down a few more streets and pulled into the side lot of Hollic's Restaurant. A furniture store sat next to the restaurant, on the western side. Just beyond the furniture store, a gas station and tire shop shared a separate building at the end of the block. The cabby coaxed the taxi across the half-filled lot, to the other side of the eatery. He eased up to a black Ford Edge sedan and killed the engine.

Jacobson nervously looked around. No one was walking toward them or wandering around in front of the eatery. No one peered down at him from any of the second- or third-floor windows of the building. Only a long line of parked vehicles out front and some blurred activity behind the smudged restaurant windows hinted at other signs of life.

Beads of sweat on the cabby's broad forehead glistened in the reflection of the rearview mirror. The cabby made no attempt to wipe his face. Since the windows had been rolled down a few inches, it was fairly cool in the cab. Jacobson could tell the man was sweating because he was afraid.

Jacobson had been in tense situations before and could usually tell when trouble lurked close by. In many cases, his gut had saved his life. In other circumstances, it had prevented him from making a fatal error.

He couldn't shake the strong feeling that he would soon be a dead man. It didn't matter how he analyzed the situation or how prepared he was. His instinct had kicked in. He was unarmed. He had no idea where he was. If two armed men approached the cab from different sides, he was a sitting duck. His military training would be useless.

"Where are we?"

Silence.

Jacobson took a deep breath and reminded himself that patience was the only thing that might work. "Can't you at least tell me where we are?"

"Get out, Mister."

So much for patience… "Please…just let me know what's going on, and I won't ask you anything else…"

"Get out of my cab, Mister. Please?"

"Please…listen to me. I'm not from around here. I don't know anyone. I'm kind of in a bind. I'd really appreciate anything you can tell me…"

"Out."

"What are you afraid of?"

The cabby groaned. "Just get out. Now--okay? There's your new ride." He jerked his head toward the right.

The black Ford Edge sat off by itself, the office building on their right dimming it from the late afternoon sun. The darkness covered it in a heavy shroud.

It looked like a hearse.

***

The dark-haired man kept the big utility van moving in the heavy westbound I-70 traffic.

Laura sat next to Momma in the back seat and desperately tried to piece together what happened. She'd been watching Momma closely, alert for any recurring symptoms from whatever Sam had slipped in her coffee. There were none. Momma appeared to be just fine.

It made no sense. But that shouldn't surprise her. Things hadn't made sense since she and Momma had been attacked on Chestnut.

What in heaven's name was going on? What was Sam involved in? Why all the lies, the deception? Why did he drug Momma?

Most important of all, who was *this* man?

Who was he and why did he just save them?

"We can't thank you enough for helping us," Momma said, smiling at the man's reflection in the mirror.

He merely nodded and kept his attention on the road ahead.

Laura couldn't take her eyes off him. Her thoughts went into immediate overload. There was something about the way he moved--the grace, the coordination... The ease and speed with which he'd overpowered the man back at the house...

He's the one...the man who helped us before, on Chestnut...

Laura couldn't think of anything else. It was true that neither she nor Momma had gotten a good look at the man during that ordeal, but nothing else made sense. This *had* to be the same man.

But if she was right, it raised another batch of questions.

"You don't...work for Sam, do you?" she asked.

He shook his head.

"How did you know where we were?"

"I was watching from across the street when Weiss took you out of the Police Station."

"You...helped us before, didn't you?" Laura couldn't stop her heart from racing. "On Chestnut. That was you, wasn't it? You put them both down. Those two guys. You put them down...like it was nothing..."

After a long pause, he nodded.

Bingo... Laura wanted to rejoice but realized that it only raised more questions.

"You're not wanted by the police...are you?" Momma asked softly.

"No."

Laura sensed that he didn't want to go into further detail.

"How did you bring me back so quickly?" Momma asked. "I was obviously drugged. Your touch...it brought me right back..."

"It was no big deal. You were probably given some mild sedative. I just restored the circulation in your wrists and hands. It brought you right out of it, didn't it?"

Momma turned to Laura. Laura could tell Momma didn't believe what he'd just said. Neither did Laura. Momma had practically been comatose. She hadn't been able to raise her head from the couch. It would take a little more than just rubbing her wrists to bring her out of it, wouldn't it?

"Who *are* you?" she asked, her fears growing. "And how do you know these people?"

He continued staring straight ahead as he drove.

Laura wondered what he was thinking. She hoped he wasn't figuring out some lie to keep them quiet for the time being. Thanks to Sam, they'd been deceived enough for one day.

"My name is Desmond Roth," he said a little later. "I personally know the man these people are working for."

***

"This is it, then?" Jacobson sat back in his seat. He didn't want to leave the safety of the cab. "No answers? No explanations?"

"You got it." The fear showed clearly in the cabby's blinking eyes. His hand shook as he turned in his seat and held out a key.

Jacobson reluctantly took it. "Like I just said, I have no idea where I am or what I'm supposed to do…"

"I don't care, Mac."

Jacobson suddenly discovered that he was more angry than frightened. He was a grown man. He'd been to Saudi, for God's sake. He'd seen and done things he hoped he'd never have to see or do again. But right now he felt like a stupid kid being dropped off in the middle of nowhere. The feeling was infuriating. And embarrassing.

"Out, Mac. I gotta get out of here."

The cabby's voice snapped Jacobson out of his self-pity. He wanted to grab him by his scrawny neck and choke him until the man gave him *some*thing...

Control yourself. You're a grown man. Act like one.

His limbs suddenly heavy, Jacobson got out and slammed the door shut.

"I got a wife and kids..." The cabby trembled as he squinted up at Jacobson through the open window. "I got ten years to go before I can retire. I can't get any more involved in this. I'm sorry, Mac, and I hope everything turns out okay." Then he slammed the cab into gear and hurried away.

A wife and kids.

You know damned well what this man is going through. The only difference is that you're obviously in this much deeper than this guy. Let him go.

Jacobson's heart sank as the cab pulled back onto the main drag.

You're a grown man. Focus on the task ahead.

Twenty feet away, the black Ford Edge sat silently, waiting to devour him.

***

210

"I personally know the man these people are working for..."

Barbara could no longer look at the man's reflection in the mirror. His last statement had brought back her suspicions in full force. She glanced at Laura, who hadn't moved. Barbara could tell by her daughter's taut expression that she was thinking the same thing. They'd been pulled into something frightening, and it felt like they wouldn't be able to come out of it.

But too many things just didn't add up. This man had risked his own health and safety to help them out on Chestnut. He'd had done the very same thing just a few minutes ago in Bridgeport.

However, that business with Sam's friend had been much more dangerous. The man had a knife and was pointing it at Laura's face. Barbara couldn't help wondering how close she and Laura had come to dying if this man hadn't come to their aid.

He didn't know them--why would he risk his life?

Was he actually helping them? Or was this something else entirely?

She'd seen movies and news stories about criminals and double-crosses, stings and seizures. Is that what this was all about? Were she and Laura mere bargaining chips in someone's power struggle? Was this Sam's scheme? Or were there even more people involved?

This man helped me, brought me back from a frightening darkness...

That was the one thing that kept her from letting her fear take over. She just couldn't believe this man was a criminal.

The quiet buzzing of a cell phone startled her. Desmond Roth pulled it from his jacket pocket. Although the phone was hidden from view, Barbara guessed he was texting someone.

Her suspicions came thundering back.

***

Sam Albright elbowed through the heavy Mall crowd.

Nothing out of the ordinary. Albright hadn't seen anyone answering to Weiss' description of the suspect. Mid-thirties, six-one. Slim, muscular build. Brown hair, green eyes. Facial features resembling the actor Christian Bale. Most likely dressed in good clothes.

Excellent description, but in this case, not good enough. No one fitting that picture had crossed paths with him since he'd come in. He hoped the information was accurate.

There was no reason for it not to be. Weiss came with great references. All of them did, actually. Albright had made a lifelong habit of surrounding himself with dependable talent. There could be no room for error in something of this magnitude. If the man coming after Barbara *was* in the area, Weiss, Milan, or Levinson would surely spot him.

This was why these men had been sent here in the first place. When a deal this size was going down, top-notch talent was essential. You couldn't take chances with billions at stake.

He found a vacant spot on the other side of the fountain. Since it was the dinner hour, the place was packed and wild with high school kids. Just ten feet away, a group of sloppy-dressed, tattooed punks giggled loudly. Their blood-shot eyes suggested they were high on something.

Albright pressed the number for Crowley. It was picked up on the second ring.

Where r u? Albright typed.

SUV, came the reply.

Need u @ Mall. ASAP.

???

Contact spotted. W, M, and L watching.

What about women?

W/Dev. We do them after we find contact.

Copy.

Once we find contact, we go back & question women, do them & clean up. Gotta talk 2 Dev.

Copy.

Albright buzzed Devlin's line. Hopefully, everything was going all right back at the house. He hadn't approved of how Devlin had manhandled Laura at the front door, but that would probably keep her from acting up again.

The phone was picked up on the second ring as well.

U @ house? Albright typed.

Yes.

Women OK?

Yes.

No trouble?

No.

213

Stay @ house. Keep women quiet. If girl is problem, tie her. No trouble. Got it?

Yes.

Albright pocketed the phone. Everything was happening as it should. It wouldn't be long now.

***

"Mr. Roth," Momma said, "how do you know Sam? How are you involved in this?"

He didn't reply.

Laura could tell he was holding back. But it didn't matter; they had to know what was going on. They'd been kidnapped, taken from their home, and placed in the center of a nightmare. Momma had been drugged. Laura had been manhandled and threatened with a knife.

"Sam told us about a hired killer," she said. "He said this killer was sent here to kill Momma. Do you know anything about that?"

"There's no killer."

"Are you sure?"

"Positive."

Laura and Momma exchanged stunned looks.

There *was* no killer. That should make them feel better, but once again it only raised more questions. Sam had been lying all along. Laura had already figured that out, but it didn't explain why such a story had been fabricated in the first place.

"Why would Sam lie to us?" Momma asked. "Why would he tell us such a ridiculous story?"

He didn't reply.

"*Please* tell us what's going on." Momma's voice trembled. "If you know anything about this…"

214

"You do know, don't you?" Laura asked. "That's how you knew when and where to rescue us. And how you knew what was going to happen with those two muggers. You knew what they were going to do, and when and where they were going to do it. That's the only possible way you could have saved us. Tell us how you knew about all this, Mr. Roth."

He still didn't reply.

Laura decided right then that she'd had enough of all this uncertainty. It occurred to her that she and Momma might be going about this the wrong way. She realized only then that they probably weren't asking the right questions.

"Where are you from, Mr. Roth?"

Silence.

Momma leaned forward. "*Please* tell us..."

After a long, uncomfortable pause, he said, "Orlando, Florida."

***

Gazing numbly at the Ford sedan, Brad Jacobson forced his brain to start looking at things rationally again. It was a *car*--not a hearse, or some metal-plated monster waiting to devour him. It had no mind of its own, no blood lust or predatory instinct. And only a neurotic with an overactive imagination would think otherwise.

He studied the key the cabby had given him. The overwhelming urge to toss it consumed him.

Like it or not, I have to follow through with this.

He went back to staring at the key, wondering... The cabby was nervous and scared; he might have accidentally given him the wrong one. This would change everything. *If I can't get in the car...*

He'd be forced to call another cab and return to the airport. *Sorry, but the man who picked me up gave me the wrong key...*

It sounded ridiculous.

His hand shook uncontrollably as he moved the cursed silver object toward the slot in the door. It took him several tries.

The door clicked open.

A splash of cold fear washed over him. Trembling, he opened the door, got behind the wheel and shut the door. The object on the passenger seat startled him, and he immediately pulled back, bumping his head on the window.

A black plastic case sat on the seat. He'd seen similar cases before and had a good idea what lay inside. He just didn't want to find out for sure. But he had no choice.

The metal snaps gave him an electric jolt the moment his fingers touched them. He toughed it out and flicked them open. Then he sat back and stared at it, wanting it to evaporate. He tried turning away, but he just couldn't stop staring at the damned thing.

Open it. You know you want to.

Yes. He did want to. In fact, he could think of nothing else. He knew what he'd find but reached for it anyway. His body turned to ice the moment he touched the lid.

Gasping, he pulled away as if a deadly snake lay coiled up within it, waiting to strike.

But it wasn't a snake; it was something much worse.

A ring of cold sweat encircled his neck. The bright image of Jen, Wendy, and Amber flashed before his eyes. A giant bubble of heat exploded in his gut, and he sat back and forced himself to breathe. He couldn't end his life this way--not with three beautiful ladies in his life. He'd do this and then try to forget all about it. He'd do it because he had to, because he'd be crucified if he didn't.

He wiped away the hot tears blurring his vision, took another deep breath and eased open the case. The short coppery hairs on the back of his neck bristled.

An AR-15 .223 5.56 NATO Bushmaster tactical assault rifle, complete with red dot, battery-operated ACOG-type sight, single 30-round box magazine, silencer, and standard XDS bipod, slept comfortably in its gray foam bed.

The object lying before him meant death. This had nothing to do with finding someone and bringing him back to Orlando. This meant finding someone and killing him.

He gazed numbly at the cursed thing and struggled to turn it into something else--something other than what it was. He closed his eyes and tried thinking of other things. The trip back. Touching down in Orlando. Going home to Jen and the girls.

Sighing deeply, he opened his eyes and felt the cold sliding down his back again.

It's not going anywhere. It's right here in front of you, and nothing you can do will change anything. It's here for a purpose. You're here for a purpose. Like it or not, you've got to use this thing. You've got to use it and then find some way to forget about what you've just done. You know you'll never be able to forget something like that, but it's the way things are. So suck it up and get this done!

Somehow, he'd get through this. He'd get through it and return to his family. And when it was all over and the dust finally settled, he'd find some way to nail the bastard responsible for putting him through this.

But all the while his eyes stayed fixed on the weapon, his attention drifted over to the other item in the case.

A small white envelope sat on top of the shiny plastic stock. His hand quivered as he fumbled for it. It took him forever to open it without making a mess of it.

Inside was a short, hand-printed note, with a small close-up color photo of a man's face. The note included detailed directions, a map, and a time: *7:00 P.M.* Four words were printed neatly in pen beneath the man's clean-shaven chin: *ONE SHOT TO HEAD.*

Jacobson stared at the note until everything grew hazy. The pressure consuming him increased, making him light-headed. His gut churned loudly. He turned in the seat, forced open the door, stuck his head out and threw up.

***

Barbara sat frozen in tense silence, her full attention on the man in the front seat. This nightmare had just turned even more bizarre.

218

Desmond Roth is from Orlando...

Could this explain why she'd sensed Joe's presence? Could it explain the reason for her strange dream?

Did this man have some sort of connection with Joe? Had he talked to Joe recently? Had Joe mentioned her? Their marriage? Their life in Manville? Had Joe talked about Laura? Her accident?

She was being ridiculous. Why would Joe talk to this man or anyone else about her and Laura? They were out of his life. He'd probably stopped thinking of them years ago.

And what made her think this man even knew her ex-husband? Orlando was one of the largest cities in Florida. Millions of people lived there or had family or friends living there. Orlando had been an immensely popular tourist spot since the mid-seventies and was still one of the most visited places in the world. Even with the last couple of recessions, Orlando continued to enjoy a heavy influx of daily visitors.

But she couldn't ignore the last two weeks. There had to be a reason why she'd dreamed about the man who'd deserted her and her daughter. And there had to be an even better reason why this mysterious man had suddenly come into their lives...

"You did say Orlando, didn't you?" She had to be certain she'd heard him correctly.

"Yes..."

She sensed the anxiety coming from him. She remained silent, afraid to ask anything else. But before she could ask the next question, he said, "I met Joe about a month ago."

Barbara's heart began pounding loudly. *He knows Joe. He actually knows Joe.* Her suspicions were right after all.

"How...do you know him?"

He remained silent.

"Are you and Joe in the same business?"

"No."

"You never told us what business you're in."

"No. I didn't."

They'd come too far to stop. Just a few more questions could explain everything. She hesitated; she wasn't sure if she wanted to hear some of the answers. But she had to know.

"What kind of work are you in, Mr. Roth?" Laura asked.

No reply.

The fear returned. Barbara suddenly realized that she might have been wrong about him. He knew these people, didn't he? That could mean that he actually did work with them. But if he did, why did he keep rescuing them?

More importantly, where was he taking them?

She refused to believe he was a criminal. She could tell he had a conscience. There was a sense of goodness about him, a sense of peace. Yet he obviously didn't want to tell them anything else.

What could be so bad that--

No. Barbara couldn't believe that--not for one moment. This man was *not* the hired killer Sam had told them about. She and Laura had talked about this before. A hired killer murdered people for money.

Besides, he'd told them there *was* no hired killer.

That in itself was no assurance. She shouldn't assume that he was telling them the truth about all this, should she? If he'd actually been hired to kill her, it would be stupid--as well as dangerous--for him to tell them why he was here.

Killers wouldn't want their victims to know what was going on. Their victim's guard had to be down. This way, the victims could be taken away and killed in some private spot without any fuss. It was much easier this way...

Stop this. You're driving yourself crazy.

This man was *not* a hired killer. A hired killer didn't *help* people...

So...who *was* this man?

"How...do you know Joe, Mr. Roth?" Barbara could barely hear her own voice.

When he failed to respond, another cold wave wrapped itself around her.

Silence isn't good. In fact, silence is very bad.

She'd ask him one more time. If he didn't respond...

"Mr. Roth," Laura said quickly. "Is my father...still alive?"

The sudden silence was deafening.

"Oh my God..." Laura's voice had become a whisper.

Barbara's heart sputtered. Her eyes glistened as she brought her hands up to her face.

***

Sam Albright squeezed through roving clots of shoppers, until he reached the rest rooms. His cell buzzed just as he went in.

The large brightly lit room smelled strongly of a minty air freshener. One man faced a urinal, zipping up. Albright slipped into a stall, closed the door, and pulled out the cell.

It was Miles Lester.

"What's up?" Albright asked.

"I thought I'd let you know what's going on with those two the Manville cops nabbed."

That was something Albright didn't want to think about. Those two idiots nearly ruined everything. Hopefully, Lester acted quickly before they opened their mouths to the Manville cops. "How bad is this?"

"I sent an attorney there to represent them. They're out of lockup."

"How long did that take?"

Lester chuckled. "Less than ten minutes after my attorney went in with the papers. He told me the trip was unnecessary. The Mayor had already been ordered off the case."

Albright sighed in relief. "The big man works fast, doesn't he?"

"You could say that…"

"What were the charges, by the way?"

"Before the call came in, the boys were told to plead to mischievous activity. Mickey Mouse stuff. The fact that there were no witnesses besides the women helped considerably. And as long as the women remain unavailable, there's no case."

"They're unavailable, all right."

"Good deal. I hate complications just as much as you do."

"Any idea what the boys already told the cops?"

"No need to worry about that, either. They both said it happened too fast."

Albright suspected Lester wasn't telling him everything. It sounded too convenient. "They didn't see their attacker at all?"

"They said everything was a blur."

"That's *it*?"

"Whaddya mean?"

"You sound like you're holding something back."

"Why would I hold something back?"

"You tell me…"

"Those two are bouncers. They push people around for a living. They get into fights nearly every night. Hell, all three of them have had their brains scrambled or pounded dozens of times. It happens."

"It still sounds like you're leaving something out."

Lester took a breath. "Well…in a nutshell, they haven't been the same since. They've both been real quiet since that ruckus. Pellinger hasn't said two words since they left the Police Station."

"Is that normal for him?"

"Pellinger's a quiet guy to begin with. He served in Iraq, so he's got some issues. But this seems more serious."

"How about the other boy?"

"He's been in a daze ever since."

"Miles, tell me what you think is going on."

"What I think isn't really relevant."

"Tell me anyway."

"Something happened earlier today to another one of my guys. It really got me thinking."

"Was this that busboy you hired?"

"That's what I'm talking about."

"What happened with him?"

"The same damned thing."

"He ran into the same man?"

"We're not sure, but judging by what's happened, I'd vote yes."

"What else could've happened?"

"Here's what we know. The kid followed a man to the Catholic Church outside of Manville. He was supposed to stay there and wait for his relief. He decided to go back to work instead."

"Just like that?"

"This kid makes minimum wage busing tables at the Buffet Garden. He went back to work rather than stay in his truck another fifteen minutes. When I spoke with him, he said he cared only about getting back to work."

"Weird."

"How many kids that age would rather bust their balls in a hot kitchen for minimum wage rather than sit in a truck for two days and watch two women for a thousand bucks a day?"

Albright was right; this made no sense at all. "What the hell are we dealing with, Miles?"

"I don't know, but whatever it is, it's scaring the living bejesus out of me."

CHAPTER ELEVEN

Joe's dead. My God...

"I'm sorry." Desmond Roth pulled off the shoulder and parked the SUV. As traffic whizzed by, he turned around in his seat. "There was no other way for me to tell you."

Barbara sat back and wiped her eyes. Beside her, Laura had taken a Kleenex out of her bag and dabbed at her eyes and mouth.

Joe was dead. It was all over. There would be no more waiting for that long overdue phone call...or post card...or birthday card for Laura. The painful part was gone now, and that portion of their lives, however sad, could finally be put to rest.

"When...did it happen?" Laura asked in a soft, broken voice.

"Two weeks ago."

A flurry of images filled Barbara's mind.

Joe died two weeks ago.

His spirit came to see me. He's been trying to communicate with me, trying to tell me something important.

Was it to ask for forgiveness? Or was there some other reason?

Her gaze went back to the man watching them from the front seat. Once again her suspicions rose.

"What happened?" she asked in a broken voice. "*Please* tell us..."

Desmond Roth shrugged. "According to what he told me, his problems began the day he drove to Florida five years ago."

"He told me he'd been offered a new job." Barbara discovered that the memories remained painfully vivid--as if it had happened just days ago. "He'd been selling insurance since college and wanted out, but the job market had slumped in this area. The only things available were jobs he had no interest in."

"I was still in high school." Laura wiped her nose with her Kleenex. "But I could feel the change in him. The fire had gone out of his eyes. At first I thought it was me. I'd just been through a couple of wild years and was always getting in trouble. I really thought I had something to do with it, but I was too full of myself at the time to actually pay attention to what was going on..."

"It had nothing to do with you, baby."

"Or you, Momma?"

That was a good question. Joe was burned out, but she'd often wondered if that had been all of it. Perhaps if she'd been more supportive...if she'd taken the time to talk to him during those quiet moments after dinner, when she suspected something was bothering him...

She'd also been working at the time and, consequently, had little time for things other than fixing dinner and trying to keep the house neat and clean. She'd always been too busy to notice Joe's quiet moods, especially during those last few months. At the time, she'd attributed his silence to fatigue and stress--and, of course, the burnout. She hadn't even bothered asking him what was really wrong.

"I don't know, baby. If I'd been more attentive, maybe... If we'd talked more..."

"Dad wasn't around much then. And when he was, he didn't talk very much. It was almost like...like he'd already left."

"That's a good analogy, baby. He seemed a thousand miles away."

"You tried finding him at first, Momma. I remember."

If only that had been the case... She'd rebelled when Joe first told her. She'd told him he was being selfish and cruel for even considering leaving. He'd wanted her to reconsider, to perhaps come down later on and join him. Her reply had been very simple: don't go. She'd sensed failure in his plan and somehow felt that if he left, she'd never see him again. The last thing she told him was that once he left, he shouldn't bother coming back.

"I tried calling him," she told Laura. "For several weeks I tried. After nearly a month, my calls stopped going to his voicemail, and then his cell phone was no longer in service. I tried a few more times and then gave up. It broke my heart, but the fact that he never returned my calls proved to me that he no longer wanted me in his life. The next time I tried to contact him was through my attorney."

"How did he find Dad?" Laura asked.

"I don't know, but it only took him a few weeks. He must have had some connections in Orlando. What happened, Mr. Roth? Did he tell you what he did when he went down there?"

"He'd made friends with someone in this area. This new contact had associates in Orlando, and they wanted him down there immediately. He was given a new car and told he could use it to drive down to Orlando."

"What *was* this new opportunity?" Laura asked.

"He was told it was to maintain the books for some large Orlando-based company. Joe didn't want to do it at first because he hadn't done bookkeeping in a long time. But he was offered a lot of money and decided to go ahead with it."

"Joe hated bookkeeping," Barbara said. "He preferred dealing with people."

"He was backed into a corner," Mr. Roth said. "His career had bottomed out. He felt he had no other place to go. He was afraid to tell you because the bills were piling up and he was finding it harder to pay them."

"He handled everything," Barbara said. "He'd done all our bookkeeping since we were married. I knew things were getting tight, but...he never told me the extent of the debts."

"He originally went to Wheeling to get a high-interest loan from some unscrupulous people. That put him in contact with the man who offered him the new job."

"Dad went to the *Mob*?" Laura asked. "For *money*? Did you know this, Momma?"

"Of course not."

"He didn't tell anyone," Mr. Roth said. "He was embarrassed, for one thing. He hated himself for letting it get to that point. He saw no other way out of it."

"But how did he intend to pay off the debt?" Barbara asked.

"He didn't get that far. This Mob affiliate heard about his situation and decided to use him to pay off an old debt of his own. He took Joe aside and told him about the opportunity in Orlando. He said that if he took it, all his debts would be paid off."

"And Joe believed him?"

"He didn't think he had much of a choice. He took the car and drove it to Florida. When he got there, he found out that the car had been reported stolen. OPD rushed in and found nearly a million dollars in drug money hidden in it."

"My dear God!" Barbara brought her hand up to her mouth.

"He had no idea what they'd done, of course. He'd gone in blindly. A man does strange things when he's desperate. Once he found out how much trouble he was in, he also learned that the people he was involved with had pulled some strings and got him off the hook. As a result, he was on their payroll and had to do everything they said. That's how these people recruit their employees. Joe couldn't even tell you what happened without endangering both of you."

"He couldn't have called?" Laura asked.

"He was probably told that if he tried getting in touch with you, he'd live to regret it."

"So that's what he did down there?" Laura asked. "Worked for these people?"

"They hadn't lied about the Accounting job. They hired him to keep two sets of books for them. The man he was working for is powerful, successful and well-connected. He's also very dangerous and deals in matters that frequently involve kidnapping and extortion. Murder is also high on this list. Contract stuff involving government figures, dignitaries, developers..."

Barbara found all this difficult to believe. "And Joe actually *worked* for this man? All the time he was in Florida?"

"Until two weeks ago."

Silence.

"What happened?" Laura asked. "What changed all this?"

"He'd had enough and wanted out. He felt badly for leaving you, and he really wanted to see you again."

"Did he say that, Mr. Roth?" Barbara whispered. "Those exact words?"

"Yes. He made plans to come back. A one-way ticket to Pittsburgh was found in his suitcase."

"Mr. Roth...who *found* his suitcase?" Barbara had difficulty pulling the words out of her throat.

"The Orlando Police."

She shivered. "Tell us...what happened..."

"It was a highway accident. His car skidded off the road and smashed into a streetlamp."

Barbara buried her face in her hands. The tears were a mixture of grief and sorrow, with slivers of anger mixed in. Anger for what happened...and for what didn't have to happen.

I wasn't the reason Joe left, but I did nothing to keep him here. I did nothing to support him, help him through his problems. I even showed anger when he told me his plans. And because of my negligence, my selfishness, the man I once loved is dead.

"Oh, Momma..." Laura wrapped an arm around her and pulled her close.

"I tried getting him out of Orlando," Mr. Roth said. "I met with him that night and tried taking him to the airport, but they found him before I could get him on the plane. They weren't looking for me, so I came here to tell you what he wanted you to know. He'd already asked me to, in case he didn't make it himself."

"Why, Mr. Roth?" Laura asked. "Why'd you do it?"

"He needed help. He didn't have anyone else."

"Who was he?" Barbara desperately needed to know the man responsible for all this. She had to know the name of the man who'd taken Joe away from her and Laura. "This hoodlum. The one who got him into this mess."

"It wouldn't be wise for me to tell you anything else. For your own protection, I really don't--"

"Please...*tell* me!" Barbara edged quickly toward hysterics.

"His name," he said, "is Sam Albright."

***

Trapped in a long line of slow-moving traffic, Brad Jacobson followed the procession onto the exit that led to the Ohio Valley Mall. Evening rush hour traffic remained heavy. Endless rows of parked vehicles engulfed the food courts, creating a blinding sea of metal and glass.

Carefully switching lanes, Jacobson veered onto the straight stretch that went past the brightly-lit front entrance. According to the written instructions provided, this area was the kill zone. The target would be there at precisely seven o'clock. A sixty-second window had been provided for the kill shot. He had no other option.

Directly across from the entrance, eateries peppered the vast concrete thoroughfare. McDonald's, a bakery, Cracker Barrel, two coffeehouses and an assortment of other fast-food places hustled to handle the crowds. Due to its location, the McDonald's seemed the perfect spot. Delivery trucks and dumpsters provided seclusion on one side of the building. Most of the activity was confined to the other side, toward the front. Customers came outside munching burgers and slurping large drinks.

His first order of business was to make several loops around the area and select a spot about a hundred yards away to watch the activity. A hundred yards would give him enough time to escape in the confusion. When everything felt right, he'd drive to the chosen site, park at an appropriate angle and set up. Since he'd been given just half an hour to pull this one off, he had to scramble to make sure all factors were perfect.

This felt unreal--almost dreamlike. After his last kill in Saudi--a suicide bomber at a distance of nearly four hundred yards--he promised himself that he'd never again take a life in such a cold, ruthless manner. As a law enforcement officer, he'd been forced to kill in the line of duty, but his victims had all been heavily armed, and were trying to kill him. But now, the mere thought of positioning an unarmed man in the crosshairs of a high-powered rifle nauseated him.

He gave the photo another thorough examination. The man was distinguished-looking, in his mid to late forties, slightly balding, clean-shaven, and well-dressed. Wealth, arrogance, and success showed clearly in the small dark eyes. This man was no doubt just as corrupt as the bastard ordering this.

It made no difference. He'd been chosen to do the hit. If anything went wrong, he'd be just as dead as the man he was ordered to kill.

A brief glimmer of light flickered in his brain at that moment, giving him a shred of hope. *If you do this right, you'll live to see another day.*

This thought alone would give him the chance to hunt down the man who'd planned this.

Forcing his mind on the task at hand, Jacobson turned right at the intersection and began searching for the perfect kill spot.

***

Joe's dead and Sam's the one responsible...

The van had become dark and cold, with everything closing in on her.

Barbara closed her eyes and listened to the frantic thumping of her heart. She tried telling herself this was just a bad dream. But she knew better.

233

Sam had caused all this. The man she'd considered a very good friend had turned their lives into a nightmare. This was the same man who'd given her a very good job and was always there for her and Laura whenever they had a problem.

But now that she'd learned the full story, it made her flesh crawl. Sam had sent Joe a thousand miles away, to work for a group of very bad people who kept him prisoner for five years. And now Joe was dead.

The last five years had finally been explained. The strange way Sam had squirmed his way into their lives, their home. Helping them. Being supportive. Staying close.

"He's been with us almost from the beginning," she said. "Not long after Joe left, Sam bumped into us at the Mall. He handed me a twenty-dollar-bill and said it had fallen from my handbag. Like an idiot, I believed him."

"You were distracted, Momma. We both were. We'd been wandering around in a daze ever since Dad left."

She still had to accept her own accountability. How could she have gone so long without seeing things for what they really were? How could she have not seen the deceit in Sam's eyes?

"He *bought* me, baby. For twenty dollars. That's what it amounted to. We let him become part of our life…for *five years!*" The repulsion had become a blistering coal in the pit of her gut. If Mr. Roth hadn't already started the van back up and rejoined the heavy, fast-moving traffic, she would have asked him to pull over again so she could open the door, stick her head out and rid herself of the disgust in her stomach.

"Momma, you're being too hard on yourself."

"I should've seen it, felt it. I should've asked myself why he was always so interested... It couldn't have been because he thought so much of us. Why all this time, Mr. Roth? Five years is a long time to keep close to someone."

"These people like to keep a close watch on their investments."

"*That's* what we were? Investments?"

"It's what Joe was to them. That's why there were no phone calls, not even when Laura was in the hospital. They didn't want either of you to know anything."

Barbara felt her heart sinking again. *Poor Joe... He couldn't even find out about Laura--not even when she really needed his support.* "But someone obviously told him about Laura's accident..."

"It was probably Albright."

"Why would Sam tell him then forbid him to call her?"

"It was most likely Albright's boss who made him back off. Joe told me he made one call and was warned not to make another."

"You haven't told us everything, have you?" Barbara asked.

"About six months ago, funds came up missing, and a small staff of accountants was brought in to locate the leak. Since Joe was the one keeping the books, he was their number one suspect."

"Joe was no thief." The accusation made her head hot. "He was honest to a fault. I'm surprised these people couldn't see that."

"Honesty doesn't mean anything to them. They care only about profits."

"Did they ever find out who was stealing their precious money?"

"Joe was sent to a different company for a while. The skimming stopped almost immediately. Everyone thought it was too much of a coincidence, so they continued their investigation very discreetly. The skimming eventually started back up. This was about the same time Joe decided he'd had enough and wanted out. They put down his strange behavior as a sign of his guilt. This convinced them that he'd been sending the money here all along."

"You mean, to *us*?" she asked.

"Is *that* what all this is about?" Laura asked. "They actually think *we've* got all this money they think Dad stole?"

Barbara couldn't believe this. "I divorced Joe. When I didn't hear from him for two years, I divorced him on grounds of desertion. Didn't anyone know that?"

"You have a daughter together," he said. "Family ties would keep both of you highly suspect."

"Why didn't they just search our house?" Barbara asked. "They wouldn't find anything and would know for sure that he wasn't sending us anything."

"I'm sure they've already done that," he said.

"But...we haven't seen any sign of--"

"These people are good. I'll wager your place has been thoroughly searched at least a dozen times in the past six months."

Barbara shivered at the thought. *They've been in our home. Going through our rooms... our dresser drawers... our private things...*

A fresh surge of nausea erupted in her throat. It took her a moment to find her voice. "You don't think Joe...you don't think he actually took money from those people?"

"He told me he didn't, and I believe him."

His statement quickly dissolved her growing anger. It gave her comfort to know that Joe hadn't been alone in his last days. Someone had reached out to him, listened to him.

"You said you tried helping him," she said.

"Yes."

She had to know why. And how. And what really happened.

So many questions... It was important to gather her thoughts so she could ask them coherently. Concentrating had become difficult. But what mattered most was that Joe had left them not because of anything she or Laura had done, but because he was ashamed of himself for his failures in business. He'd wanted only to fix things...to get the bills paid so he could build a new future for himself and his family.

A cell buzzed. She cringed in her seat.

He glanced in the mirror. "I have to take this."

"Is that Sam?" Uttering his name instantly brought back the anger.

He studied the display and nodded.

Barbara gritted her teeth. Her stomach twisted in knots.

Sam Albright, when this is all over, you're going to wish you never laid eyes on either of us!

***

Sam Albright had been growing extremely uneasy during the last fifteen minutes. The talk with Miles Lester had made him even more eager than ever to find some way of walking away from this mess. Whoever they'd been looking for was extremely dangerous. Anyone who could put the fear of God into two tough young bouncers--as well as Miles Lester, who was no shrinking violet himself--was someone to avoid at all costs.

He glanced at his watch. Where the hell was Crowley? He should've heard from him by now.

Albright had to warn the big ape about what was going on. Then he'd contact the others to tell them he and Weiss were returning to Bridgeport. Crowley, Milan, and Levinson could take care of this mysterious badass who was spooking everyone. These boys did this sort of thing for a living. The three of them should be able to handle one man.

Sam was a businessman; he didn't hurt or kill people. Like all successful men, he paid to have his dirty work done.

Questioning the women remained their number one priority. Since they were running out of time, he had to contact Devlin and let him know he and Weiss were on their way back to Bridgeport. They needed answers quickly and could no longer stall

238

for time. He couldn't risk Big Al stepping in and blowing this mess wide open. The big man tended to go to extremes when he was stressed, and took no prisoners. Albright hadn't heard from him for some time but knew a call from Orlando was inevitable.

He got behind a slow-moving procession oldsters shuffling along past the stores. He pulled out his cell and punched Crowley's number.

Where r u?

Pulling off I-70.

How long b4 u meet w/W?

10 min. Traffic heavy.

Drive over 2 Big K. W in sedan 10 rows down.

Albright clicked off. Good deal. Once Crowley got here, things would go much easier. Crowley was a beast--he could go up against a grizzly. He wouldn't have a problem with a man who could outwit a couple of oversized punk kids.

He was about to put the cell back into his pocket when it buzzed.

It was Weiss, and he sounded excited. "I think I just spotted him, boss."

"Where?"

"In the parking lot. Looks like he's headed straight for the front entrance."

***

Mr. Roth pocketed the cell and followed the long line edging down the straightaway leading to the Mall complex.

Laura found it difficult to believe what the man had said, but after hearing the full story, she realized that much of the pain and agony plaguing

239

her and Momma the last five years could finally be put to rest. Laura discovered that it no longer hurt quite as much. Dad had actually tried finding out about her while she was in the hospital and would have called her back if he'd been able to.

But Dad was dead, and it was all because of Sam. Laura felt herself tensing up again. This anger, she discovered, was much worse than anything she'd ever felt before.

You've got to hold it together. Momma's going through hell right now and needs you beside her. She needs you to be thinking clearly.

She moved closer to Momma and placed her hand on her mother's forearm. It helped, but she knew she couldn't keep the anger and the hatred in check for very long.

Mr. Roth kept with the flow. It was well into the dinner hour, and the fast-food courts were packed. He followed the traffic down the main thoroughfare, and they were soon going down the straight stretch running past the front of the complex.

"Why are we here?" she asked.

"Albright thinks I'm here. He and his friends are looking for me."

"Why would he think that?" Momma asked.

"I don't know. But I intend to find out."

"What did Sam say?" Momma asked.

"He wants Crowley to meet one of the others outside the building."

"Who's Crowley?" Laura asked.

"The man whose cell I've been using."

"Where is *he*?"

"Don't ask."

It was becoming clearer to Laura that this was something much too complicated for her and Momma to understand. But at least she could figure out *some* of it. "Let me guess. You took care of this Crowley just like you took care of the scary guy back at the house?"

He nodded.

"How can you do all this yourself? I mean, there are so many of them…"

"Like I said, don't ask." He stared straight ahead at the huge complex looming before them. "I've got to find somewhere safe to drop you two off. I can't do it at the Mall. I don't know where Albright has his men stationed."

"You're walking into a trap, aren't you?" Laura asked.

"Probably."

"So why do it?"

"If I don't, they'll kill someone. I know how these people operate. They won't leave until someone's dead."

"Even the wrong person?" Laura asked.

"I'm afraid so."

"How many are there?"

"I'm guessing five or six. I've already put two out of commission, so that leaves three, possibly four."

"They're all criminals, aren't they?" Momma asked.

He nodded. "What makes them so dangerous is that the ones calling the shots hold key government positions. They get things done very easily and don't have to worry about people getting in their way."

"Politicians?"

"Many of them, but that doesn't matter right now. All I care about is that innocent people could be hurt or even worse. I can't let that happen."

"You never did say what you did for these people," Laura said. "How could a man like you work for them?"

"I can't go into that right now. I've got to find a place to drop you off. The people we're dealing with--"

"They're monsters," Momma whispered fiercely. "Sam Albright is responsible for ruining my life. He's also responsible for destroying my daughter's memories of her father. Joe's dead because of him."

Laura took Momma's hand. It was very warm and tense.

"I need to look Sam in the face," Momma said, her voice still a harsh whisper. "I need to tell him exactly what he did to me, to Laura, and to Joe-- especially Joe. I think I should be given that chance."

He didn't reply.

Momma stared at Mr. Roth's reflection in the mirror. "Please tell me you think I'm right. It's important to me."

"This has got nothing to do with your being right. It's--"

He stopped talking and began staring at the crowded lot to their right, on the other side of the McDonald's Restaurant.

"What's wrong?" Laura asked.

He didn't speak.

Laura could sense a cold darkness emanating strongly from the man.

CHAPTER TWELVE

Brad Jacobson gazed into the crosshairs of the scope for the tenth time since he'd set up.

A steady crowd, mostly women, flowed through the main entrance. The shoppers leaving the building immediately scattered and wandered off.

So many people...

Why the hell did he have to pick such a busy spot for a kill?

But at least he'd found seclusion. Using the scope, he'd calculated his position at a hundred and fifty-seven yards from the entrance. This would ensure a successful hit and easy exit, as well as diminish the possibility of collateral damage.

Due to passing traffic, he'd placed the rifle case flush on the back seat before adjusting the bipod. He then removed his sport jacket and folded it into a small square, positioning it on the case. This added nearly six inches of height to his vantage point and gave him a less obstructive view by keeping the traffic out of the line of fire. This new position also enabled him to leave the window open just four inches. With the tip of the suppressor inside the sedan, no one would see anything unless they walked up to the window.

The AR-15 claimed an effective range of around 550 yards. At less than one-third that distance, he'd have no problem.

At 6:48, reality set in. His nerves began quivering and he found it difficult to breathe. He kept reminding himself that this would soon be over. Then he could drive back to the airport and return home.

You've got a wife and family waiting for you. Once you're with them again, you can forget all about this...

Could he? Could he actually forget about this? Could he honestly forget that, as a police officer, he was about to gun down an unarmed man in a crowded shopping mall?

No. Unfortunately, that will stay with you. All you can do is make sure you don't put anyone else in jeopardy. Once this is all over, you can concentrate on hunting down the man responsible.

He was satisfied that he'd chosen an area with little activity. At least he didn't have to worry about people strolling past. Folks didn't like getting too close to dumpsters.

Somewhat calmer, he settled into a comfortable position, his left leg bent beneath him on the seat, his left side supported by the back of the seat. His body shook as his left hand gripped the hard, cool stock of the rifle. It felt like dead flesh.

Get hold of yourself!

He had to take a few more deep breaths before he could move his right hand closer to the trigger guard.

Reality set in again. His vision went double as the dark, blood-soaked images splashed before him...

Saudi. Death. Blood. Thunder. The earth shaking in terror.

The face of the suicide bomber flashed brightly in his head, the boy's large black eyes glazed and empty as he approached the U.S. Army barracks. The boy moved stiffly, his bulky sand-dusted jacket unable to conceal the vest of explosives strapped to his skinny torso as hot snorts of desert breeze nudged the corners of the fabric, making them flutter. The kid, barely a teen, was around five-three and maybe eighty pounds, soaking-wet. His smooth, olive-skinned cheeks remained grim as he gazed at the bright, cloudless sky.

Four hundred yards away, twenty-one-year-old Brad Jacobson crouched in his minaret perch on top of the crumbling mosque and waited. It didn't matter what he saw in the boy's eyes, what he felt or didn't feel. All suicide bombers had to die; this kid was no exception. Jacobson pulled in some hot, musty desert air and nearly choked on its bitterness.

Doesn't matter how young the boy is. He's a walking time bomb and will slaughter a platoon of fifty men and women I've been living with for ten months if I don't take him down right now.

Then, with one last breath of hot terror, he sighted the boy's face in the crosshairs and gently squeezed the trigger...

You're in Ohio now. It's almost twenty years later and you're a sniper again...

His hands wrenched away from the rifle. His heart pounded mercilessly. *You have to do this... There's no other way...*

His arms trembling, he forced himself to grip the weapon. *Do it quickly and forget about it.* He grasped the underside of the stock. *This target may*

246

not be a suicide bomber, but he's still a very bad man. He gently touched the trigger guard with his palm. *No better than the bastard ordering you to do this.* He held his breath and moved his face closer to the scope. *One less criminal to worry about later on.* Pressed his eyelid gingerly against the eyepiece. Gazed numbly at the crosshairs.

The soft sound of a footfall on the pavement close by made his heart skip a beat.

A large dark mass blocked the window--and the shot.

Jacobson couldn't move. His thoughts raced. He was caught red-handed. Someone was standing right there.

The grim reality of the situation ripped through him.

I'm caught...and now I'm toast.

But as bad as that was, it wasn't his main concern. The image slamming through him right now was even worse. *If I'd pulled the trigger...if my finger had even twitched...*

"Unlock the door," the man said.

Snap to. This is reality, so wake up, for God's sake.

He sat up and struggled to pull himself together. It was all over. He reached across the back seat and unlocked the driver's door. The other man opened it, climbed inside and pulled the door shut behind him. He positioned himself behind the wheel and turned to face Jacobson.

The man held something in his right hand. A Glock. It wasn't pointed at him, but Jacobson could

247

sense that he'd come close to being shot. This man wasn't just an innocent shopper.

"Who are you?" the stranger asked.

"It...doesn't matter." The words made his throat burn. "Just...get it over with. You'll be doing me a huge favor."

"What are you talking about?"

Something didn't feel right. An armed man showing up right now wasn't exactly a good thing. Even so, Jacobson sensed no impending doom or danger--only warm relief. He'd been stopped from murdering someone. It didn't matter who the target was or what was at stake; this *was* a good thing. Despite everything that had happened in his life, Brad Jacobson hated taking a human life.

"Have you come here to kill me?"

"Do we know one another?"

"No..."

"Then why would I want to kill you?"

It all registered at once: this man was not a killer and hadn't come to kill him. Jacobson quickly discovered that the fear had gone completely.

Had he suffered a heart attack and died, but hadn't yet realized it?

Maybe he *had* died and was in the process of reaching that place where souls found peace. This man could be an angel--or guardian--and had come to make sure he didn't get lost on the way.

An angel with a Glock?

"You all right?" the man asked. "You look kind of...spacey."

Spacey was a good word. It sounded better than clueless, or zombie-like. But it didn't justify the cold, dark, empty feeling taking over right now.

Jacobson surveyed his surroundings. He still sat in the back seat, the AR-15 resting on its bipod, inches from his grasp. He was still sweating, still shaking. The only thing that had changed during the last few minutes was the stranger sitting in the front seat.

No, he wasn't dead. The rifle beside him reminded him why he was here.

And so did the dashboard clock.

It was now past seven, and he hadn't done what he was supposed to do.

The big man had obviously heard what happened. This man had been waiting nearby for instructions. When he was told about the fuckup, he was ordered to come right over and finish the job.

But something was definitely off. A professional would have already killed him.

"What's your name?" the man asked.

"Jacobson. Brad Jacobson." He was surprised he was able to get it out coherently.

"What are you doing here?"

"What do you think?"

The man glanced at the rifle. "I noticed the setup right off. I'm just wondering what's going on."

Jacobson saw no animosity, no evil in the man's face. And he felt only that same calmness when he looked into the man's clear gray eyes. "I was supposed to...kill someone." Despite the gravity of the situation, he found it surprisingly easy to talk to this man. "At seven o'clock. I haven't done it. I'm now on borrowed time."

"You're a professional killer?"

The words sliced through him. His throat filled with hot bile.

"Actually, I've been a police officer with OPD for the last fifteen years."

"An Orlando cop?"

"Hard to believe, huh?"

"Who are you supposed to be killing?"

"I wasn't told very much about the man."

"Who are you doing this for?"

"I don't know his name. In fact, I don't know anything about him. All I do know is that he's the biggest bastard I've ever been involved with."

The man nodded. "And he's your handler?"

It sounded even worse when someone else said it. "He somehow found a way to put a death-grip on my testicles. And he hasn't eased up on the pressure one bit."

"Tell me more about this. What were you told?"

"It doesn't matter now. I've already--"

"Tell me anyway."

What harm would it do? It certainly wouldn't make things any worse. "I've got instructions and a picture."

"Let me see."

Jacobson found that he actually *wanted* this man to know what was going on--although he had no idea why. But it didn't matter. He'd been caught; he'd run out of options. He took the instructions and photo from his jacket and handed them over.

The man glanced at the photo and read the instructions.

"Know him?"

"I've seen him before." The man glanced at his watch. "It's almost ten past seven."

Jacobson's cell buzzed. The fear thundered back, and he trembled.

The man turned in his seat. "How would you like to get your testicles back?"

Jacobson didn't know what to say, how to react. Was this some sort of sick joke? Was it a dream?

Or was his death theory more accurate than he'd imagined?

"I d-don't…know what to…"

The stranger held out the gun, butt-first. "Let's start it off with an even trade. The phone for the Glock?"

"Are you…are you *serious*?"

The stranger's gaze didn't flinch as he moved the gun closer.

Jacobson saw nothing dark or sinister in the man's eyes. Before he realized it, he'd already dug the cell out of his pocket and handed it over.

***

Frustrated, exhausted, and in need of a strong drink, Sam Albright followed the crowd back inside through the Mall entrance. After passing several stores, he left the flow and veered to the right, stopping in front of the pet shop window.

Weiss' call just five minutes earlier had been a total bust. Albright was almost positive Weiss had been mistaken when he'd said he'd spotted someone near the front entrance. He'd then suggested Albright get over there and make sure he was seen. Weiss had said the man would panic when he saw Albright. He'd turn around and slip back into the crowds, or hurry back to his vehicle. Weiss would be close and would have no problem getting him.

Albright hadn't liked Weiss' reasoning. He didn't want to confront someone who could easily defeat two strong young bouncers. Weiss should have waited for Crowley to show. Then the two of them could have handled this man.

This just didn't feel right. Albright couldn't understand why the man would go to the Mall in the first place. Laura worked at one of the coffeehouses on the property--not in the Mall itself. At this hour, Coffee Masters was closed. This man would sense a trap. He'd already slipped away before the cops showed up on Chestnut--why would he risk exposing himself here?

In any event, Albright was getting tired of all this. After nearly five years of slaving away for the sake of this condo project, they were no closer to finding Joe Neilson's stash now than they were before.

For weeks he'd been debating with himself about closing the Manville office and handling his affairs from Wheeling. But he knew he had to wait. Ten million in missing funds was nothing to sneeze at. Big Al's offer of a twenty percent finder's fee would more than compensate for the five years he'd spent babysitting Barbara and Laura. But what really made this venture of paramount importance was the fifty-fifty partnership in the Bridgeport Renaissance condo project he'd been promised for helping Big Al snatch up the properties.

Albright had done some highly unethical bargaining to keep the bidding closed while the funds transfer was being arranged. He'd gone out on a limb for this, scraping together funds he and Miles Lester had collected laundering money from Lester's shady investments.

Big Al owed him.

This mess had to be totally resolved before they could proceed with the project. Joe Neilson's skimming had compromised the deal on several different levels. Valuable documents had gone missing along with the money and would destroy everything.

The stranger from Orlando had found out about this and flown here to confiscate the money and documents from Barbara Neilson. Albright figured it was someone who'd befriended Neilson--a spy in one of Big Al's businesses, most likely. Or just one of the many hundreds of employees Big Al had either fired or blacklisted. Once this man had found out all he needed to know, he boarded the first plane to Pittsburgh. He might have even been the one responsible for having Neilson killed.

Albright had employed a team of top men to thoroughly search the Neilson home one afternoon each week during the last few months. He knew Barbara and Laura weren't clever enough to outwit a team of former FBI surveillance experts. Local mail drops were scanned by a Post Office contact. Barbara Neilson's safe deposit box at the local bank was examined by a bribed bank officer, revealing nothing. The stolen merchandize was apparently being stored elsewhere.

Albright was convinced Barbara had been contacted by her ex-husband. He was also convinced the man from Orlando knew enough to put everyone away. It was vital to question Barbara and Laura Neilson as soon as possible. Once the money and documents were located, the women would no longer be needed, and the Renaissance project could proceed as scheduled.

Albright checked his watch. Time had run out. He had to call Devlin. If the sick bastard was allowed to work freely, they'd have their answers long before he and Weiss returned to Bridgeport.

Albright grabbed his cell.

***

The stranger pulled a small black metal box from his jacket pocket. Attaching a wire to it, he inserted the free end into the cell phone.

Jacobson had seen this same equipment before. The technology was currently being used by the DEA in drug cases, and was highly effective in dealing with drug traffickers, and informants requiring total anonymity. The FBI used a similar device in kidnapping cases. This one was much smaller. Jacobson guessed it was a newer model. "Is that a voice modifier?"

"It's a version of the MorphVOX. This one's an earlier model with a few added tweaks."

Jacobson wondered if this man was actually an FBI agent, or with the DEA. It didn't really matter. All he cared about was what the man was doing, and why. He could tell that the man did not mean him any harm. This man hardly acted like a criminal. He'd traded Jacobson the Glock for the phone. That was something a criminal would not have done.

The man pressed a couple of switches and held it out. "Say something."

"I sure hope it doesn't rain while I'm here," Jacobson said nervously.

The man pressed another switch, set the box on his right thigh and put the phone in front of his face. "This is Jacobson."

"What the fuck happened?" came the familiar voice, loud and clear. "And why did you take so damned long to answer the phone?"

Jacobson flinched when he realized the phone had been placed on speaker.

"What's that?" the stranger said.

"Don't play stupid, cowboy. You know that crap doesn't work with me. You fucked up, so dump the attitude and tell me exactly what happened."

"What would you like to know?"

"I told you not to play stupid. You flew up there to do a job for me. I bought you a ticket and had everything arranged down to the letter. You failed."

"How's that?"

Another pause. "You wouldn't by any chance be *taping* this conversation, would you, cowboy?"

"Why would I do that?"

"Let's just say I don't like the sound of your voice. Your attitude sucks even worse than usual."

"There's nothing wrong with my attitude."

"We've been through this before. It's fifteen minutes past seven, for Christ's sake, and you didn't do what you were supposed to do."

"Really?"

"You bastard. Did you forget how powerful I am? How many contacts I have?"

"How can I? You remind me every time you open your big mouth."

"You son of a bitch. You can't talk to me like this. I'm putting out the word. You're a walking dead man. Your family's also dead. Your bimbo wife? Those two brats? Bye-bye…"

Jacobson sat back in the seat, closed his eyes and forced himself to keep quiet.

"You honestly think you can threaten me like that?" his companion said.

"No one crosses me and lives to talk about it."

"What exactly do you intend to do to my family?"

"You actually think you can tape all this? What good is a fucking tape when you're dead?"

"Pretty good if I make copies…"

"It's illegal, brainiac. A dumb cop like you should know that. Have you forgotten Florida law? Taping a conversation is inadmissible."

"I'm not in Florida right now, I'm in Ohio. You ought to know that. You sent me here. You just said you did, didn't you?"

"Doesn't matter where you are, cowboy. Courts won't take this seriously. They're swamped as it is."

"Maybe so, but the man you hired me to kill just might take this seriously. I understand he's pretty important up here."

"Now how would you know *that*?"

"If he wasn't, you wouldn't want him out of the way, would you?"

"If you think you can blackmail me, you bastard, you're even stupider than I thought."

"I wouldn't call it *blackmail*..."

"What *would* you call it?"

"Insurance. Self-preservation. I plan to keep copies of this conversation in several safe places for a little while. I'd say thirty years would be a reasonable period of time. You might still be around, but you'll be living in a rest home, caterwauling for the closest available nurse to wipe your ass for you."

"You bastard--"

"And while I've got this stored in a safe place, I'll want something from you in exchange. You wouldn't want me to forget about this arrangement and accidentally release the tapes before the allotted time, would you?"

"*Now* what the hell are you talking about?"

"I want my record expunged."

Jacobson opened his eyes and sat up.

A chuckle. "Now why would I want to do a stupid thing like that?"

"You've got until eight o'clock to gather up every single shred of evidence you've got on me

257

and send it directly to my desk at the Police Station by special messenger."

"Listen here, cowboy, and try to understand what I'm saying. Even if I *wanted* to do something that stupid--which I don't--it's not enough time..."

"With *your* contacts? You could probably have it delivered there in ten minutes, tops."

"It doesn't matter. I just said I won't do it."

"I'll be making a call to OPD at precisely eight o'clock. If a certain package hasn't arrived by that time, the man in this photo gets a copy of this tape. At eight-fifteen, I'll call again. If I find out that it still hasn't arrived--"

"I don't care how many fucking calls you make. It won't hold up in court. Besides, no one'll be able to make anything stick."

The stranger paused for only a moment. "Does the name Joe Neilson ring a bell?"

"What about him?"

"I think I need to remind you of a few things."

"That loser's dead, cowboy. Car accident, as I recall. Stupid fuck got behind the wheel drunk. It was in the papers. Hell, everyone knows that."

"Maybe...but what everyone *doesn't* know is that Neilson kept two sets of books when he worked for you in Orlando. Does anything about *that* ring a bell?"

"Neilson didn't have anything when he bit the dust. The cops checked. Nothing in his apartment. Nothing in his bank account or safe deposit box. The bank president happens to be a friend of mine. He also checked. Zilch."

"You didn't find anything because Neilson gave all his valuable stuff to a trusted friend before he died. Wanna guess who he gave it to?"

A sudden silence.

"Still there?"

"You're bluffing, cowboy."

"How would I know about those books, then?"

"Neilson didn't have any friends down here. Like I said, you're bluffing."

"Then I wouldn't know what's in those books, would I? I wouldn't know names like G. J. Allen, who supplied muscle for you last year, when you needed to get two major land deals pushed through even though the EPA was bogging you down with red tape. And what about Jorge Grayson? I understand he supplied hitters for you and your associates on a monthly basis just a couple of years ago. And of course, we wouldn't want to leave out Frank Bollinger, who can manipulate the stock market better than anyone…"

"Enough!"

"It's all in Joe's book. Everyone will know what you've been doing for the last several years. Would you like to guess what your friends and associates will do once they find out about this book?"

"How the fuck do you know all this, cowboy?"

"All you need to know is that the book is in a safe place. And it'll stay right there while you clear my name. Meanwhile, you'll stay away from me and my family. And also Joe Neilson's ex-wife and daughter."

"You can't get away with this, cowboy. I'll ruin you…"

"Eight o'clock."

"That's *not enough time*!"

"Those are my terms. Get busy making your famous phone calls. You're wasting valuable time."

"Damn you!" *Click.*

He lowered the phone and sat back.

Jacobson hadn't moved. He couldn't believe what he'd just heard. "That was the most amazing thing I ever heard…in my entire life."

"Let's hope it worked."

"I just hope he leaves my family alone…"

"As long he thinks you're in possession of a book that'll get him killed or put away for years, your family's safe."

"*Is* there such a book? Or were you just leading him on?"

"The book exists. Whether he's convinced you've got it is another thing entirely."

"When will we know?"

He consulted his watch. "In just about forty minutes."

CHAPTER THIRTEEN

The approaching darkness pushed firmly against the windows of the crowded eatery, reminding Barbara of their desperation.

She and Laura sat at a table about twenty feet from the entrance. Barbara didn't even notice the swirling tendrils of steam rising from the coffee cups on the table between them. She hadn't noticed much of anything since Desmond Roth had dropped them off.

He'd left to take care of something urgent. He told them he'd be back--that they should stay there until he returned. They'd be safe as long as they stayed in a crowded place.

Safe. Somehow that simple word had lost its meaning. Would she and Laura ever be safe again? Would they be able to survive this nightmare? Could they return home and resume their lives as if this had never happened?

Right now, it seemed unlikely. Her sense of stability had been wrenched from her in the last few hours; she didn't think she could ever get it back. Then she wondered if it had even been there in the first place. The last five years had become some illusionary charade based on lies and false hopes.

The guilt came thundering back. It wasn't all her fault, but that no longer mattered. The damage had been done. If only Joe had confided in her... If only he hadn't kept their problems bottled up inside him...

Problems were a part of life. But when you loved someone, you were never alone, and nothing

261

was ever truly hopeless. It was much easier to solve a problem when it was shared...when there were two of you talking about it, seeing it through.

"Momma? Are you all right?"

Barbara found it difficult to look her daughter in the face. Laura was the one who'd suffered most. Because of the mistakes Barbara and Joe had made, their daughter had been robbed of the last few years of her childhood.

I shouldn't take the blame for this. I can't and I won't. I feel that it's my fault, but I have to keep reminding myself that it isn't.

The man responsible for all this was just a couple of hundred yards away, walking around in the Mall. He'd destroyed her family, and he'd done it all for money. He'd betrayed her and Laura, and right now he and his friends were looking for Desmond Roth, the man who'd rescued them. And from what she'd just learned in the last couple of hours, Sam was going to order his men to kill Mr. Roth the moment he saw him.

"Momma? Please say something..."

"It's all been a lie, baby. The last five years. Nothing's been real."

"It's not your fault."

She sat back in her seat. "It sure feels like it is."

"If Mr. Roth wasn't lying to us, Sam planned this from the beginning. From the time we first met him at the Food Court."

"Mr. Roth wasn't lying, baby. I can tell."

"I know, Momma. I saw it in his eyes. He's a good man."

"It's very strange. When we were with him, I had this feeling…"

"Did it feel like everything might turn out all right?"

"Yes."

Laura sipped some coffee. "I think there's something really special about him."

"There's something very strange about his hands, baby…"

"His…hands?"

Barbara couldn't forget the warmth flowing through her the moment he touched her. Everything had instantly turned very bright. All the darkness that had been smothering her simply vanished. There was something very special about his touch…something she'd never experienced before.

"I don't know what it is, baby, but it's definitely very special."

"Well, whatever it was, it brought you right back."

"It really did."

Laura patted Barbara's wrist. "When we see him again, I'd like to ask him more about that. And also about Dad."

"I just hope we see him again."

"You think we might not?"

She thought of Sam and the other men looking for Mr. Roth. It gave her a sinking feeling. "It's possible."

"He told us about the others. When I think about these people, who they might be, what they might do… It's scaring me, Momma."

Barbara slid out of the booth. Her mind was made up--she had to find Sam. And she had to find him before he found Mr. Roth.

"Momma? Where are you going?"

"You stay here, baby."

"Momma, tell me what's going on…"

"I have to find Sam. I'm going to tell him I know what he's done. I'm going to look him right in the eye when I tell him."

Laura struggled to get up. "But Momma…he's got friends everywhere. They'll *never* let you get away with this."

"I don't care. I owe this to your father. And to Mr. Roth. Maybe it'll scare Sam off. If it gets them to leave the Mall without hurting Mr. Roth or someone else--"

"But they're *dangerous*, Momma. Besides, Mr. Roth told us--"

"Stay here. I don't want you involved."

"I *am* involved, Momma!"

"*Please* stay here, baby."

Laura didn't move or flinch. "I want to be with you. Whatever happens, we're a team. We always have been. Ever since Dad left, it's been just you and me. I have a stake in this, too. I *can't* let you do it alone…"

Barbara gazed into the large, frightened green eyes. She no longer saw the weak, frail young girl she'd nearly lost just a couple of years ago, at a time in her life when she feared she'd lost everything. Right now she saw sincerity, determination, and the same strength she'd seen in Joe when she'd first met him and found herself falling in love with a man destined with a bright future--a man full of confidence, ideas and plans.

"Momma?"

Choked up with pride and love for her beautiful daughter, Barbara reached out and grasped Laura's cold, trembling hand. "Let's go look for Sam, baby."

***

Roth sat in tense silence behind the wheel of the black Ford Edge sedan, waiting for the cell phone to buzz.

It was 7:45. He was pretty certain Al Knepp would call back. He'd known him for many years. He knew how the man thought, how he worked. He also knew that, like all power-crazed bullies, Knepp would do whatever was necessary to divert the heat from himself. He wouldn't be where he was today if he scared easily, but he also knew when to hold on and when to cut his losses.

Jacobson got out of the car, slipped in back and began disassembling the rifle and putting the components back in the plastic case. The man was obviously nervous, and wanted to keep his mind busy while they waited.

Roth turned in his seat. "Did you bring gloves, by any chance?"

"I've got a handkerchief." Jacobson pulled it out of his pants pocket and began wiping everything down. Once he'd finished, he left the case on the seat, got out and climbed in beside Roth. He hadn't spoken, and remained pensive while watching the steady flow of headlights passing the Mall entrance.

Roth could tell Jacobson was agonizing over what he'd almost done with the rifle. Being a police officer, Jacobson had no doubt killed before. The man was probably an expert shot. This would explain why Knepp had chosen him for this. But there was no doubt that Jacobson didn't have the heart for a cold-blooded killing.

At 7:55, Jacobson stirred in his seat. "The man you just talked to...you obviously know him."

"Yes."

Jacobson continued staring at him. Roth could almost hear the man's thoughts. Jacobson was wondering about him, his background. How he knew about this. "Do you...work for him?"

"No." Details weren't necessary.

"I guess I'm just trying to figure out what's really going on...why you're helping me..."

"I've got my reasons."

"But...how did you know I was here?"

"I didn't."

"Then how did you--"

The cell buzzed, making Jacobson jump.

Roth glanced at his watch. "Two minutes early. A good sign." He brought the phone to his face and made sure the modifier was set, the phone still on speaker. "Jacobson."

"I sent the package to OPD. It's everything I've got on you."

Jacobson sighed deeply and relaxed.

"You sent it to my desk?" Roth asked.

"It's what you told me to do, wasn't it?"

"I've got to check this out."

"Cut the dramatics. I told you--"

266

"I know what you told me. I don't trust you."

"Cowboy, what good would it do for me to pull a double cross?"

"None whatsoever."

"You're really getting on my last nerve, you know..."

"They've got meds for that. Now listen up. I'm going to call OPD and find out for sure. Then, if everything checks out..."

"Goddammit!"

"Give me fifteen minutes and call me right back--is that clear?"

"You bastard..."

"Got it?"

A sigh. "I got it."

"One other thing."

"Now what?"

"There better not be copies."

"There aren't any damned copies!"

"Not even for insurance?"

"I've been in this game a long time. A lot of suckers are out there, so why should I waste my time on a stupid cop with an attitude?"

Click.

Roth switched off the modifier and handed the phone to Jacobson. "Call your office. Is there someone you can trust?"

Jacobson took the phone. "My partner."

"We have just fifteen minutes before he calls back. Get on it."

Jacobson's eyes glistened as he pressed the numbers.

***

His back to the passing crowd, Sam Albright moved closer to the pet store window and pressed the number for Devlin. As he waited, he glanced at the window and saw a frightening illusion in the reflection of the glass.

Standing just a few feet behind him, two women watched him intently. At first glance, they looked almost like Barbara and Laura ...

No way. Barbara and Laura were in Bridgeport with Devlin, and in just a few minutes, they were both going to be--

"Something wrong, Sam?"

He whirled around. It only took him an instant to realize he *hadn't* been imagining things. His eyes *weren't* deceiving him. The two women actually *were* Barbara and Laura.

He stood there, frozen, and barely felt the cell phone in his hand.

How the hell did these two get here? It made no sense. Barbara shouldn't even be able to *stand,* let alone talk. Just an hour ago, she was lying on the love seat, barely conscious from the strong drug he'd slipped in her coffee.

He had to forget about that for now. It wasn't important. There was only one thing that really mattered.

They knew. By some quirk of fate, they'd found out everything. He could tell by the glaring anger in their unflinching eyes.

But how? Devlin was the only one they'd seen, and he knew very little about what was going on. Even if he did, he wouldn't tell them anything.

Devlin didn't talk much to his victims. He was much more interested in torturing them.

So how the hell did they get here?

He began shaking. He lowered his arm and nearly dropped the cell. He'd heard a click a moment before his arm fell. Devlin, no doubt. They'd obviously distracted him and knocked him out, although Albright couldn't imagine how they'd done it. Devlin was a monster--a force of nature. No normal human being could put him down--especially a middle-aged woman and her handicapped young daughter.

He cleared his throat, but nothing happened. A feeling of light-headedness had swept through him. He leaned against the storefront window for support.

"We know what you did, Sam," Barbara said. "And what happened to Joe. We also know what you've been doing to us the last five years."

***

"What's up, BJ? And where the hell have you been all day? Chief said something about a family emergency, but not much else…"

Jacobson trembled the moment he heard his partner's voice on the line. This was the most important call he'd ever made in his life. He just *had* to get this right… "Where are you now, Billy? Somewhere private?"

"What the hell's going on?"

He should have known Billy would be suspicious. The man was a cop--a damned good one.

"Just tell me where you are."

269

"I'm in your cube. No one else is around."

So far, so good. "So you're alone?"

"Christ, Brad, you're beginning to scare me."

"Did a package come for me just a few minutes ago?"

"It's sitting right here. The messenger brought it to me, but left as soon as I signed for it."

"Did you open it?"

"It's got your name on it. You know I wouldn't--"

"Open it right now."

Ten agonizing seconds of silence.

"There's a thumb drive in it."

"Anything else?"

"Just the flash. And there's no return address."

"I need to know what's on it."

"One sec..."

Jacobson wanted to come out of his skin. He glanced at the man beside him. For some reason, his companion didn't seem nervous at all.

"I'm in," Billy said.

Jacobson's guts churned hotly. The flash drive was open.

"Tell me what's on it."

"A short list of files. Just numbers and dates. The date on top looks vaguely familiar, but I can't exactly pin it down..."

"The Medina bust I made almost two years ago."

"That sounds about right."

Jacobson swallowed audibly. They'd nabbed Medina in Orlando, while the perp was doing business with a local dealer. The deal went sour, the dealer was murdered, and Medina was caught. The case was iron-clad. Medina was caught in the motel room with the stiff, a suitcase crammed with stacks of hundreds and six kilos of cocaine, valued at $150,000. The case progressed well but was dismissed just two weeks after Jacobson was contacted by phone by an anonymous caller. The message delivered was short and simple: "*Back off and forget about Medina.*"

"What else is on the flash?"

"A transcript dated April tenth of last year."

The short hair on the back of his neck bristled. April tenth was the date Medina was released and fled the country. "Open it."

"One sec, here we go... It's a conversation with Medina and someone listed only as One. I assume EM is Medina, since his first name was Emilio."

"One?" He turned to the man beside him. "Who'd be referred to as "One"?"

"The big man, obviously."

"Read it," Jacobson told Billy.

"The whole thing? It's, like, pages--"

"Read fast."

A pause. "Isn't Alan your middle name?"

"Why?"

"There's a "BAJ" mentioned a dozen times."

His pulse raced. "Read more."

"Medina is telling One to find some way to kill the case."

"What else?"

"One says he's got somebody in one of the local hotels who can move some dirty money quickly. He said he can deposit it into BAJ's

271

checking account." A pause. "Brad, what's going on? You realize what this means? If anyone sees this..."

"We'll talk about this later."

"Is *this* why Medina walked? Everyone thought the bastard bought the judge and a couple of jurors. But you've been acting really weird the last few weeks. What's going on? And where the hell are you?"

"How's it sound?" his companion asked. "Legit?"

"It's all on the drive. No names, but I'm sure it's all I'll need to clear my name."

"Brad...who's there with you? Are you all right?"

"Right now, Billy-boy, I feel better than I have in a long time. In fact--"

"We've got to talk about this. The cartel took care of Medina, but that doesn't mean this is just gonna go away..."

"We'll talk later. I promise." He turned. "There was a drug case we did. Just a couple of months after we nailed the big guy, I discovered twenty-five K in my bank account..."

His companion wasn't listening. He'd pulled a cell out of his jacket pocket and held it against his ear. His expression tightened.

* * *

Albright could actually feel the seething hatred emanating from Laura's glistening eyes.

"You killed him," she whispered through wet eyes. "You killed my father!"

"You used me, Sam," Barbara said. "You used both of us." She took another step toward him. "We came to tell you that we know what you've done. Sam Albright, you're going to pay for this."

"We have proof," Laura said. "You're going to prison, and you're going to stay there a long, long time."

A dark blur emerging from the crowd caught his eye. It was Weiss. In seconds he'd moved in closely behind the women before they'd even noticed.

"Hello again, ladies." Weiss kept his face close between them. The black snub nose of the man's automatic pistol pressed against Barbara's jacket, just above her right hip.

Weiss moved in closer. "I think we should look for a nice quiet place to continue our chat."

"Momma?" Laura turned to her mother.

"If either of you screams or does anything stupid," he whispered, "I'll put a bullet in Mommy's spine. If she survives, the two of you will have matching parking spots at the Mall."

"I think...we'd better do...as he says, baby," Barbara whispered uneasily.

"Smart lady." Weiss coaxed them forward.

Albright brought up his cell. "Everything's okay," he whispered. "The women are here with us. We're bringing them back. You'll have free reign as soon as we get there."

Without waiting for a reply, he pocketed the cell and followed Weiss and the women down the crowded hall, to the exit doors.

***

273

Weiss' sedan sat in the fire lane, oblivious of the crowds walking past. Sam's BMW waited behind it, its anonymity enhanced by the darkness of the night.

Barbara's limbs turned to ice when she and Laura went out into the cool night air and saw the two cars parked there. She found that she could not move.

Something pressed roughly into her lower back. Weiss stood behind her, his foul breath singeing her cheek. "Keep moving, lady…"

A heavy wave of despair rocked through her. In high school she'd learned about a self-defense move where you brought the outside edge of your shoe savagely down your attacker's shin and then stomped his instep with your heel. But it would only work if you knew exactly where your target was.

Although she felt the gun touching her side, she couldn't determine the placement of Weiss' feet. Since he was so close, they were probably less than a foot behind her. *Just a slight twist, then raise your leg and bring it down hard…*

Then what? Run? Leave Laura here to deal with them?

She would *not* leave her daughter alone with these monsters.

Weiss said he'd shoot her if they resisted. She had no doubt that he'd shoot both her and Laura if given the opportunity. He had the dark, hooded eyes of a killer.

Laura gripped her hand. The frozen panic on her daughter's delicate features showed clearly in the light of the Mall entrance. Laura's gaping eyes seemed to say, *Momma, please tell me what to do...*

She had to be strong. This could be the end of the road for them. Their last day on earth. She had to find some way of keeping these monsters from killing them.

If only they'd stayed in the eatery...

"We'll be okay, baby," she whispered, and hoped Laura believed her.

Weiss poked her again. "*Move...*"

Laura squeezed her hand--which made her feel better--and they shuffled down the walk.

Sam hurried past and opened the rear door of the BMW. The man sitting behind the wheel got out and went back to the sedan. Sam and Weiss stood behind them, shielding them from view of the crowd as she and Laura climbed in the back.

The door thumped shut.

Barbara felt trapped. She'd been in this car before, but now it felt totally different. It had grown smaller and much more confining. The air had become stuffy, making it difficult to breathe. It was her imagination, her fears transforming into claustrophobia.

Nevertheless, it felt so *real*...

Sam got behind the wheel. Weiss slid in beside him, pulled his door shut and twisted around in the seat. His gun appeared between the seats, pointing at her. Sam put the car in gear and, creeping out of the fire lane, eased into the slow-moving stream.

"Where...are you taking us?" Her voice sounded weak and distant.

No reply.

The fear set in again. She struggled to convince herself Sam could not be as evil as she imagined. He'd always been so *good* to her and Laura...

She realized now that whatever had happened during the last five years happened because of Sam's plan. Having Barbara and Laura constantly under his thumb was the most efficient way of monitoring any contact with Joe.

But she refused to believe he'd want to have them killed.

She was deceiving herself. These people had no qualms about killing anyone. They'd had Joe killed. Once they realized she and Laura couldn't give them what they wanted, they'd also be disposed of.

They're monsters. Rich, intelligent psychopaths who played deadly games and placed no value on other people's lives.

She and Laura had become obstacles and had to be dealt with.

She promised herself she would not give in. As long as she had a breath left, she was going to find a way out of this. Sam had to have some shred of decency clinging somewhere within him. All she had to do was find it and bring it out. "You don't want to do this, Sam."

He said nothing.

"You really don't..."

"You called the shots." He was staring straight ahead. "You know too much."

So much for that last shred of decency...

"Momma?" Laura squeezed her hand once again. "What's gonna happen...to us?"

"Shut up," Weiss snapped.

"I don't know, baby."

"You heard me." The gun stayed on her.

Her heart pounded heavily as she held her daughter's cold, trembling hand. When the gravity of their fate finally sunk in, she closed her eyes and began to pray.

***

"What's up?" Jacobson could tell by his companion's expression that something was very wrong.

His companion stuffed the phone into his pocket and turned on the ignition. "We have to go."

"Gotta go," Jacobson told Billy. "Guard that flash drive with your life." He turned off the cell and placed it in the cup holder on the dash. "Does this have anything to do with why I was sent up here?"

The man eased the car out of the spot and waited patiently for a break in traffic. The parking lot had filled even more during the last half-hour with the dinner crowd and hordes of eager shoppers. "Sam Albright is the man you were ordered to kill. He's very big in this area and a business associate of the man who's been jerking you around in Orlando."

"Just another big-shot rivalry thing, obviously. What's going on right now?"

"Two women are in serious trouble. Albright just kidnapped them from the Mall. He's taking them back to Bridgeport."

"Why?"

"I dropped them off at a restaurant, but they apparently left against my wishes, went into the Mall and confronted him. He'll take them back to Bridgeport, get whatever he can from them and then dump them. Albright's dirty and is dealing with hired killers. We can't let him get away, and we can't let them hurt the women."

Jacobson picked up the Glock and checked the mag. His adrenaline had already kicked in. He felt whole again and was more than ready to kick ass.

***

The streetlamps lit up strips of the busy highway on Mall Road. At the intersection, the traffic split up. The stranger kept with the flow moving northwest. Signs showed Interstate 70 turnoffs straight ahead.

Jacobson gazed at the steady stream of taillights directly in front of them. "Do you know which car we're looking for?"

"Not exactly."

"Then how can you be sure they're ahead of us? It's dark, and there's too much traffic to keep tabs on anyone."

"They don't have much of a lead on us, and they can't get very far in this traffic."

Jacobson stared dumbly at the man. If he hadn't personally witnessed that cell phone business earlier, he would have figured the man a local nuthouse escapee. Jacobson had dealt with crazies before and knew how to recognize the signs. This man wasn't crazy.

But he couldn't stop wondering who he was.

The soft, familiar buzzing brought him around.

His companion grabbed the cell phone from the cup holder and eyed the display. "This is for you."

Jacobson's pulse hammered. "It's...him?"

"He's right on time, too."

Jacobson froze. His throat had gone dry. His former handler was on the phone. The time had finally come.

The phone was held out. "You can make this as enjoyable as you like."

Jacobson felt as if he was being handed a winning Lotto ticket. But it was much better than that--his freedom was being given back to him. His life. His world. His happiness.

The phone warmed his palm. Jacobson put it up to his ear and was surprised that his hand was dead-steady. "Jacobson."

"Well? Do we have a deal? I came through on my end."

Jacobson couldn't help smiling. "As long as you don't have copies lying around somewhere."

"What good will copies do me? Talk, cowboy. Tell me what's next."

"I'm trying to decide."

"Decide *what*, for Christ's sake? We had a deal!"

"I've got the files. They're all I need to clear my name, should the opportunity present itself. And I guess you already know that it's pretty incriminating for you, right?"

"My name isn't mentioned, cowboy."

"My bank and account information sure as hell are."

"Like I said, you can't nail me for anything."

"You're right. But now I can finally explain how twenty-five K mysteriously found its way into my account last year."

"If you don't want it, give it away."

"I already donated it to my favorite charity."

"I always knew you were a soft touch. What about Albright?"

"What about him?"

"Don't be funny."

"You mean you want me to make sure he doesn't know what you had planned for him when I flew here?"

"That's something else no one can pin on me. That bastard's got nearly as many enemies as I have. It comes with the territory."

"Then why the concern?"

"I don't like loose ends. You should burn the instructions and photo. It would simplify things for all of us."

"Especially for you?"

"Whatever…"

"What about the rifle and scope? Suppressors are illegal, you know."

"Leave the case in the trunk of the rental, dammit. Do I have to tell you everything? Park the rental where you found it and walk away. Find a cab. Just make sure that you and I don't clash horns again. Next time, I might not be so fucking charitable."

Click.

Jacobson closed the cell and placed it in his lap. "That idiot thinks I'm going to burn the evidence, leave the rifle in the trunk and park this car where I found it."

"Let me take a wild guess…you don't intend to do as he said?"

"There's no way I'm going walk away from a car with a sniper rifle and ammo sitting in the trunk. But at least I've got all the evidence I need now."

"You'll be back with your family before you know it."

He quickly forgot about the car, the sniper rifle, and the man responsible for all this. He couldn't believe he'd gotten his life back. And it was all because of this man, who he didn't even know. "I hope you realize that I'll never be able to thank you for all you've done… "

"You're not getting sloppy on me, are you?"

"I can't help it. If you only knew--"

"You can thank me later if you have to. Right now, we've got more important matters to tend to."

Jacobson sat back and collected his thoughts. The man was right. Two women were in serious trouble; he needed to focus. "Tell me exactly what we're doing. I'm totally involved in this, too."

"About five years ago, these people got their claws into a man named Joe Neilson and stuck him on their payroll. Neilson was paid to keep two sets of books, which enabled these crooks to stay out of trouble. When Neilson got tired of keeping their asses clean, he put the incriminating evidence on a flash drive and tried to disappear."

"Where do you come in?"

"They suspected what Neilson was doing and brought in a wet boy to take him out. I got wind of it and tried getting Neilson out of town, but they got him anyway."

"How'd you get wind of it?"

"That's a separate story. I'll tell you about it later. *If* I get the chance."

Something the man just said about Neilson sounded familiar. "Does this have anything to do with a drunk driving fatality that happened a couple of weeks ago in East Orlando?"

"You heard about it, then?"

"I heard about it because Homicide got involved. Too many things didn't add up. They figured it was staged."

"It was."

"So tell me about the two women."

"They're Neilson's ex-wife and daughter, and they're in deep trouble."

"I'll wager Albright and the others think these women have the drive Neilson made."

"That's about the size of it."

"So now we're looking at a snatch and dump job." Jacobson brought up his cell. "What jurisdiction is this?"

"Belmont County. We've probably reached the St. Clairsville city limits by now. I'm not certain where they are now, but they're definitely heading back to Bridgeport. They'll no doubt dump them when they've finished questioning them."

"Before I get hold of the locals, what can you tell me about these women?"

"Their names are Barbara and Laura Neilson, and they're both residents of Manville. Barbara's the mother; she's in her mid-forties. Laura's in her early twenties and has a spinal injury. Her dad told me she was nearly killed on I-70 a couple of years ago by a meth head. Poor girl's been in constant pain ever since. She can hardly walk."

The thoughts of a disabled young girl being pushed around made his blood boil. Jacobson forced himself to focus as he pressed 911.

CHAPTER FOURTEEN

Laura knew she should be scared. Having a gun pointed at you should terrify anyone. It frightened her when Sam's psycho friend pointed a knife at her face. This was worse--a gun was much more dangerous than a knife. And it made things even more horrifying when you knew that the man pointing the gun at you was crazy.

But Laura suddenly discovered that she wasn't frightened at all. A sense of calmness, of tranquility, had settled in around her, and she no longer experienced that same icy feeling of blind terror that gripped her in the Mall, when Weiss had snuck up to them. Only moments ago, she thought she'd heard a voice telling her everything would be all right, and that she and Momma would not be harmed.

Was it Mr. Roth's voice? Was he looking for her and Momma?

Her imagination was running wild again. He probably thought they were where he'd left them. He wouldn't even know anything was wrong until he went back and saw that they were gone. Even if he guessed Sam and Weiss had found them, he wouldn't have any idea where they were being taken.

She refused to give up hope. The voice sounded convincing. She truly believed everything would turn out okay. But she also thought their fate could use a little help.

She had to find some way of stalling for time...

Sam swerved sharply to avoid something in the road. The right side of the big car thumped onto the shoulder. She and Momma were jerked back in their seat. Her lower back twanged a nerve, and a loud squeal escaped her throat.

Momma gripped her arm. "You all right, baby?"

"Shuddup." Weiss' voice sounded like the growl of an angry dog.

Momma shot him a glare. "Don't be so heartless. Can't you tell when someone's hurting?" She turned back to Laura. "You need your meds, baby?"

She took a deep breath. "I…think so, Momma."

"This is crap," Weiss said.

"Ease off," Sam said. "The girl has pins in her spine."

"I've got a plate in my head. You don't hear *me* whining about it..."

"That explains quite a bit," Momma muttered.

"Watch it, lady..."

Laura wanted to smile.

"I said, ease off." Sam glared at Weiss.

"Are they in your bag, baby?"

Laura nodded.

"Want me to get them for you?"

"It's all right, Momma. I think I can find them. If only the road wasn't so bumpy..."

Momma took her bag and opened it.

"Watch it," Weiss said.

"Don't get tense," Sam said.

"She could have a piece--or maybe a blade--hidden in there."

"Don't be an idiot."

The BMW hit a dip in the road. Laura leaned back and gasped.

"Sam, *please* be careful!"

"Can't help it."

"I'll be all right, Momma. This road...I just need a moment..."

"Pull over, Sam."

Sam continued driving.

Ignoring Weiss' gun, Momma leaned forward. "Laura and I need you to stop!"

Laura felt a sense of genuine pride. Momma took no prisoners when Laura's safety was in jeopardy.

"Barbara, I can't just *stop*..."

"Just for a moment--please? She has to take her meds. And she needs to relax her back. I can't possibly find anything in the dark--not in a moving car."

"I'll find her damn meds." Weiss switched his gun to his other hand. "Hand over the bag."

"If you even *try* touching this bag," Momma whispered, "I'll break your fingers!"

Weiss pulled back.

"Barbara..."

"Sam, I don't care where you're taking us or what you're planning to do. My daughter needs her meds. For all that's holy and decent, *please stop this car*!"

"This is crap!" Weiss swatted the back of the seat.

"There's a turnoff up ahead," Sam said. "It's some sort of family-run grocery store setup. I'll pull off for a minute or two. Then we've got to get back on the main road."

"Thank you."

Sam had pulled out his cell and held it close to his ear as he drove.

"Who you calling, boss?" Weiss asked.

"I've got to tell Crowley what's going on."

Laura's spirits lifted. *Sam's calling Crowley. That means he'll be talking to Mr. Roth!*

"Boss, he never showed back at the Mall."

"He never got with you at all?"

"Not a word."

"He was probably fighting the mall traffic while we were getting in the car. Maybe he got with Milan when he didn't see you. I'll find out what happened. Then I have to call Devlin and find out what happened in Bridgeport." He glanced at his rearview. "You wouldn't want to tell me what happened back there, would you, Barbara?"

"Not really," Momma said flatly.

Laura almost smiled. Momma would never cooperate with these people.

Sam shrugged. "Didn't think so. Anyway, I'll let Crowley know what's going on." He slowed down and put on his blinkers.

***

An endless sea of RV's and trailers sat in adjoining lots on the northern side of the long, winding stretch of National Road. The heavy flow of traffic heading west abruptly slowed.

287

Roth applied his brakes and kept a close watch on the activity ahead. Erratically blinking brake lights penetrated the darkness in front of them. Someone was making a turn. His inner voice suggested it could be Albright.

"Looks like someone's turning," Jacobson said.

"I think it's Albright."

"How can you be sure? We're way too far back."

"Just a hunch." He'd concentrated on Laura a couple of minutes ago, pushing a suggestion

(*stall*)

at her image. She'd obviously received it and somehow convinced Albright to stop.

"This whole thing is doing a number on my head," Jacobson said. "But since I'm obviously just here for the ride, I'm gonna have to take your word for it."

Crowley's phone buzzed. Roth pulled it out of his jacket pocket. It was Albright.

"We're making a pit stop," Albright said.

Using his newly-developed powers, Roth lowered his voice to approximate Crowley's raspy, low-pitched Brooklyn-accented timbre. "Where?"

"Weiss and I are heading west on National Road. Laura needs her meds. You still at the Mall?"

Good girl, Roth thought.

"Yeah. What about the others?"

"Levinson went to Wheeling. You and Milan return to Bridgeport. We'll meet there later."

Roth pocketed the phone. "I was right. Albright's stopping so Laura can take her meds."

"How'd you know he'd do that?"

"I guessed. She's in a lot of pain, and this road is no doubt making the drive difficult for her."

Jacobson shook his head. "You ought to play the Lottery. By the way, that voice thing. Who was that?"

"One of Albright's men."

"Where's *he*?"

"Don't ask."

"Can I ask how you did that thing with your voice?"

"Just a little something I picked up."

"You sounded totally different."

"The guy I mimicked is an enforcer. He doesn't talk much, just grunts once in a while. Mimicking him was a piece of cake."

"Maybe you can start your own nightclub act with your winnings from that Lottery ticket."

About a quarter of a mile before traffic had slowed, they'd passed a sign on which *Brehn Road* was painted in block letters. Roth could tell by the size and shape of the sign that it was a country road and wouldn't be heavily traveled.

"Are we gonna turn?" Jacobson asked.

"We've got to do *some*thing. Otherwise, we'll lose them."

"He'll spot us if we get too close."

"I know."

"But if we hang back..."

"I know that, too."

A large lighted building sitting off to their left came into view. Roth put on his blinkers and made a quick turn, taking the Ford Edge sedan into the big paved front lot of the local fire station. He swerved, circling back around to face National Road.

About a quarter of a mile straight ahead, headlights showed slipping through the trees as it climbed the winding country road extending north of the main highway. It made a sharp left and went a short distance before stopping behind a grove of trees.

"What is that place?" Jacobson asked.

"It could be a country store, or private residence."

"Got a plan in mind?"

"Albright won't give Laura much time to take her meds, so I've got to get there before they take off again. Contact the locals again, get them here and stick around until they show."

"I didn't come all this way to stand around with my thumb up my ass while you do all the good stuff. I *am* a cop, you know." He picked up the Glock. "And I'm damned good with one of these."

This wasn't the time to argue. "All right. Once you give them our twenty, cut across the road and use the woods to work your way up that hill. Stay on this side of the road and make sure no one sees you."

"Where will you be?"

"I'm gonna circle around them. If they kill me, do whatever it takes to get the women safely away. They're blameless and don't deserve any of this. Albright said Weiss is with him, so be extra cautious. Weiss is a cold-blooded killer, and he's always armed."

"You sound like you know him."

"I know his work."

"You have a gun?"

He patted his jacket pocket. "I'm good."

"Just so I know...do you plan to take down Weiss?"

"I'm going to try and take him alive."

"A cold-blooded killer?"

"He's valuable. I'm pretty sure he can be tied directly to your former handler."

"Still...a cold-blooded killer?"

"Bringing him in should be interesting-- wouldn't you say?"

Jacobson frowned. "A tad suicidal, actually. But as I said, I'm just here for the ride."

"Would you believe me if I told you I'll be okay? That I won't even need a gun?"

"Mister, after what happened in this car an hour ago and the things I've just seen you do, I'll believe just about anything you say."

Roth opened the driver's door. "Don't worry. I can do this."

"I'll be close, anyway."

Roth circled the front of the sedan and waited for a break in traffic. Then, dodging passing cars, he cut across the busy highway and slipped into the dark mass of the woods.

***

Ignoring Weiss' gun, Laura used both hands to push open the back door of the BMW.

"I didn't say you could get out of the damned car." Weiss kept the gun pointed at her. "You can take your meds right there, in the seat."

291

"I have to get out and stretch." She wanted to grab his stupid gun and beat him in the head with it. "If you have to shoot a crippled, unarmed girl to feel like a real man, go right ahead. I'm not moving too fast for you, am I?"

Weiss grunted.

"You'll have to shoot me, too," Momma said flatly.

Gripping the armrest, Laura stepped carefully onto the sloped, uneven pavement and leaned against the side of the car. Momma got out carrying Laura's bag.

Sam slid out, circled the front of the BMW and stopped a few feet away, separating them from the front entrance of the dairy store that sat about two hundred feet from where they'd parked. Inside, customers could be seen milling around behind the windows.

Three cars and two pickups sat in the small gravel lot in front of the white one-story block building, close to a thick grove of buckeyes separating the woods from the west side of the store.

The mere presence of others nearby made Laura feel a little safer. Five vehicles meant at least five potential eyewitnesses. The cashier, who could be the owner of the red pickup parked in front of the dumpster at the other end of the building, would also complicate matters. Eyewitnesses would prevent Weiss from being reckless. Laura could tell he was cautious but sensed that he wouldn't hesitate to shoot her and Momma if they pushed him too far. She saw no need to do anything stupid and decided to stick with her original plan. Stalling seemed the smartest thing to do. She had to do whatever it took to keep from getting back in the car.

"Let's get this over with." Sam nervously scanned their surroundings. "Take your meds, stretch your back, and get back in the car." He gave them both a cold glance. "Just don't try to run or do anything stupid."

Laura laughed. "Does it look like I can run *any*where?" She couldn't believe he'd said such a ridiculous thing. But it told her how desperate he was.

"Just remember what I said."

Laura rested her palms on her knees and carefully lowered her torso, an inch at a time, until her hair brushed the pavement. She stayed in this position for about thirty seconds, until the blood rushed into her head and the pressure in her lower back eased up. Then, inching her hands up her thighs, she slowly straightened.

Momma had opened Laura's bag. She frowned at the streetlamp on the other side of the lot. "I need more light."

Weiss reached into his jacket pocket. Producing a slim penlight, he flicked it on and aimed the beam directly at Laura's face.

She turned away quickly and gasped when a blade of sharp pain sliced across her back.

"*Please!*" Momma held up an arm, shielding herself and Laura. "That was really stupid and inconsiderate!"

"You wanted light." Weiss shrugged. "You got light."

"We won't be able to find anything if we're both *blind*, you know."

"I'm *so* goddamn *sorry*..." Weiss scowled.

"Control yourself, dammit." Sam sounded even more nervous. "Let them find her meds so we can get back on the road."

Grumbling, Weiss directed the slender beam of light at Laura's bag. As soon as Momma's hand disappeared inside, he said, "That hand *better* not come back out with a piece in it." He kept his own gun pressed against his right thigh, out of sight of the store.

"You've seen *way* too many bad movies," Momma replied. "Besides, if I *had* a gun, I would've shot you long before now."

Weiss glared.

Momma found the meds and pulled them out. "Just one, baby?"

"That should be enough for now, thanks."

Momma carefully twisted off the child-proof plastic cap, tilted the vial and shook one out onto her palm.

Laura reached out to take it. *Make it look good, girl...* Just as she touched her mother's hand, she groaned and twisted sharply to her left, knocking the vial out of Momma's grasp.

Pills flew everywhere. Some landed on Laura's arm and rolled off. Others slid down Momma's shoulder and onto her forearm, spilling to the pavement and disappearing underneath the BMW.

Darn!" Laura frowned. "I'm so *sorry!*"

"That's all right, baby." Momma dropped to her knees and placed Laura's bag on the ground beside her. "You gonna be okay while I look for them?"

"I'll be all right, I guess."

"What the hell was *that* for?" Sam asked.

"Just a twinge. I get them all the time. It comes from having my spine cracked and held together with titanium pins. But don't worry, I'm okay. And thanks for asking."

"Leave 'em," Weiss told Momma. "Shove one down her throat and let's get the hell out of here."

"These pills are horribly expensive," Momma said testily. "Give me that light. It'll only take a minute to recover them all."

"She ain't gonna need--"

"Shut up and give her the light." Sam glared at Weiss.

Laura caught a flicker of movement out of the corner of her eye. A figure had come out of the woods about fifty yards away. Moving briskly, it disappeared behind the dumpster before reappearing briefly and vanishing once again behind the building. She hadn't been able to see who it was. It couldn't possibly be an employee coming back from a break. What would an employee be doing in the woods?

About two minutes later, just as Momma had collected the last of the pills, the figure appeared from the opposite end of the building. It was much closer than before. Laura could see that it was a fit-looking man in a jacket. Moving swiftly, the man slipped between the vehicles parked in front of the store and crept straight toward them. As soon as he'd reappeared, he became Mr. Roth.

Laura wanted to leap for joy, hug Momma and tell her everything would be all right again and that they had nothing to worry about.

But when Mr. Roth was just twenty feet away from Sam, Weiss cocked his head, spun sharply on his heel, and aimed his gun at Mr. Roth's face.

***

Roth stopped cold. He cursed himself for not being more careful. He should have expected Weiss to have razor-sharp reflexes. High-profile crooks like Albright would employ only the best protection.

Albright stood a few feet behind Weiss, out of the range of fire. Laura and her mother clung to one another behind the open rear door of the BMW.

"Who the hell are you?" Weiss' eyes glinted in the darkness.

"Just a passerby, you could say."

Weiss kept the gun trained on Roth's forehead. "Never saw you before, but you don't look like no passerby to *me...*"

"I've seen *you* before," Roth said.

"Oh? And where the hell was this?"

"At the Manville Police Station. You were taking these nice ladies outside and putting them in your car. Remember?"

"Yeah. I vaguely remember."

Albright had been watching Roth closely. "You're not by any chance from Orlando, are you?"

"As a matter of fact, I am."

296

Albright straightened. He regarded Roth for a few moments. "*You're* the man everyone's been talking about?"

"Everyone's talking about me? And what are they saying?"

"For starters, they're saying you overpowered two nightclub bouncers in seconds. They're also saying you did things to their minds. I don't know exactly what's going on or what you did, but apparently they're not the same anymore."

"Maybe they just needed a slight attitude adjustment."

"Apparently it was a little more than that..."

Roth smiled. "I sound impressive, don't I?"

"You really did--at first."

"Something changed your mind?"

"It seems to me that a man of your skills...well, someone like you wouldn't put yourself in such a dangerous situation--wouldn't you say?"

"What do you mean?"

"The gun pointed at your head. You've noticed it, haven't you?"

"It would be difficult not to."

"This has to be extremely embarrassing for a man like you."

"I don't consider it embarrassing at all. I've got some important things to do. That's why I stopped by."

"You're saying you *voluntarily* decided to join us?"

"Why else would I walk right up to a man holding a gun?"

"Sounds like you've got some sort of death wish," Weiss said.

"That's not why I came over."

Albright's expression remained grim. "Mister, I could care less who you are, where you're from or what you can do. The only thing that matters to us is what you've got. I'm sure you know what has to happen next."

"Why don't you give me a little hint, so I know what we're talking about?"

"Let's not insult one another. Joe Neilson stole something very valuable from an associate of mine in Orlando. Are you going to tell me you weren't with Neilson before he died?"

"I was with him, all right."

"Then you know exactly what we want."

"As a matter of fact, I do."

"I'm glad you've decided to cooperate. We know he gave it to someone. He didn't have it on him."

"I'd say that was pretty smart of him."

"Smart or not, it's caused many of us much anguish. If you don't mind, you can just hand it over right now and the matter will be settled. It's getting late. Weiss and I have things to do."

"That's right. You've got two kidnapped women to deal with. I'd say you're in kind of a tight spot right now, too."

"What makes you think these women are here against their will? Barbara works for me. I've been looking after them."

"Yeah, I know why you've been looking after them, all right. And judging by their body language, they know, too."

"Mister, I don't really know what you're talking about."

"Then let me spell it out. If they're not here against their will, why are they so terrified?"

"What makes you think they're terrified?"

"Why don't I just simplify things by asking them if they really want to be here?"

Albright rubbed the back of his neck. "I don't have time for this. Hand it over. Now."

"What makes you think I brought it with me?"

"Drop the innocent act. Even if you didn't bring it with you, you have it hidden somewhere. Logic tells me that since you don't live here, you're probably keeping it in your car or hotel room. Please spare us the aggravation and tell us where it is right now. I guarantee you things will be much more pleasant for all of us if you comply."

Roth had seen Laura straighten when Albright mentioned her father's name. She no longer looked terrified. Even in the darkness, he could see the anger flickering in her eyes. Laura was one tough lady. Her father would have been very proud of her.

"No offense, but I find it hard to trust someone who pushes women around and uses psychopaths for trigger men."

"Watch it..." The gun in Weiss' hand twitched.

"If this makes things any easier," Albright said, "I'll settle for the intel right now. The money can come later, after we establish some sort of rapport between us. I know this rapport will have to be short-lived, but I'll settle for anything I can hang my hat on--for the sake of my business interests, of course."

Roth smiled. "Are you referring to the ten million you were told was sent to the women by Joe Neilson?"

Albright sighed. "We both know what we're talking about, so why don't you just drop the act so we can end this fairly quickly?"

"I hate to burst your bubble, but there *is* no ten million."

Albright stiffened, but quickly recovered. "Listen to me, whoever you are...I was specifically told Joe Neilson--"

"You were told wrong. Tell me something...were you told about this just a few months ago, when certain funds came up missing?"

Albright didn't reply.

"You don't know Knepp very well, do you? It's the oldest con in the book, and he's been using it for years. He tells his associates about missing funds and gets them all worked up about it. What did he offer you as a finder's fee? Twenty percent? Twenty-five? He's been stringing you along. The ten million was probably just another of his ploys to get you to stay close to Barbara and Laura and make sure nothing was sent to them that would worry him. It worked, didn't it?"

Albright stood with his arms at his sides. He was shaking. "I don't believe you..." His voice was a harsh whisper.

Roth shrugged. "I don't care. Just try finding ten million bucks that never existed in the first place. Believe me, it'll be helluva trick if you do."

Albright took a deep breath and continued watching Roth closely. After another deep breath, he found his voice. It was shaky and laced with pure anger. "Mister, I'm tired of your bullshit, and one way or another, I'm going to find out what's going on. I've got two men standing by who are well-trained to handle such delicate matters." He raised his left arm and displayed the cell. "Both are tough, very strong and determined, and know how to question people. I don't think they'll have any trouble with you. They're much more formidable than punks barely out of high school. If you still want to play the stupid innocent, that's entirely up to you. But let me give you a piece of advice: it isn't always possible to ask important questions without someone getting hurt. Just bear in mind that these men sometimes get so involved in their work that they often forget when they're supposed to ease up." He waved the cell at Roth. "Now...shall I call them? I can have them both here in fifteen minutes."

Roth shrugged. "I'm not going anywhere right now."

Sighing, Albright pressed a number on his phone.

The cell in Roth's pocket buzzed.

Albright stiffened.

Roth grinned. "Want me to get that?"

Albright's gaze jumped from Roth to his own shaking hand, which held the cell.

"Boss?" Weiss hadn't taken his eyes off Roth. "What the hell's going on?"

Albright quickly brought the cell in front of him and worked it again.

The cell in Roth's other pocket buzzed.

"Who would you like to talk to?" Roth asked. "Crowley? Or Devlin? If I remember correctly, I've got Crowley in my left pocket and Devlin in my right." He paused. "Or is it Crowley in my right? Sorry. I get easily confused these days. It must be the jet lag."

"B-Boss?"

"What did you do...to my men?" Albright asked in a soft, unsteady voice.

"They were working too hard. I gave them some time off."

Trembling, Albright gawked at Roth. "We've got to get out of here." He shot a glance at Weiss. "Quietly. There are people inside the store..."

"Got that covered." Weiss's free hand disappeared inside the side pocket of his jacket. His hand came back out, gripping a silencer. He continued aiming the gun at Roth as he carefully screwed it on.

"We can't risk that here," Albright said. "We've got to take them to Wheeling. I'll call Levinson. He should already have things ready." Albright turned back to his cell.

It was time to shake things up even more. Roth suspected Jacobson wasn't far away. "How much did Big Al pay you to set up Albright?" he asked Weiss.

"Shuddup."

"He contacted you long before seven o'clock, didn't he?"

Weiss' gaze shifted to Albright, who stood very still, watching him. To Roth, Weiss said, "Now how would I know anything about that?"

"I don't know. How would you?"

"Weiss?" Albright hadn't moved.

"He's talking crap, boss."

Roth said, "Albright, I'll bet you have no idea just how close you came to taking one in the head tonight."

"What the hell are you talking about?"

"Let me make it simple. Were you told to go out through the front entrance of the Mall at precisely seven o'clock and stand there off to the side for a minute or so?"

Albright didn't reply.

"Who told you to go outside?"

"W-Weiss? What do you know…about this?"

Weiss kept the gun pointed at Roth. "Milan told me he saw someone outside. I told you that."

"What's this have to do with Big Al?" Albright asked.

"Tell him, Weiss. Tell him the big man called you a while ago. It wasn't because he was irritated that Albright couldn't get these ladies to talk-- although that did irritate him quite a bit. But this was set up long before the women were even taken to Bridgeport. This was set up before you even got to Manville, wasn't it? The only thing you were waiting on was when and where. Big Al knew what was going to happen, but you knew only a few minutes before seven, when he called and told you.

He told you to lure Albright over to the front entrance--that someone suspicious was seen heading toward the front. A fake description was even provided to make it more legitimate. This would kill two birds with one stone. Big Al had already set up Albright for the hit. I know, because the hitter was sent here from Orlando three hours ago. Big Al doesn't like taking chances--especially with a project worth eight figures at stake. He wanted this hit set up no matter what happened or didn't happen. It didn't even matter if the women talked-- Albright was on his way out anyway. Big Al doesn't like owing people."

"Weiss?"

Roth turned to Laura. He lowered his voice and held out his hand. "Come here, Laura. I won't let anything happen to you or your mother."

Laura slowly straightened.

"Weiss?" Albright's voice sounded strained. "I need to know about this *right now!*"

"Baby?" Barbara was staring at Roth, her eyes as large as silver dollars.

"I trust him, Momma." Steadying herself, Laura stepped past Weiss and shuffled awkwardly toward him.

"*Please* don't, baby..."

Weiss was still gawking at Albright. "Boss, I dunno what the hell this asshole's talkin'--" He stiffened when he noticed Laura moving behind him. He spun around and jerked the gun at her. "I told you not to move!"

Laura's eyes glistened as she hobbled toward Roth.

I can't *be wrong about all this*. Roth struggled to stay in control. *I just* can't *be...*

The same soft, relaxing essence that had drifted into his mind that night in the burning church one year ago entered his thoughts once again. He knew right then that everything would turn out all right.

"You stupid bitch..." Weiss aimed and pulled the trigger.

***

The abrupt *click*! could barely be heard above the sounds of the passing traffic at the bottom of the hill.

Forcing her eyes shut, Laura held her breath and froze. For long, agonizing moments she waited for the excruciating storm of pain to slam through her.

She felt nothing.

Her hands shook as she gingerly felt her clothing. Dry. The area around her stomach was dry. Her shirt and jacket were also dry. No cold. No blood. No stickiness.

It finally registered, and she started breathing again. No pain. No wound.

Then she heard Weiss' voice behind her. "What the *fuck...*?"

This made no sense at all. Weiss obviously knew how to use his gun. How could he miss such a close, slow-moving target?

Her heart thumping wildly, she opened her eyes.

Mr. Roth stood in the same spot, just five feet away, reaching out for her.

Keep moving, Laura. I won't let anyone hurt you or your mother.

His lips hadn't moved, but she'd clearly heard his voice.

How was this possible?

She'd obviously forgotten much of what had happened today. This man had saved their lives-- not once, but twice. He'd also communicated mentally with her during the last half-hour.

But the only thing that mattered was that Weiss hadn't shot her. He'd aimed and pulled the trigger, but the bullet hadn't hit her. She wasn't certain what just happened, but she was almost positive that Mr. Roth had something to do with it.

Just a few more feet, Laura...

Taking a deep breath, she forced her stiff legs to move again. After half a dozen or so short, awkward steps, she reached out for him and felt the pain slicing into her back and hip. But the moment her fingers touched his palm, a warm tingling sensation scurried up her arm and settled in her shoulder. The tingling eased gently down her back, relaxing her and numbing the hot, jagged pain in her spine.

He pulled her gently toward him. Despite the sudden jerking motion, she felt no pain. She also found it strange that she could stand up straight and distribute her weight equally on both legs. She hadn't been able to do this since before her accident.

For one moment she remembered Momma saying something about this man's hands...that something was special about them... But the moment she tried remembering exactly what Momma had said, her thoughts shifted, and she found herself wondering what Mr. Roth was going to do next.

Once they faced one another, he shifted, blocking her from Weiss. "You all right?"

She could see his face for only a few moments in the dimness of the distant streetlamp. Then he began getting blurry and soon blended into the darkness of the night.

"I'm fine..."

Everything grew soft and warm. She suddenly couldn't remember where she was or what she was doing here. She looked down and saw that she was holding onto someone's hand. Then she raised her head to see the man's face, but his features were hazy and out of focus. The back of her mind still functioned, and she knew Momma was somewhere close...but everything else had gone all screwy, and she began wondering if she was dreaming.

She tried distinguishing the blurred hand holding her own, but the darkness prevented her from seeing it clearly. Even so, she could tell there was something unusual about it. It was very warm, large, and very strong. She sensed that as long as she held it, everything would be fine. Nothing bad would ever happen again. She also thought she saw some sort of bright light somewhere in the back of her mind, a shimmering brilliance that brought about an incredible sense of warmth and well-being. This made no sense. How could holding someone's hand make her feel so euphoric?

I've got to see it...

She pulled it toward her, squinting in the darkness. She wasn't sure if she was seeing things or if the darkness was playing tricks. There was some sort of brightness in the center of the man's palm. It looked like flame emanating from his flesh, escaping from an opening about the size of a quarter...

She was about to ask about it when he turned it over and tightened his grip on her hand.

"You'll be okay from now on." His voice sounded as if it was part of her own mind. *"You and your mother will be just fine, and soon all you'll remember about this night is that there will be no more nightmares..."*

I'm dreaming... I'm imagining weird things, hearing strange voices...

Then she heard the man's voice again. This time, it rang loudly over the sounds of the passing traffic. At first she thought she knew who it belonged to, but as soon as she tried pinning it down, her mind blanked it all out, and she found herself wondering what it was about the strange man's palm that had intrigued her so much.

"Come here, Barbara!"

She snapped to and suddenly realized that the man standing beside her was calling out for Momma.

***

Her body still shaking, Barbara began breathing again only after she saw Laura peering around Mr. Roth's shoulder. Her baby daughter was still alive...and apparently unharmed.

Then she noticed jolts of sharp pain in her palms. She'd apparently closed her hands so tightly that her nails had penetrated the flesh of her palms. It took all her strength just to force her hands open. Ignoring the pain, she took in a deep lungful of fresh evening air. Feeling stronger, she forced her gaze from Weiss. It took every ounce of self-control within her to fight down the urge to run up to him and bury her nails in his face.

She couldn't succumb to the rage. Laura had *not* been shot. Right now, she was standing next to Mr. Roth, and she looked dazed...

Well of course she's dazed, silly. Weiss just shot at her--who wouldn't be in shock after something like that?

"You'll both be okay," Mr. Roth said, staring at her.

In the next moment, the fear--as well as the rage--dissolved.

She believed him. He'd never lied to them. He'd rescued them twice before. He just rescued Laura--although she had no idea how he did it. But he did, and that was all that mattered.

If he could protect Laura, he can also protect me.

Forcing her eyes straight ahead, she veered around the open door of the BMW and began walking toward them. Just as she passed Weiss, she heard him shift his position on the pavement.

Then she felt the long tube-shaped barrel of his gun pressing against the back of her head.

She gasped and stopped cold.

"Trust me, Barbara." Mr. Roth's soothing voice reassured her.

"Don't move, lady. I mean it."

"He won't hurt you," Mr. Roth said.

Weiss huffed. "You don't know me very well, do ya?"

"Aren't you curious why you didn't hit Laura?"

"Gun jammed. That happens when you buy a cheap Russian knockoff."

"Sure it was the gun?"

"*Course* it was the damned gun. I guess it didn't like the silencer. But it doesn't matter. It won't happen again."

"You actually think you should shoot someone right here? With people in that store?"

"He's right, Weiss." Sam's voice sounded unsteady. "We can't do this here. We have to get out of here. Besides, there are things you and I need to discuss."

"Boss, I won't have to do it at all if the three of them get in the damned car and do as they're told. You're not gonna do that, are ya?" he asked Mr. Roth.

Mr. Roth smiled. "You know better than that."

"Then I guess I've got to put out this nice lady's lights so you start taking me seriously."

Barbara felt her composure crumbling.

Just then, Mr. Roth said, "When are you going to kill Albright?"

Albright gulped audibly.

"The big man already knows that the other guy he sent here didn't go through with it. It doesn't change anything, because he still wants the man dead. This means *you've* got to do it."

Weiss didn't reply.

"Weiss? Is he...telling the truth?" Sam's voice had become weak.

Weiss still didn't speak.

"You'd better figure something out," Mr. Roth said. "You know how the big man gets when he pays good money for something and gets nothing in return. What did he pay you for Albright in case the first hit didn't take? Five figures? Or six?"

"You're talking out your ass."

"Weiss...*talk* to me!"

The barrel against Barbara's head twitched a little. Barbara watched Mr. Roth, who was now staring at Sam. No words were exchanged, but she could tell by the intensity in Mr. Roth's eyes that he was somehow communicating silently with Sam.

A moment later, Barbara heard Sam running away. She was afraid of moving but could tell by the diminishing footfalls that he was heading for the grove leading to the woods on the far side of the store.

"Now, Barbara," Mr. Roth said softly.

Trembling, Barbara hurried toward Mr. Roth. Her heart was thrashing loudly, but she forced herself to keep moving. He reached out, grabbed her arm, circled her and used his body to shield her.

Behind them, Weiss yelled, "All three of you are dead!"

Mr. Roth spun around to face Weiss. Behind him, Barbara huddled close to Laura and felt the familiar warmth moving up her limbs. It was just like before, when the man had brought her out of her daze in Bridgeport. The bright light returned, and a feeling of calm enveloped her. Then she heard his voice. It sounded like it was coming from her own mind.

"You and Laura are going to be just fine. Your darkness has been lifted. All you'll remember is that your pain is gone, and will never return..."

Everything grew hazy.

In the distance, she heard someone behind her say, "Drop the gun, Weiss. *Right now!*"

Barbara turned around. Everything was blurry and dark, but she could vaguely see the other man's arm shaking. She heard him grunt and thought she saw him bring up his other arm to steady his gun. The darkness increased, and the gun disappeared, but she guessed that it was still pointed at them. Then she heard his voice. It sounded like it was coming from miles away.

"What the fuck is going on...?"

Something clattered on the pavement. The man stood there, shaking. In the next moment, the darkness swallowed him up, and all she saw was the dark shape of the man standing directly in front of them.

Rustling in the bushes nearby drowned out the traffic sounds. She heard footsteps. A loud, sharp click that sounded like a gun filled the night air. A strange, unfamiliar voice yelled: "Freeze! I'm a police officer, and I'll shoot you if you move!"

Then silence.

Barbara turned back to where Laura was standing. She was still dark and blurry, but Barbara could tell it was her beautiful daughter standing close, smiling at her. There was something different about Laura that she couldn't quite grasp.

Is it Laura?

Is it really my daughter? Or am I hallucinating?

Then it dawned on her. Laura was standing tall and straight, and Barbara could tell by her daughter's beaming smile that she felt no pain.

What's going on?

Where are we?

And why are we here?

"Momma?"

Barbara reached out and wrapped her arms around Laura. Laura's arms encircled her waist.

The warmth of the night was like a comforting blanket fluttering around them. Barbara felt as if she'd just awakened from a deep sleep.

The distant whine of sirens penetrated the cool breeze.

CHAPTER FIFTEEN

Relaxing in the passenger seat of the Ford Edge, Roth waited for Jacobson to return. Roth was tired, but his fatigue had vanished instantly when he saw Laura and her mother following two officers over to the squad car parked in front of the dairy store.

Laura was walking like a normal person. Free and easy, with long strides.

And without a limp.

Jacobson had brought the Ford over from the fire station a few minutes ago and parked it beside the red pickup, at a safe distance from Albright's BMW. He'd asked Roth to stay in the car. He needed some time alone with him to get things straightened out before they reached the Station. Jacobson had no doubt seen and heard everything from the bushes and had a barrage of questions. He was a cop; he'd want everything explained in full detail.

Once Weiss was cuffed and shoved into the back seat of a squad car, Jacobson hurried over and got behind the wheel. He flicked on the ignition, put it in gear and followed the procession down the winding hill, back onto National Road.

"I guess you didn't need that gun after all," he said flatly.

"I didn't think I would."

"You wanna tell me what you did back there?"

"For instance?"

"Let's start with Weiss. Any idea why a professional gunman would botch a simple shooting? Not once, but twice?"

"He told me it was because his gun was a cheap knockoff. It's possible, isn't it?"

"In some circumstances."

"Just some?"

"A professional gunman using a cheap knockoff?"

Roth sighed. "He probably wanted something untraceable."

"Maybe…but that wouldn't explain that other deal, would it?"

"Which deal would that be?"

"I just can't figure out why a man like him would suddenly start shaking, then drop his gun and stand there like a dazed idiot while the cops walked right over and calmly arrested him."

"Any ideas of your own?"

"Actually, I'm more interested in what *you've* got to say about all this."

Roth could tell the man wanted to know everything and wasn't in the mood for excuses. But that didn't matter. Roth had other things on his mind. There was still much to do. He had to return to Orlando and couldn't afford to waste the rest of the night sitting in a Police Station, answering questions. "I take it we're going directly to the Station?"

"First I need to find out some things from you. I just hope you won't be quite as vague…or defensive…as you're being right now."

Roth couldn't tell Jacobson that he wasn't going in with him. This wasn't the time for that. Jacobson had to know a few things first. "I guess I can do that," he said.

"Great. First of all, I really have to know what happened with Weiss. If he spills his guts when he comes out of it, I don't want to look like a stupid idiot who just came to town for the scenery."

"I don't think Weiss will remember what happened."

"Care to explain that?"

"I guess you could say I put the man in a trance."

"Judging by how he was acting, I figured it was something like that. You wouldn't want to explain how you did it, would you?"

"I would if I could."

Jacobson shook his head. "Judging by what I've seen you do since I met you, I have this sinking feeling you're actually telling me the truth."

"I am."

"Well, at least in this case, we might not have to worry. Even if Weiss does snap out of it, he and Albright will be too damned busy trying to avoid life sentences for the kidnapping and attempted murder of two innocent women."

"Everything'll turn out all right, then."

Jacobson stared straight ahead at the taillights of the cruiser three car lengths ahead. "I'd consider it a tremendous favor if you told me who you are and why you really came here."

Roth sat back. "My name is Desmond Roth, and I personally know the man who's practically been running things in Central Florida the last fifteen years or so. This is the same man who sabotaged the Medina case, deposited that dirty money into your checking account, and put you on his payroll."

Jacobson was silent for several moments. When he turned to Roth, he was glaring. "I figured you knew this bastard. I kept hoping you didn't, but too many things wouldn't add up otherwise. Please tell me you don't work for him and I'll be extremely happy that I won't have to bring you in as an accessory."

"I don't work for the man. Never did, never will."

"Who is he, then? And how do you know him?"

Roth stared at the taillights straight ahead. "The man's name is Alvin Knepp. He's my brother."

***

Sitting in the back of the police car, holding Momma's hand, Laura found that she couldn't get her mind to stop spinning.

What happened back there? That man who helped us--where did he go?

Most of all, why am I not hurting?

That was the most important question of all. It was as if she'd just opened her eyes and found herself walking with Momma over to this car. She was *walking*--not limping, stumbling, or staggering. *Walking*, like a normal person. Walking like she was actually *healthy*--without crushed vertebrae, or pins in her spine.

I haven't been able to walk or move this way since before my accident.

When the cruiser first pulled away, Laura was afraid to move, to shift her position in the seat. She was terrified that the pain would come back. But her curiosity soon got the better of her. She began squirming a little in the seat, twisting slightly, shifting her torso, turning her head.

Nothing happened. There was no pain. No discomfort whatsoever.

It made no sense.

Neither did the huge blackness filling her head. The last thing she remembered was that man coming out of the dairy store to help her and Momma...

That brought back some of it, making her feel a little less like a complete idiot. Sam had brought her and Momma here, to take her meds. Then Laura had stumbled, making Momma drop the meds, which infuriated Sam and his friend. And when Sam's friend Weiss tried shooting her, someone rushed out of the store and got between them. She vaguely remembered Sam getting scared and running away, but that was when things turned blurry again.

You're tired. You're also extremely confused. Your fractured spine no longer hurts, and you can't understand why.

"Momma?"

"Yes, baby?"

"I took my meds just a few minutes ago, didn't I?"

"Why do you ask?"

"It's gone, Momma. The pain...there isn't any..."

"That's good, isn't it?"

"Yes, but something's different."

"How?"

"I don't know. I just feel *different*..."

Momma smiled and squeezed her hand. "I could tell you weren't hurting when we walked to the car, dear."

"You could?"

"Of course. You didn't lean on me. I can tell you're feeling much better."

"I didn't limp, Momma..."

"That's wonderful, baby."

"I haven't walked like that in...in..."

"Since before your accident. Yes. I know."

"Why is this happening, Momma?"

"Don't question it. Just enjoy it."

She *was* enjoying it. She couldn't help it; the feeling of being without pain for the first time in two years was so *fantastic*... But she just couldn't stop wondering why it had happened.

"Momma...you remember that man who helped us back there, don't you?"

"Of course, dear."

"Where'd he go?"

"I don't know. I thought I saw him walk off with that policeman. The one who came out of the bushes and arrested Weiss."

Laura forced the images to come back. Sam and his friend Weiss were both standing beside Sam's car, watching as Momma gave Laura her meds. Momma opened her bag...

But I didn't take the meds because I moved the wrong way and bumped into Momma...and the meds scattered all over the ground.

If I made Momma drop the meds, did I have time to take one first?

She *must've* taken one. Otherwise, where had the pain gone?

Just then, something else flickered briefly in her mind.

"That police officer who came out of the bushes, Momma. Did you see where he went?"

Momma was silent for a moment. "I'm not sure, dear. I think he might have gotten back in that sedan he brought over when the others were looking for Sam."

Laura sat up and stared at the driver's reflection in the rearview mirror. "Officer, what happened to that man who helped us back there?"

He glanced at her from his rearview mirror. "What other man, miss?"

"He helped get between us when Weiss was trying to shoot us."

The two officers exchanged confused looks.

"We didn't see anyone else, miss," the passenger said. "Weiss and the officer were the only two there, besides you and your mother."

"He was there, believe me," Laura said.

"We believe you," the driver said.

"Then where *is* he? If you didn't see him..."

320

"He might have gotten in the Ford sedan with the officer from Florida," the driver said.

"That man is from Florida?" Momma asked.

"That's what he told us."

"What's he doing here?"

"That's what we intend to find out as soon as we get back to the Station."

Laura gawked at Momma. She could tell Momma was thinking the same thing.

What was a police officer from Florida doing here?

"We need to thank him," Momma said.

"I also want to thank that other man." That same image flickered in Laura's head. "The one who came out of the store and helped us."

"He'll probably be at the Station when we get there in a few minutes, ladies," the driver said. "You can thank him then."

Laura twisted around in her seat. The dark sedan followed them. Laura thought she saw two shadows, but it was much too dark to be sure.

She turned back to Momma. Still no pain. This was very, very strange.

"You okay, dear?"

"I think so, Momma. But I just don't understand this."

"What don't you understand, baby?"

"As I said before, the pain's gone. I mean completely. Totally gone."

"The shock of all that's happened...maybe it somehow interfered with your back injury."

Her heart sank. "Then the pain...might come back?"

321

Momma gently stroked her wrist. "We'll worry about that when and if the time comes."

Momma was right. There was no need to worry about that now. There were other things to be concerned about.

She and Momma sat in silence for a few minutes.

Something else flashed in Laura's mind. "Momma, that man who helped us out of Bridgeport...do you remember him?"

"I remember him taking us out of the house and driving us to the Mall. He was the man who told us about your father."

"He was from Florida, too, wasn't he?"

"I think he said that, yes."

"He knew Dad."

"He said he did."

"Dad's really dead, isn't he?"

"Yes, baby."

"Sam was responsible, wasn't he?"

Momma shrugged. "Yes, dear."

Laura tried remembering the man, but most of it was blurry. She couldn't even remember what he looked like, or how he knew where to find them. "Did he tell us his name, Momma?"

"He might have, dear, but I can't remember."

"Do you remember what he looked like?"

"No. I guess I was too stressed. He just drove us to the Mall, told us about what happened with your father, then dropped us off at one of the fast food places. Then he was gone."

That sparked something else, but it was also blurry. "Momma, someone else helped us in town, at lunchtime, when we were mugged. It was another man. It wasn't the same man who brought us to the Mall, was it?"

"I don't think so, dear. I think the Sheriff told us it was probably some ex-military guy passing through town who happened to be there at the right time."

"I don't remember what he looked like, either."

"I only remember that it happened too fast to remember *anything*," Momma said.

"But what about the other man? The man who came out of the store. Why can't we remember him?"

"I don't know, dear. A lot of things happened to us today. Just sit back and try to relax and forget all the bad stuff, okay?"

Laura sat back and tried to do what Momma said, but her mind just wouldn't turn off. Too many things just didn't make any sense. What she remembered most was that Sam was a very bad man and that he'd been responsible for Dad not being able to come back to Ohio.

He was also responsible for Dad being dead.

"They'll catch Sam, won't they, Momma?"

"I hope so, dear."

"I want them to. I really want Sam to suffer for what he did."

"Me, too."

"Does that make me bad, Momma?"

"No, baby. It makes you human." Laura patted Momma's hand.

The officer in the passenger seat turned and smiled. "Once we reach the Station, we'll get you some nice hot coffee and you can sit down and rest."

"Thank you," Momma said.

Laura didn't reply. She was desperately trying to remember the man who'd helped them outside the store. She couldn't wait until they reached the Police Station so she could thank him for what he did.

***

"That bastard...he's your *brother*?" Jacobson jerked in his seat. The sedan swerved, bumping the shoulder. His expression, a mixture of surprise and rage, could clearly be seen in the darkness of the cab.

"My stepbrother, actually," Roth said. "My mother and Knepp's father met and married about three years after my father died."

Jacobson stared straight ahead. Roth could tell the man was trying to understand, to process the situation. After about a minute, he took a deep breath and glanced at Roth. "I need to know more. How close were you two?"

"Not close at all. Once I got to know the man, I despised him."

"At least that's *some*thing... What was his father like?"

"I didn't see much of him. He was quiet and reserved, and always working. He ran his own consulting business and put in a lot of hours. He seemed to treat my mother pretty well, so I had no complaints with him. She didn't do well being by herself, so that's why she didn't stay a widow very long."

"How'd your father die?"

"Heart attack. Heart disease was common on his side. It didn't help that he smoked and liked his blood-rare steaks. He was fifty-one."

Jacobson went silent again. Roth could tell he was trying to sort it all out. "How old is Knepp?" he asked a minute or so later.

"He's nine years older than me, which makes him close to fifty. He was already out of college when Mom married his dad. I was just starting high school, so I never really got to know him. I saw him briefly in the summers and on holidays, but he always had something going on, business-wise. The age gap was too wide for us to actually socialize or get to know one another."

"Any regrets?"

"Need you ask?"

"I guess I was hoping for some sort of revelation. Something to indicate a childhood trauma that made him the way he is."

"Like I said, I hardly knew him, so I can't say what happened before he joined my family. I'm fairly certain that he came packaged that way."

"What makes you say that?"

"Success came naturally to him. By the time I graduated from high school, he'd already set up a law practice in Miami and built up an impressive list of high-profile clients. He was a millionaire by the time he was thirty. By the time he was thirty-five, he'd become a multimillionaire specializing in real estate and land development projects as well as major land deals popping up in different parts of the state."

"That's a pretty damned quick rise to success."

"By the time he was forty, he'd become a billionaire who'd amassed a client list of the most successful developers in the state. He'd also bought up prime Miami property, businesses, and office buildings. He snatched up business interests in other areas of the state as well. He set up a base in Orlando and bought up a hundred acres of prime real estate in the Disney area. He bought a hotel, a golf course, stores and other high-priced stuff."

"He sure was busy."

"Success was his obsession. He couldn't stop buying and selling. Once he'd snatched up what he could, he began hunting other valuable bargains. Along the way he bought a couple of police chiefs, a detective agency, real estate developers, City Councilmen, Selectmen, and small groups of policemen in Orlando, Winter Park, and Casselberry. He bought people who knew things, saw things, and heard things. Anyone of value was up for grabs, and when he wanted something, he negotiated and snatched it up. When an obstacle blocked his path, he got out his checkbook and bought it. If he couldn't buy it, he had it removed."

"Did you two ever have a falling-out?"

Roth felt the heat of anger coming back. He took a moment before responding. "Something far worse happened."

***

Roth enlisted in the Navy at eighteen and became a SEAL at twenty-one. When he came back home years later to bury his mother, Knepp met him at the airport in a stretch limo and had his driver take them to Winter Park, where their parents had been living since they were married. Roth learned much about his stepbrother that same day, during the thirty-minute ride to the house.

"How's Dad doing?" Roth asked.

Knepp poured brandy from the bottle he'd taken out of the portable wet bar between the seats. "He's dealing with it. She'd been sick for some time, he told me. She started going downhill fast the last year or so."

"I wrote her a few times. She never said how she felt, but I could tell something was wrong. She didn't sound like her usual cheerful self."

"The old man's holding up, but you can tell he's wrecked." Knepp took a swig of the brandy and stared at his glass. "I figure he'll probably last another year or so, but not much longer."

Roth stared at Knepp. "You don't sound too broken up."

"About who? Your mom? Or my old man?"

"She was your mom, too."

"Not technically, but in answer to your question, I don't get too worked up about this sort of thing. Everyone eventually gets his ticket punched. The old man's getting on up there. You were in Iraq. You know damned well that no one lives forever."

The iciness emanating from his stepbrother chilled Roth to the bone. He knew right then that their mother's death, her funeral--everything about this sad event--was nothing more than an inconvenience for Knepp. The man simply had more important things on his mind.

Knepp sipped his brandy. A moment later, he looked Roth in the eye. "So...I guess you're finished with all that Navy gung-ho shit?"

It took Roth nearly a minute of intense deep breathing before he was able to respond in a civilized manner. He didn't know if it was Knepp's tone that had torqued him up or the term Knepp had used to describe Roth's service. In either case, he'd become extremely uncomfortable in the other man's presence and felt the barriers going up. "I was discharged--if that's what you meant."

"That's what I meant."

"What the hell was it you did for them? I've heard all sorts of things about SEALS and these covert spy games everyone's playing nowadays. Care to tell me if any of it's true?"

It was at that moment that Roth realized he'd already begun to despise his stepbrother. "Yes. I care."

"C'mon, now. We're practically related. You can tell me... "

"No. I can't. And if I could, I wouldn't."

***

"I don't believe he actually had the balls to ask you about that," Jacobson said, shaking his head as he drove.

"Knepp honestly believes he's entitled to anything he wants. That includes getting into people's business. But that's beside the point. That small half-hour exchange told me everything I needed to know. I realized right then that I didn't like him and could never trust him. He was my stepbrother, but we were no more than strangers, and would always be that way."

"But asking you about Black Ops... Seriously?"

"As I said, he expects people to tell him whatever he wants to know."

Jacobson waved it aside. "Let's get off this. It's really pissing me off. What happened after your mother's funeral?"

"I had some money saved and found a small place of my own in Casselberry. The Navy had educated me in engineering, so I planned to use my background to pursue a career in building and design. Knepp found out what I was doing and offered to give me a referral. One of his associates had contacts with a designer firm that could help me get started. I didn't want to owe him a favor, but he was insistent, convincing me of the advantages of working with such a prestigious firm."

"How'd that go?"

"The week I started working for them, I spent five straight days running personal errands for the higher-ups. I knew right off that I'd made a huge mistake in accepting Knepp's offer."

"How'd Knepp take the news?"

"The day I decided to put in my resignation turned out to be the same day Knepp called and asked me to meet him for lunch at Leed's Oyster Bar at Church Street Station in Orlando. By the time I got there, Knepp was already sitting at a corner booth, sipping a vodka martini. It turned out to be his third, and he had three more before I left."

"Did he normally drink this much? Or was something wrong?"

"Apparently one of his biggest associates, a major land developer, was having problems with a business rival. According to Knepp, this rival was embezzling huge amounts of money from local business owners and using it to finance a drug trafficking network he'd built up over the last year. It had been growing by leaps and bounds for six months and was directly responsible for the deaths of two high school kids in the Winter Park area. Knepp told me this man was using local kids as drug mules. When the parents found out what was going on, they got the local cops involved. The man in charge panicked and started making phone calls. Some important clients got wind of things and began calling in favors to close down the operation, and several kids came up missing."

"I don't remember anything about teens going missing under those circumstances," Jacobson said. "Where exactly did this happen?"

"The College Park area."

"When?"

"Eight years ago, supposedly."

"Supposedly?"

Roth closed his eyes and took a breath. The memories came back anyway, bringing with them the unresolved anger and the regret. "Knepp told me that this man was untouchable. He had some key OPD people in his pocket and they were keeping everything under wraps. Without proof, of course, everyone's hands were tied. The man had a pretty tight gig going on."

"Where was he going with all this?"

"Where do you think?"

"You mean…"

"He wanted this man out of the way."

"And he asked *you* to do it?"

Roth stared at the taillights directly in front of them and thought about that day and how it had changed his life forever. "Not in so many words."

"What words did he use?"

"He said, "You were Black Ops. You were taught some nasty shit.""

"Damn. Who the hell are we talking about here?"

"Knepp told me this man's name was Curtis Saunders. He lived in a prime section of Winter Park. He was fifty-four, married for thirty years, and had three kids. He owned large blocks of stock and had substantial holdings in real estate. He played golf on weekends and specialized in buying up foreclosures at huge discounts and later reselling the properties at reduced prices, mostly to ex-servicemen, or those on fixed incomes."

"What about the drug trafficking network?"

Roth sighed. "There wasn't any."

"I figured as much."

"What Knepp neglected to tell me was that Saunders was a churchgoer, gave money to several charities and donated much of his time to Catholic Church activities. He didn't embezzle money from local business owners and had nothing to do with drug trafficking. Apparently the man's only *sin* was that he owned a parcel of property in downtown Orlando and did not want to sell it to Knepp under any circumstances. He'd heard that Knepp wanted to buy the property so he could turn it into a string of topless bars."

"And *that's* why he wanted this man dead?"

Roth could only nod as the familiar storm of intense rage plunged through him.

***

As he followed the procession of police cruisers into St. Clairsville, Jacobson knew that he had to go after Knepp as soon as he returned to Orlando. A man like Knepp was a menace to society. Because of him, the man sitting beside him had murdered an innocent human being. Roth had been lied to and coerced just as Jacobson had been.

Roth was just another victim in a long list Knepp used for his own personal gain. Because he'd been told the lives of innocent children were at stake, Roth had used his military training, employing deadly force to kill someone he believed was a very bad man.

But at least Roth had had the sense to turn destiny around to save Laura Neilson and her mom from certain death.

And me, he reminded himself. *Don't forget that.*

"How'd Saunders die?"

"Heart attack."

"You didn't act on this based solely on Knepp's word, did you?"

"Knepp showed me several photos and a short film made by someone he told me was a reliable source. Both the photos and the film clearly showed two known associates of Saunders carrying the bodies of two boys and dropping them in a freshly-dug grave in the middle of the woods."

"Known associates?"

"Both of them. I checked them out thoroughly."

Jacobson nodded. "The evidence was obviously staged."

"Knepp has a ton of connections at his disposal. He can provide photos of anyone doing anything. I just didn't know that at the time."

Jacobson didn't reply.

"Aren't you going to ask me anything else?" Roth asked.

"Should I?"

"You're a cop. You've just been told about a major crime. It's your duty to do something about it."

"I know my duty quite well." Jacobson hadn't meant to sound so angry. The frustration building within him had brought it out. "But you're right--you do know I've got to look into this, don't you?"

"As I just said--you're a cop. It's your job--your duty. You *have* to pursue it."

Jacobson sighed. Yes, he was a cop. It was his sworn duty to pursue this. An innocent man was dead because of Knepp and this man. But Knepp was his main concern, and he didn't want to cause Roth any more trouble. The man had been through more than enough.

But the fact remained: Roth had killed an innocent man.

"I don't think I'll tell Orlando about Saunders--not yet, anyway."

"Isn't that slightly unethical for someone in your position?"

"In this case, it's my duty to go after Knepp. He's the same bastard who put that sniper rifle in my hand and ordered me to kill Albright. If I can nail Knepp for just a couple of felonies, I might be able to work the Saunders murder in such a way that--"

"I'm still responsible."

"I'm aware of that. But if I can nail Knepp for enough felonies, he might flip when I drop the Saunders case in his lap."

"Knepp's slippery. He knows nothing can tie him to that."

"It's worth a try, isn't it?"

Roth didn't reply.

He knows that it's murder, no matter who else was involved or even who planned it. But I've got no choice...

Roth sat back. "Anyway, I'm glad I told you what actually happened."

"What was the first thing you did when you found out?"

"When the truth came out, I suspected Knepp had done things like this before. I also knew that it was my duty to do whatever I could to stop him. The fact that he was extremely wealthy and well-connected meant nothing to me. I spent the last several years doing things to his businesses that cost him anguish and a great deal of capital. I was only one man, with limited resources. My SEALS training evened up the game a bit, but I still acted alone. I couldn't in good conscience bring anyone else into this."

"What'd you do?"

"In the beginning, I used my surveillance and tactical training to bug his phones and offices, tape conversations and compile a long list of names and firms he did business with. I made phone calls and canceled or changed times of meetings, contracts-- anything that would hit him hard. I have a couple of friends who were dynamite hackers and called in some favors. I figure my efforts probably cost him millions in lost revenues from canceled contracts and business deals."

"Did he ever find out what was going on?"

"He found out a couple of years ago, actually, when people began canceling future dealings with him or harassing him about missing shipments of contraband. He suspected me, of course, and put out contract after contract, upping the amounts whenever someone failed. I had to go into hiding, but again, my training came in handy, and I had no trouble slipping beneath his radar. The contract on me had climbed up to a million dollars, with a bonus of a hundred K if the actual killing was videotaped."

"That's cold."

"Knepp was furious. Like I said, I'd cost him millions. I'd hit him where it hurt most."

"So what happened?"

"An out-of-towner came into the picture. He'd been a hitter for one of the Colombian cartels and was responsible for more than fifty hits, among them foreign diplomats, several U.S. Governors and a couple of Congressmen. The man is known only as Black. He was paid two million dollars to kill me."

"What happened?"

Roth shrugged. "He fulfilled his contract."

"He what?"

"It happened last June, almost a year ago."

**

When they were about a block from the St. Clairsville Police Station, Jacobson slowed and stopped at the yellow light. He was confused and didn't know how much of what Roth had said was true. He liked Roth and was extremely grateful for what the man had done. The man had saved his life and career.

But he just couldn't believe what the man had just said.

He fulfilled his contract...

That just didn't make sense. And it made him wonder. If Roth was lying about that, what else had he lied about?

The light changed. Instead of heading straight for the Station, he pulled over to the curb and put the sedan in park. Then he turned in his seat and stared at the man beside him, desperately trying to see something in the clear gray eyes that would tell him what was going on.

"You said Black fulfilled his contract?"

"I did."

"A professional hitter?"

Roth nodded.

"The contract was for you?"

"Right."

"I don't understand."

"It's just as I said. Black fulfilled his contract."

"But...you're still here..."

"Yes. I am."

"And you're still alive."

"That, too."

"Hitters generally don't leave their marks alive."

"Agreed."

"And when they fulfill their contracts, as you just said--"

"You're a good man," Roth said suddenly.

Jacobson blinked. "How's that?"

"I said, you're a good man. A good cop. You're a credit to your profession."

"Well, thanks, but that doesn't really explain--"

"And you're going to walk inside that Station in just a few minutes and tell them everything you know, right?"

"Yes...but what I'd like to know right now is what you meant. I just don't understand. How did Knepp's hitter fulfill the contract Knepp had on you?"

"Would you agree with me if I said there are things you really don't need to know?"

Jacobson tried once again to read Roth's expression. Once again, he found it impossible. "In some cases..."

"Just some?"

"I think I should know everything there is about this. After all, I was brought up here and tossed right into the center of it. I have no choice. Yeah, I need to know everything."

"Yes," Roth said, "you're a very good cop."

Jacobson knew right then that something strange was going on. Roth wasn't answering his questions anymore. He was acting weird, and his voice sounded different. It was softer, with an almost dreamlike quality.

Just then, Roth reached over and placed his left hand on Jacobson's right forearm.

Jacobson didn't have time to question the action or react in any way. His hand and forearm immediately grew very warm. A strange tingling ran up his arm. Dizziness enveloped him, and he fell back into the seat. He closed his eyes.

Then he heard a voice. It was soft and mellow, and sounded like it was coming from the back of his mind.

"You're going into that Police Station and tell them everything you know," the voice said. *"Sam Albright and Al Knepp have been working on a condominium project in Bridgeport. They bought up a block of houses just off State Road 40. Albright ordered Barbara and Laura Neilson taken there to be questioned about money they thought Joe Neilson had taken.*

"You did this on your own. You couldn't go through with the Albright hit because you're a good cop and will not under any circumstances break the law. A stranger happened by at the right time and enabled you to see what you were about to do. That was when you realized just what was at

stake. When you return home, you're going after Knepp and will bring him down."

Jacobson opened his eyes and realized that he was crossing the street. Had he zoned out?

Too much on my mind, obviously. I'm tired, and I want to get back home.

He had the strangest feeling he'd forgotten something…

Wait a minute. Wasn't there someone with me?

Yes. The man who helped Laura and Barbara Neilson. The man who came out of the dairy store and shielded them from Weiss.

He was supposed to come with me and give his statement…

He turned. The Ford sedan was parked along the curb. But it didn't look like anyone was sitting in it.

Where'd that guy go? Weren't we just talking about the case?

Of course they were. How else would he know about Albright and Knepp? How else would he know about the Bridgeport project?

But where the hell *was* that guy?

He hurried back to the car, reached for the door and pulled it open.

No one was sitting in the passenger's seat.

A thumb drive lay on the console between the seats.

CHAPTER SIXTEEN

Alvin Knepp nervously paced his comfortable air-conditioned Disney Village office and forced himself for the third time in the last hour to refrain from grabbing the Crown Royal bottle from his desk drawer. He needed a clear head for whatever bit of business he faced. It was much too early in the day to lose his edge.

However, this waiting was getting on his last nerve. Two days had passed, and still not one word from Miles Lester. He was still trying to recover from the blow that bastard cop Jacobson had dealt him. Jacobson had not only sabotaged the Albright hit, he'd also gotten hold of Joe Neilson's sensitive intel. He had no idea how Jacobson had done it. None of Knepp's snitches or shadow people had seen anything that would suggest Jacobson had contacted Neilson. There was no evidence anywhere to suggest Jacobson even knew Joe Neilson existed.

So how the hell did Jacobson know about the intel?

Something had gone seriously wrong. There was no way in hell that Jacobson could get his paws on that intel. It made no sense.

Other things made even less sense.

Why would Jacobson fly up to the Ohio Valley if he had the evidence all along? Why would he let Knepp or anyone else push him around? Anyone possessing such a powerful bargaining chip would have made a stand long before getting on the plane. Jacobson would have told Knepp about the intel the moment he'd acquired it. It would have saved him a lot of aggravation. But Jacobson had boarded the plane, found the right cab, driven to the kill site and waited for the designated time of the hit. Other than not actually going through with the hit, Jacobson had done everything he'd been ordered to do.

Had Jacobson planned this all along?

Or had he stumbled onto the intel by accident?

Briefly he wondered if Barbara Neilson had given it to him when Weiss was arrested. It was possible, wasn't it? How else could Jacobson have gotten it?

That didn't make sense, either. For that to have happened, he would have had to have met Barbara Neilson before Albright took her to Bridgeport.

But why would Jacobson let Weiss take her and her daughter out of the Manville Police Station in the first place?

Jacobson had obviously planned all this from the start. He'd somehow found out about the intel and decided to use it to clear his name. All the while, he'd been shadowing Albright and saw an opportunity to get the others out of the picture. A simple call to the St. Clairsville Police would enable him to rescue Barbara Neilson and her daughter and nail both Weiss and Albright for the kidnapping. In just a few hours, he'd cleared his name, rescued two women from two kidnappers and scored points with both the Manville and St. Clairsville Police Departments. He'd flown back to Orlando a damned hero.

The worst part of all this was that Jacobson still had the intel.

The bastard would pay dearly for this.

Knepp glanced at his Rolex. His call from Columbus was long overdue. His contacts had been instructed to give him a full report of the Albright fiasco long before now. That idiot Weiss would ruin everything if he opened his big mouth. St. Clairsville had Weiss in custody, but that would soon change. Once Columbus had given the order, Weiss would be released on bail, taken to Pittsburgh, and flown to Orlando for a serious debriefing in one of Knepp's warehouses. With Weiss out of circulation, Jacobson would have lost much of his credibility.

His cell buzzed. He fished it out of his jacket pocket and checked the display. It was Lester calling, hopefully with some sort of report. Lester would also pay dearly for taking his damned time to call.

Knepp pressed a switch on the scramble box on his desk. "Talk to me."

"Sir, I've just had half a dozen of my men working their asses off, trying to figure out what's been going on in St. Clairsville since Weiss was brought in..." Lester sounded even more anxious than usual.

Knepp wasn't in the mood for excuses. If Lester couldn't give him what he needed to know, Knepp would pull a couple of his Ohio Valley investments that would cripple Lester's empire in just days.

"I honestly don't give a healthy shit about the state of your men's sorry asses. I need answers, and I want them now. Where's Albright?"

"This morning he was arrested by the Wheeling cops and turned over to the St. Clairsville PD for questioning. He's already contacted his attorneys, but he's facing multiple felonies, and since a double kidnapping is one of the charges, they're not giving him his usual VIP treatment--"

"Good. That's one question answered. At least we know where the asshole is. Now all you have to do is get him out of there."

"Pardon?"

"You're directly responsible for Albright being arrested in the first place."

"But sir...I had nothing to do with--"

"You and Albright have been partners for years. Albright became a liability the moment he showed me that he was unable to get answers from Barbara Neilson. You were the one who supplied Crowley and Devlin. Those two didn't deliver-- through no fault of their own. Albright didn't want Devlin to question the women. This was his fault, but since you were also involved, this reflects directly on you. Deal with it."

"But sir..."

"I don't need any more bullshit--especially from a worthless hick about to lose everything if he doesn't follow my instructions." Knepp pressed another switch on his scramble box. "Get Albright out of there. I don't care how you do it. I want him in Orlando in three days, or the next bastard I put on my hit list will be you--get it?"

"But--"

Knepp clicked off, stripped the cell and dumped the components in the trashcan beside his desk. He stepped behind the desk and opened a drawer. After that bit of nonsense, he decided it wasn't too early in the day after all. Dealing with incompetent idiots frequently called for desperate measures.

He brought out the Crown Royal, poured two inches into a glass, sipped, and poured more. He turned and gazed out the tinted window, at the lush, trimmed grounds of Disney Village, and hoped that the beauty of the sunny day would expel the frustration eating away inside him. He'd get this sorted out eventually. He had money and unlimited means at his disposal; he'd learned many years ago that with those two commodities, nothing was ever out of reach.

I'll find out what happened if it's the last thing I do. I'll find out who made a mess of everything, and when I do, I'll make sure that whoever is responsible is buried in cement twenty feet underneath the foundation of my next building project.

Knepp finished his second drink and sighed. One more would make him feel just fine. He turned around. He was just about to reach for the bottle when he noticed someone standing in the doorway, watching him.

It was a dead man.

***

As Desmond Roth faced his stepbrother for the first time in years, he discovered that he felt no anger, no animosity. No fury or rage whatsoever, even though he now shared the same room with the man who'd not only tricked him into killing an

344

innocent man, but also paid a professional assassin two million dollars to have him eliminated.

That no longer mattered. Perhaps it was because Roth knew Knepp's time was up and that he was about to lose everything. The fact that Roth had been instrumental in making it all happen also made things much more tolerable. He'd sabotaged Knepp's Bridgeport plan. He'd also rescued Barbara and Laura brought down one of Knepp's business partners and three highly-paid henchmen.

Last of all, he'd wrenched Brad Jacobson free from Knepp's control.

Knepp stood there frozen, his gaze on Roth. His grim features had paled. His right hand had stopped moving toward the bottle of Crown Royal on the desk blotter. Knepp let it drop to his side.

Roth could almost hear the gears grinding in the man's brain.

Knepp's surprised state lasted only a few moments. He finally took a deep breath and opened his mouth. "Is that...*you*?"

Roth wanted to smile. "I've never denied it."

Knepp shook himself and pulled in another deep breath. He placed the empty glass on the desk beside the bottle. His gaze hadn't left Roth.

"You're...dead."

"Am I?"

"You have to be... I arranged it."

"And yet I'm standing here."

Knepp slowly circled the desk. "Black...told me he killed you."

"I'd say he was wrong--wouldn't you?"

Knepp's eyes glowered. "Black was paid *two million* to kill you. He's reliable. A pro. He's been in the business for years. What the fuck happened?"

"Why don't you ask him?"

"I'm asking *you!*"

"What did he tell you?"

"He told me he trapped you in a damned church."

"He did."

"He told me he brought along a small team of ex-military mercenaries with him. He used--"

"C-4. I was there. I clearly recall the fireworks. I had a ringside seat."

"He sent me the whole thing on disk. And on two thumb drives. And color pictures. I've got copies of everything in this office. I have the originals in a couple of my safe deposit boxes in my personal banks." Knepp's face relaxed slightly. "The fire was damned impressive."

"Yeah, it burned pretty bright. Too bad you weren't there."

"Let's stop the bullshit. What the fuck happened and how are you here?"

"The fire apparently wasn't quite impressive enough."

Knepp's face reddened instantly. "The damned building was torched down to the timbers! *No one* could have gotten out!"

"No one?"

"No one, dammit!"

Roth shrugged. "As you can see, I managed to slip out. I needed a breath of fresh air."

Knepp ignored the quip. "But *how?*"

Roth smiled easily. "I guess you could say I had a little help."

***

Roth's military training had taught him everything about hunting. As a result, he instinctively knew when he was being followed. This sense had been growing the last couple of days. It had become so intense that he was convinced another assassin was looking for him. For the next five days he stayed on the move, switching vehicles often and keeping close to crowds--a task easily accomplished in the Central Florida area.

On that final day, Roth sensed that someone had tracked him down to a Motel 6 on the outskirts of Casselberry. He snuck away and spent the next day on the road, maneuvering through heavy traffic and using the main highways, but after several hours of playing cat-and-mouse, he continued to see clear evidence of a tail. His gut told him there were at least two different vehicles keeping him in sight.

He turned off the main highways and kept on country roads for more than an hour and ended up in the Conway area three or four miles south of Orlando. He pulled into a crowded shopping center, crossed the lot, and followed the alley running directly behind the stores. At the far end, the alley became a winding country lane that went past a small trailer park and ended two miles later, in the middle of a clearing that led to an open field, taking him through a parcel of woods not yet cleared by developers.

At the other end, facing another secondary road, a church sat behind a grove of pines and some large oak trees. The paved lot out front was empty, the building totally dark. Roth parked in some overgrown bushes behind the church. Using some tools from his emergency kit to force open a window, he crawled inside.

He waited a few minutes. Then, hearing nothing, he thought he'd successfully eluded his tail. Since he had only his hunting knife and the small .22 snub-nosed automatic he'd kept for protection from his military days, he hoped he had nothing to worry about. His plan was to keep watch for an hour or so. If no one showed, he'd sack out in a pew. He was exhausted and needed a recharge. Once refreshed, he'd head straight for the airport. Knepp wouldn't stop sending killers after him. Roth's only chance was to disappear.

But after just twenty minutes, Roth sensed someone outside. Through a crack in the front door, he peered out at the darkness and saw the square shape of a vehicle parked across the field, behind some pines. From a window facing out back, he spotted three dark figures moving among the bushes and realized he was surrounded.

He discovered very quickly that he had no time to work out a backup plan. The deafening explosions plummeting into the church walls told him his killers fully intended to destroy the church, and that he'd be dead in minutes. Something was tossed onto the roof. Another explosion followed, and the wooden rafters splintered and collapsed.

Large swirls of flame dancing overhead overwhelmed the confined space.

In minutes, the smoke had flooded the area. Wild flames climbed the rafters, feasting hungrily. Large chunks of charred wood plummeted to the floor. The stained-glass windows exploded. Colored shards danced, splashing in a blinding starburst. They fell, glittering and winking as the slithering serpent of smoke rolled over them, covering the floor in a dark gray shroud.

Roth had taken off his jacket and covered his head with it to protect him from the smoke and the fumes. He'd also brought along his earplugs, which he'd used for emergencies in his military days, to protect his ears from the deafening percussion. He got down on his elbows and knees and began crawling on the stone floor in hopes of finding a way out of the building. He knew that if he did manage to make it outside, Knepp's men would get him immediately. But he had no other option. He could get to his gun as soon as he was safely out of the building and take out at least one of them. He promised himself he wouldn't go down without a fight.

He moved slowly, an inch at a time, reaching out for obstacles before proceeding. The jacket helped, but the smoke had taken over every square inch of air space. It would only be a couple of minutes before the smoke would kill him. He'd done two tours in Afghanistan, had been wounded three times and almost captured by the enemy twice, only to come home and be murdered by assassins sanctioned by his stepbrother. The irony filled him with rage.

His senses guiding him, he kept moving. More rafters collapsed, crashing to the floor dangerously close and sending large chunks of burning wood and smoked kindling hopping across the floor directly in front of him. Something heavy dropped beside him. He jerked away and doubled up, expecting the flames to leap on him. He waited tensely, hacking away inside his jacket. When nothing happened, he carefully pulled his jacket a few inches away from his face.

The burning rafters that had collapsed onto the altar lay in a massive heap just a few feet away.

But that wasn't what got Roth's attention...

***

Knepp could tell Roth wasn't telling him the truth.

Fifteen minutes after starting the fire, Black had called on a secured line and given Knepp all the details. The church had been deserted for months, with no witnesses around to present a problem. Roth's rental car was the only vehicle parked near the building, and the entrance door and church windows had been boarded up. Black had also said that there was nothing anyone could do but stand by at a safe distance and watch the flames. The violent blaze would turn everything to ash. And since the Fire Department had gotten there much too late to do anything but prevent the fire from spreading into the woods, Roth's body would be cremated beneath the enormous pile of rubble.

But Knepp's eyes told him otherwise. The man was standing less than ten feet away and was very much alive. And there wasn't a noticeable burn mark on him.

Knepp was convinced Roth had left out some major details.

"You say you had help?"

"I'd be dead otherwise." Roth's eyes seemed unnaturally clear. A strange light was coming from within them.

It's the damned sunlight penetrating the tinted windows. It's reflecting off Roth's face.

Knepp soon found that he was extremely uncomfortable in the man's presence. His thoughts began spinning with graphic details Black had sent him. Flames. Smoke. The building caving in on itself. His stepbrother trapped in the building, overwhelmed by smoke and fumes, unable to escape.

Stop this, dammit. Roth had been sabotaging my business for months. He cost me millions and needed to be taken down.

Where the hell was all this guilt coming from?

Knepp had learned years ago that guilt was unproductive and unnecessary. Weak people felt guilty. Losers. Worthless wretches with no ambition. Idiots unable to focus...or plan...or succeed.

Decisions were a way of life; they usually involved shoving obstacles out of your way. Knepp had learned early on that anything worthwhile came with an obstacle clinging to it. He'd also learned never to look back when you were pursuing your goal.

Never explain, never complain. It was a motto he'd lived by.

It was time to get back on track.

Black was a professional. He'd been a contract killer for nearly two decades and had never made a mistake. Anyone who demanded half a mill a hit couldn't afford mistakes. Black would not leave *anything* to chance--especially involving a job paying two million bucks.

But Roth wasn't a ghost--he was real, and he looked just as healthy and as formidable as he did the last time Knepp saw him.

Something was very wrong. There was a weird calm about Roth that Knepp had never noticed before. Roth also *looked* different. It wasn't only the man's eyes, or the fact that Knepp felt that disgusting sense of guilt... It was something else.

I had help...

That was the statement that baffled Knepp most of all. Roth was alone. The church was surrounded. The C-4 turned the building into an inferno of burnt timber, smoke and ash in minutes.

So how the hell did Roth get help?

"You were there alone. Black said there was no one else around. To me, this means you were alone."

"I *was* alone...in a manner of speaking."

Knepp waited for more of an explanation.

Roth said nothing else.

"Well? What the hell are we talking about now?"

Roth merely smiled.

Roth's smile was like a slap in the face, disorienting Knepp, making him see red. The smile was smug, exuding confidence. Roth knew he was in control.

What is this bastard keeping from me? What the hell is making him so goddamned arrogant?

Who the hell could "help" him? Who'd given him enough of a heads-up that would enable him to…

Knepp's mind quickly jumped into its cold, calculated logic, and when the inevitable revealed itself, his body turned hot. His mind went wild with rage. He wanted to spit blood.

"It was Black, wasn't it? That bastard *turned* on me! I paid him two million bucks and he *lied* to me! He helped you, didn't he? He got you out before he started tossing the C-4. What did you give him? What the hell did he take for stabbing me in the--"

"It wasn't Black."

"It *had* to be Black! He was the one calling the shots!"

"Maybe…but he wasn't the one in charge."

***

Engulfed in flame, the life-size wooden crucifix trembled beneath the heavy brass chain bolted to the charred rafter above it. His wet eyes blood-shot and burning from smoke, Roth scrambled to his feet. An instant later, the beam collapsed. The cross dropped straight down, its large square base crashing to the floor a mere three feet in front of him.

Roth gazed at the blackened face of the lean figure on the cross. In that one instant, he thought he saw the figure's eyes focused on him. Chills trickled down his spine, and the fear and panic enveloping him vanished.

The flaming cross began swaying. It eased forward, lowering toward Roth. Roth instinctively held out his hands, bracing for the impact. The cross continued to fall, the figure moving toward him, until Roth's exposed palms stopped its descent. Roth cried out in agony when the smoldering heat from the brass nail-heads protruding from the figure's palms met with his own, searing his flesh and forcing him to his knees.

In just seconds the pain evaporated, and a sensation of warmth scurried up his arms. The warmth moved inward, settling deep within him. The pain, the fear and the heat had vanished, and a supreme sense of peace filled his spirit.

Roth opened his eyes. The cross lay flat on the floor, face-down. Roth couldn't remember lowering it. All he remembered was the warmth flowing through him. He stared at his horribly blistered palms and wondered why he felt no pain. Then he gazed at the fallen cross and felt a strong sense of inner peace and calm.

A gentle voice inside him said, "Turn around and walk into the light, and you will no longer have anything to fear."

He turned. A strange beam of shimmering light radiated from the center of the roaring flames. The heat and the flames had become unbearably intense, forcing his eyes tightly shut. He realized in *that same instant that he didn't need his eyes to direct him--the light was pulling him in the right direction.*

He kept walking. When he could no longer feel the heat on his back or face, he discovered that the air had become clean and pure, and the smoke that had nearly smothered him moments earlier had vanished.

He opened his eyes. He was standing in the middle of the woods. The distant cries of a crowd thundered a hundred yards behind him. Fire trucks and police cruisers nearly surrounded the blaze as firefighters and police struggled to contain the fire and keep the growing number of spectators and news people at bay.

No one had noticed him leaving the burning building.

***

Knepp's initial reaction to Roth's story was anger. Roth should know better than tell him something like that. Knepp wasn't born yesterday; he'd heard just about every cockamamie story in his forty-eight years and had learned not to believe anything without investigating first.

No, this one was about as unbelievable as any he'd ever heard. Roth was trapped in a burning building. He couldn't breathe, couldn't see, couldn't move around...but he still managed to find the strength to push a damned cross out of his way and walk out of the inferno, right past the South Conway Fire Department, the Orlando news people, and a crowd of sensation-obsessed ghouls.

And no one saw him do it.

Roth was covering for Black. Nothing else made sense. Roth obviously paid him to let him go. Why else would a pro with Black's perfect record fuck up a job that paid him two million bucks?

The only thing that made this so aggravating was that Black had never bungled a job before. Once Black was given his fee, he never changed the plan--it was his personal SOP.

Knepp found it disheartening that you couldn't trust anyone these days--not even a proven hit man with nearly two decades of successful contracts to his credit.

"You must think I was born yesterday," he said. "What did you pay Black to look the other way while you slipped out of the church? How much time did he give you before he started lobbing the C-4 at the building?"

"I knew you wouldn't believe me," Roth said.

"Then why waste my time? I'm an extremely busy man."

"Actually, I came here to warn you."

"*Warn* me? What the hell are you talking about now? As I just said, you're taking up my time. What you need to put in that lame brain of yours is this: once you leave this office, another order will be put out on you before this day comes to an end."

"That doesn't concern me."

"It should. This time, I'm going to hire two hitters. I intend to offer them the additional incentive of an extra half-million if they bring me your head in a box."

Roth didn't bat an eye. Knepp wondered if the man was on sedatives.

"You heard me, didn't you? I plan to pay out an extra half-mill to see your head in a box."

"I heard every word you said."

"Well? Any comments? Concerns? Tips on who I should contact?" Knepp winked devilishly. "I *am* next of kin, am I not?"

Roth still didn't flinch. "As I said, none of this concerns me. I came here only to warn you. You don't have much time left."

Knepp had to struggle to stay in control. He wanted to rattle the man's cage but wasn't making any headway. This made no sense. If anyone knew how to rattle cages, it was Knepp. When you rattled someone's cage, it knocked them off-balance and put you in total control. Knepp had to be in total control.

Roth had obviously lost touch with reality. What the hell was going on? How could he just stand there and threaten Knepp? He'd lost it, plain and simple. The fire had fried his brain, made him delirious.

"Listen to me, dammit. *You're* the one who doesn't have much time left…"

Roth ignored the comment. "A man will be coming after you. He's a good man, and when he finds you, he'll make sure you'll go to prison, and all the money in the world won't be able to help you."

Knepp shrugged. "Okay, I'll bite. Just who the hell is this *good man*?"

"Someone capable of taking you down."

"I hate to burst your bubble, but I'm not worried. I buy *good men* all the time. They're like

357

neckties--they come cheap. I have dozens lying around. You'd be surprised just how *bad* a *good man* can get when he's offered a little pissing-around money."

"This man isn't for sale."

Knepp couldn't believe how naïve some people were. "In case you haven't figured it out yet, moron, everyone's for sale."

"You couldn't buy *me*, could you?"

Knepp laughed. Now was the perfect time to wipe the smirk off Roth's face. "Even better--I got you to get rid of someone for me. And I didn't even have to toss money at you to get you to do it."

Roth's expression didn't change. "That was only because you tricked me into doing it."

"It worked, didn't it?"

"Get your affairs in order. This man has everything on you, and by the time he's finished, you won't have anything left."

"Who *is* this asshole?" Knepp's curiosity flared.

"I wouldn't want to spoil the surprise."

"You bastard. As I said before, the next hit will be right on the mark. I'll be sure to be waiting at home when FedEx notifies me to tell me a certain box will be delivered to my door. "

"How could you, Knepp?" Roth's expression darkened, showing anger for the first time. "A middle-aged woman and her handicapped daughter? Barbara hadn't heard from her ex-husband since he left Ohio five years ago."

Roth's statement suddenly made everything click. Ohio. Barbara and Laura Neilson. Yes. It *had* to be... Nothing else made sense.

"It was you, wasn't it? *You* were the one stirring the pot up there in Ohio. *You* were the one. It's Jacobson, isn't it? *He's* your *good man*, isn't he? The idiot you actually think will bring me down?"

"Goodbye, Knepp." Roth turned to leave.

Knepp soon found that he could no longer control the rage. Roth had not only survived, he'd gone to Ohio and sabotaged even more of Knepp's interests. The Bridgeport Renaissance Project, no less. An eight-figure contract with annual dividends that would easily double its net worth every five years.

This bastard did it to me again!

Before he realized what he was doing, Knepp had circled the desk, opened the top drawer and grabbed the Llama automatic he kept for emergencies. In the blink of an eye, he had it aimed at Roth's face.

"Fuck the hitters. I'm too goddamned pissed and disgusted to waste any more money on an asshole like you. Besides, I can't wait. I've got to do this myself. I can have a clean-up crew here in ten minutes. Good riddance, Roth. Be sure to make things comfortable for that idiot Jacobson when he follows you down in a couple of days, because I intend to put a hit on his sorry ass as well."

He began squeezing the trigger.

Roth's eyes had suddenly become too bright to look at.

Knepp closed his eyes and found that he couldn't move. His hand grew numb; he felt his arm drop to his side. The Llama thumped to the floor at his feet. Knepp opened his eyes and gawked at it.

It looked evil...and frightening...

Death lay at his feet.

What the hell is happening?

Roth took three steps toward him. His face was just as serene as before. "Since you now seem to be in a more receptive of mind, would you really like to know how I got out of that church?"

Knepp found that he could barely look at the man. Roth's eyes glowed even brighter than before. This was totally unreal. Nothing made sense anymore.

Roth slowly held up his hands.

Burned flesh the size of a half-dollar showed boldly in the center of each palm. The hands themselves gave off a hazy golden glow.

It took a while for Knepp to find his voice. "W-What the hell...*is* that?"

"I'll let you figure it out for yourself."

Knepp couldn't take his eyes off Roth's hands.

What the hell had made those welts?

And what was that glow coming from them?

***

Roth took two more steps toward the pale, trembling man standing behind the desk. Knepp had grown much smaller. He no longer projected the image of success, power or evil. In an instant he'd become just another confused man facing something he couldn't comprehend.

360

Roth lowered his hands. "As I said, Black wasn't the one in charge that day."

Knepp didn't reply; he continued trembling.

Roth reached out for Knepp's shoulder.

Snapping out of his trance, Knepp jerked back. "Stay away from me!" His voice was a harsh croak. He glanced at the Llama lying on the floor. He appeared to be deciding if he should go for it again.

Roth decided to give his stepbrother one last chance. "Listen to me, Knepp. If you just let me--"

"*You* listen to *me*, asshole. I may not understand what's going on, but I know what you used to do when you were pulling that gung-ho Navy SEAL shit. I've heard all about that martial arts crap and know what nutcases like you can do to a guy. I'm not gonna let you lay a hand on me and do what you did to those hicks in Ohio. Just get your sorry ass out of here. I've got things to do!"

Without a word, Roth left the office and went down the stairs.

Outside, he stepped into the light for the very last time.

EPILOGUE

Momma placed the silver urn containing Dad's ashes on the living room mantelpiece. Standing behind Momma and Laura, his handsome, fine-featured face solemn and respectful, Officer Jacobson looked on in his neatly-pressed dark-blue suit.

The silence grew heavy. Laura fondly remembered her father as he was when she was growing up--happy and proud, full of fun and spontaneity. She reminded herself that it was important to focus on the good times--not on the depressing months after he'd disappeared from their lives.

She could tell Momma was thinking the same thing. Momma appeared tired and sad as she stared at the metal object containing the ashes of the man she'd loved for more than half her life. However, the gleam in her eyes suggested much of this love had survived and would remain forever in her heart.

Momma finally shook herself out of her silence and invited Officer Jacobson over to the sofa. Her eyes glistened, but she bravely held on to her smile for the sake of their visitor. "Would you like some coffee?"

"No, thank you, ma'am." He waited for Momma and Laura to join him before he sat down. "I can't stay very long. I've got to get back to the Police Station and give Sheriff Kloss another statement. Then I've got to drive over to St. Clairsville and speak with their Chief of Police."

"We can't thank you enough for bringing Joe's ashes."

"It was the least I could do."

Laura found herself shifting back to that strange, terrible night.

"Baby? Everything all right?"

Laura sighed. "Just thinking about it again, trying to sort it all out."

They grew silent again, the three of them drifting back to the night that had forever changed their lives.

"This whole thing is baffling," Jacobson had told them as he drove them home that night, after more than an hour of questioning at the St. Clairsville Police Station. "I was sent up here by a very bad man to do a very bad thing. Many of those details have somehow escaped my mind, but I distinctly remember someone stepping in just as I was about to do something that would have destroyed my life. I'm a cop, and I've always been blessed with a terrific memory and great powers of observation. But for some strange reason, I can't remember who this person was or what he looked like. All I remember is that he happened by at the perfect moment. Call it chance, if you like. Or maybe it was one of those things you might want to refer to as a miracle. Whatever it was, it really did something to my head."

"Had you seen him before?" Momma asked.

"Never."

"He just *appeared*?"

He nodded. "I have no idea who he was. All I remember is that he saved my life."

"Did he tell you his name?" Laura asked.

"Maybe, maybe not. When I try to remember anything about it, something in my brain darkens. Call it a mental block. Or maybe it's my subconscious trying to protect me, for some unknown reason."

"What exactly did this man do?" Momma asked.

"He freed me from the man who'd been blackmailing me."

"How?" Laura asked.

He shrugged. "The only thing I remember is that my blackmailer called me that night, but I didn't talk to him. This man talked to him and somehow got me off the hook. I don't remember the details, but I do remember calling my partner in Orlando later on to verify that certain evidence had been sent to my desk. I'm pretty sure this evidence was what my blackmailer had on me... But as I said before, everything's a blur."

"Strange," Momma said.

"Strange doesn't begin to cover it," he said.

"What happened to him?" Laura asked.

"That's something else that I can't get a grasp on. He was driving the car from the Mall and telling me what Sam Albright had done. We followed Albright's car onto National Road. Then he pulled into the parking lot at the Fire Department and told me to call the local cops. After that, everything turned cloudy. I have no idea where he went or how I got in the bushes. I remember someone coming out of the store to shield you two ladies from Weiss, but everything else is just a big dark void in my head."

Laura had been thinking about the man who came out of the store but couldn't remember anything else about him. It was almost like the three of them had been affected by the same memory lapse. She wondered if they were dealing with mass hysteria, or conversion disorder. She'd read about such things in college but had never thought too much about it. It usually happened when people were involved in some catastrophe. While the cases she'd read about dealt with symptoms such as numbness, blindness, and paralysis, memory lapse didn't seem worth mentioning. But it still struck her as extremely odd.

"You took him to the Station, didn't you?" she asked.

He sighed. "I tried…"

"What happened?"

"That's another thing. He disappeared as well."

"Wasn't he in the car with you?"

"Yes…but when I got out and crossed the street, I was alone. I went back to the car to investigate, but he'd already gone."

"Maybe he didn't want to get involved," Momma said.

"That's possible," he said.

"I really wish we could have seen him," Laura said. "I wanted so much to thank him for helping us."

"Did he tell you his name?" Momma asked.

"That's another blank," he said. "If he did tell me, I sure don't remember what it was."

"There's something about this night that just doesn't make any sense," Laura said, sitting back in her seat. "It's almost like...like something wonderful happened. Something we're not supposed to really understand..."

Now, as they sat in their living room one week later, Laura still couldn't shake that same feeling that something extraordinary had happened that day.

"What do you think will happen to Sam?" Momma asked.

"He's facing several felonies. The FBI has decided to proceed with the kidnapping charges. I was told that they took him into custody a couple of days ago. No one knows where he is right now. That strikes me as kind of odd, but I'm sure the Feds know what they're doing. He'll be spending most of his time in courtrooms for the next several months. He's got several attorneys on his side. But he's facing kidnapping charges, as well as attempted murder, so you're talking major time. Every single transaction he's ever made will be investigated. He'll have to cash in his chips and call in favors, but it won't do him much good. When the FBI and the other agencies close in, they'll find things that'll not only burn him, but also many others he's dealt with. Even if he gets off with a few years in a minimum-security prison, it'll be years before he'll be allowed to conduct business again."

"And Weiss?" Laura asked.

"He was also taken by the FBI to an undisclosed location for questioning. He'll be facing major prison time."

"What about the man who arranged all this?" Momma asked. "The man responsible for Joe's death?"

He sat forward. "Thanks to a stroke of incredible luck, we've got quite a file on him. Because of it, he was brought in for questioning."

"Who *is* this man?" Momma asked.

"His name is Alvin Knepp, and he's quite possibly the most corrupt individual I've ever seen in my life. He's into everything you can imagine-- money-laundering, drugs, prostitution, murder, extortion, kidnapping. He's one of the richest men in the country as well as one of the most well-connected. No one was ever able to connect him with any illegal dealings...until I found the file and surrendered it to the appropriate authorities."

"Has he confessed to anything?"

"Not yet, but we really don't need his corroboration--not with the file we've got on him."

"How did you find a file on a man like him?" Momma asked. "I'd think that someone in his position would be particularly secretive. Does this have anything to do with the books Joe was keeping for him?"

"I don't know if your ex-husband had anything to do with this, but that isn't important. This file was much more damaging than his illegal books. It was all on a thumb drive. The drive was sitting on the console of the Ford sedan I was driving the night I followed you to the Police Station."

"How'd it get there?" Laura asked.

"I wish I knew. After parking the car that night, I got out and started crossing the street. I suddenly felt as if I'd suffered some sort of blackout. I didn't think too much about it at the time because it had been such a hectic day. I was exhausted, so I figured it was that and nerves that got me off my game. But when I regained my senses, I remembered the man who'd ridden over with me--the man who'd come out of the store to help you ladies. I went back to the car to investigate. The man was gone, but the drive was sitting on the console."

"You don't think *he* left it there..." Laura's imagination was starting up again.

"I don't know what to think. For all I know, it could have been there all along, and I just didn't see it. But no, I don't think my passenger left it. How would he have gotten hold of it? He was just a guy who showed up at the right time and helped you ladies."

"Just like the guy who showed up and helped you?" Laura asked.

"Exactly," he said.

Laura smiled. "I think a miracle happened that day. I can't call it anything else."

***

One week later, Laura rose early, put on a sweatshirt, sweatpants, and tennis shoes, and went outside for her morning jog.

It had been more than two weeks since she'd experienced any pain in her back. Five days ago, she decided to take the gamble and start doing the same exercise routine she'd followed diligently before her accident. But she knew better than take any unnecessary risks and eased into it gradually.

She began her new regimen the morning after Officer Jacobson had brought Dad's ashes to the house. That first day, she took a leisurely walk. Since she hadn't exercised in so long, she decided to limit this new activity to a walk to the end of the block and back. She experienced no pain, only elation--possibly from the sudden stimulation of muscles she hadn't used for so long. She was so excited that she wanted to keep going. Once she reached their house, she turned around and made another trip.

Again, she experienced no pain.

She tried a brisk walk the next day, covering two full blocks before noticing that her heart rate had increased.

The third day, she covered the first block at a brisk pace and then eased into a leisurely jog. Although it had been two years since she'd been able to run, she maintained the pace for a full block. She turned around, jogged for most of the block and walked the rest of the way back to the house.

On the fourth day, when she was convinced the pain wasn't coming back, she told herself that she should no longer worry about it. Through some strange miracle, she'd become healthy again and no longer needed meds. She could not only climb the stairs, but she could also run up and down them without difficulty. She could carry bags of groceries. And grab things from the kitchen cabinets. And kick off her shoes without howling in pain. And roll around in the grass if she felt like it.

She had no intention of telling her doctors about her miraculous recovery. Doctors were scientists. They distrusted the strange and the unknown and rejected anything they couldn't comprehend. They would never consider anything that didn't exist in a medical book. She didn't want to be treated as a medical oddity.

Whatever had happened on that strange day two weeks ago was something neither she nor Momma would fully understand. Laura decided that it no longer mattered. Everything had turned out just great--why question it?

Two other miracles occurred the other day, when she'd gone back to work at the Coffee Masters. The first--and most notable--was when she marched briskly into the office, where Maddie and Carl sat at the desk, working on the laptop. Laura stood in the doorway, smiling at them. They immediately stopped talking and stared at her. For nearly a minute, no one said anything. Then something flickered in Maddie's eyes. Her mouth opened, and her jaw dropped.

"L-Laura?"

Laura couldn't help grinning.

"Is that...*you*?"

"Laura *Neilson*?" Carl was just as shocked as Maddie. He slowly stood up and gawked at her. His pen dropped to the floor.

"It's me."

"Really?" Maddie looked doubtful. "I mean...are you...*sure*?"

She laughed. "I checked the name Momma stitched on the inner lining of my underwear before I came in--just in case you'd ask."

Maddie swallowed. "Why are you *standing* like that?"

Laura spun around and held out her arms. "Is this better?"

Carl shook his head. "*Wow...*"

Maddie got up from the desk and approached her slowly. Her large blue eyes filled the sockets. Then, finally, she lowered her head and stared at Laura's feet. She gasped. "*Heels?*"

Laura nodded.

"You're...wearing *heels?*"

"Four-inch spikes. Got 'em the other day. They feel wonderful on my toes. I'm as tall as you, now..."

"Laurie...what...happened?"

"Are we still talking about the heels? Or is this--"

"Your back, Laura... Forget the damned heels. Tell us about your back!"

"I don't know. I got better. There's no more pain..."

Maddie looked skeptical. "I can see that..."

"Something else?"

Maddie shook her head. "It's not that. It is, but it isn't. It's much more than that. It's..."

"Your face," Carl said. "You look...totally different."

"Good different?"

Carl said, "Wow" again.

Laura blushed.

"There's a brightness coming from your face," Maddie said. "It's something I've never seen before. Your eyes…they're so…happy…"

"I *am* happy, guys--happier than I've ever been."

Later, after her friends had recovered, Maddie told her that the jewelry store had called the morning before and asked if Laura could come in and pick up the horseshoe ring. At least three dozen people had asked to see it during the sale, but none expressed an interest after examining it. Several had even handed it back the moment they touched it. The owner said Laura could have it for the sale price even though the sale had ended. This wasn't their store policy, but they felt they could make this one exception. The owner couldn't shake the eerie feeling that the ring actually belonged to Laura.

This morning, she jogged down to the end of the street. While taking in the fresh air of the new day, she covered the next block before turning left. She was halfway home when she passed a tall, slender man with curly white hair shoving an envelope into the mailbox in front of the two-story brick house at the end of the block. Just as she passed, he said, "That's a very nice ring."

Laura stopped cold and spun around. "Excuse me? What did you say?"

He closed the lid of the mailbox. "Just said it's a very nice morning." He glanced up at the clear blue sky and nodded. Then he grinned and shuffled down the walk.

Laura watched in shock and confusion as the man climbed the two stone steps leading to the front porch. The door closed silently behind him.

Was she hearing things? Imagining them?

She told herself this was no big thing; she just hadn't heard him correctly. How could a man his age see that she was wearing a ring in the first place? She was running, for one thing. The ring was a dark gold, and not very brilliant in the morning sun.

No, it was just her imagination trying to trick her again.

She gave the man's house one last glance. Then she resumed her jog, slowing down for the last block and walking briskly the rest of the way, until she reached the front porch.

The front door opened. Smiling, Momma came out in her light-blue flowered bathrobe. Her hair was pulled back and tied with a red rope. She held her brown coffee mug in her left hand. "You're up earlier than usual." She sipped the hot coffee.

"I felt like running a mile or so before breakfast."

Momma's eyes glistened. "I'm so glad you're doing so well, baby. Still no pain?"

"I feel great, Momma."

"And you still haven't needed your meds?"

"Not since that night we were taken to the Police Station."

"This is all so unbelievable..."

Laura smiled. "Something wonderful happened that night, Momma. I don't know what it was, but I truly believe Dad somehow found a way to come back. I think he felt badly about leaving us and wanted to come back and make amends."

"I feel the same way, dear. Even though a lot of terrible things happened, I know your father loved us both."

"I still feel him, Momma. It's almost like…like he's right here, beside me."

"When someone's in your heart, they're always with you. And I really think he did find some way of coming back after all."

Laura hugged Momma. She truly believed life would never be the same because of what had happened that day. But she had the strong feeling that whatever it was, it would always keep the darkness away.

"Think you're up to climbing a ladder?" Momma asked.

"I'm pretty sure I can. What's up?"

"I'd like to make a trip to the attic. We need to find those pictures of your father and put them all back in the bedroom and living room, where they belong."

The darkness veiling her mother's eyes the last five years had completely vanished. Laura suspected she'd never see it again. "That sounds like a terrific idea, Momma."

"C'mon in and let's have breakfast first. You're probably starving after your run."

"I'll only be a moment."

Smiling, Momma turned and went back inside.

Laura stayed on the porch, her eyes closed as she took in the cool morning air. On this particular morning, the air had a special sweetness to it. She couldn't help thinking that everything would be different from now on. And it should be, because she was different.

I don't know exactly what happened that day, but I do know that I'm not the same person I was. Maddie and Carl didn't recognize me, so I know it's not just my imagination. I'm all better now, both physically and emotionally. Something wonderful happened. It was as if something flicked on some special light switch inside me, and I intend to keep it switched on for the rest of my life.

She opened her eyes and started for the front door.

"You and your mother will be just fine," a strange voice inside her urged. *"There will be no more nightmares..."*

She stopped cold. Was it her own voice she'd just heard? Why did that message sound so familiar? Why did the voice itself sound so familiar?

She thought she caught a brief flash in her mind of a dark-haired man with clear gray eyes watching her. She turned around quickly.

No one. Her imagination again, no doubt. It was like what she thought she'd heard the white-haired man say to her.

She closed her eyes and tried to bring back the image she'd just seen.

Had there been a golden haze around the man's head?

What did that signify?

"Turn around and start your new life..."

The same voice, but with a different message.

375

Or was it?

No more darkness... Turn around...start living again...

The words were different, but the message was the same.

It was time to walk into the light. The darkness had gone, and the future looked brighter and more promising than ever before.

Feeling incredibly happy, Laura turned around and went back inside to help Momma with their new attic project.

ALSO BY DAVID BERARDELLI

THE APPRENTICE
THE WAGON DRIVER
DEMON CHASER
DEMON CHASER II
STEPPING OUT OF MY GRAVE
ESCAPE CLAUSE
FATAL INNOCENCE
COLORS
THE FUNNY DETECTIVE
"Taking On the Orlando Mob"
JUST A SIMPLE ERRAND
A Funny Detective Novel
WORKING FOR A MOB BOSS
A Funny Detective Novel
AND DARKNESS FELL
DEMON CHASER III
AFTER DARKNESS FELL
IN ANOTHER REALM